REFLECTION

A DOPPELGÄNGER NOVEL

ALLY WADLEY

Nomadic Owl, LLC

1057 Streamlet Way

Monroe, NC 28110

©2017 by Nomadic Owl, LLC

ISBN 978-0-9996897-0-7

First printing: December 2017

Visit Nomadic Owl on the world wide web at www.nomadicowl.com

*FOR MY MOMMA, WHO ALWAYS BELIEVED
ANYTHING WAS POSSIBLE, INCLUDING
WRITING A BOOK
AND FOR MY AUNT RELLE, WHO
SUPPORTED AND GUIDED ME EVEN WHEN IT
WAS FRUSTRATING*

I WOULDN'T BE ME WITHOUT BOTH OF YOU.

1

___

AFTER

There was silence. Surrounded by damp air, the sweat and dirt had formed a solidified layer of new skin.

She thought she heard a rustling, but she couldn't be sure. She wasn't sure of anything anymore. It was a realization that had come as a surprise for the girl who had always been so self-assured.

The silence was broken by another faint rustling sound. This time she was certain she had heard it. But there wasn't time to process what was happening. A deafening boom startled her to her senses.

She found that fear mixed with relief was creating an interesting emotion as sunlight suddenly flooded the dark and humid room. Disoriented, she raised her head to peer at the doorway. There was nothing but blinding light, hurting her eyes. An overwhelming sense of dread consumed her as she was hoisted from the ground into unfamiliar arms.

However, the panic didn't manifest itself into action. Inaction had become her M.O. The standard. Her powerlessness was part of her identity now.

The scent of cologne was unmistakable. It was Aqua Di Gio, to be sure. Her ex-boyfriend had worn the same scent many years ago. It was a comforting reminder, somehow.

She was being carried. Moved. But to where? By whom?

All she could currently comprehend was the light and the smell of Armani. Then, just as quickly as that understanding occurred, the light dimmed and the trees of the forest came into view.

Flashes of white and green came in waves into her visual field. She was struggling to keep her eyes open, the fatigue of her body more evident at that moment. But she slowly became aware of her feet dangling in space with each step he took through the woods. Somewhere in her semi-conscious mind, she was aware that she was being extracted from her nightmare.

What she didn't know was whether this was a rescue or not. And if the unknown person granting her supposed freedom should actually frighten her.

Yet, she felt strangely safe. A relief was washing over her and a peace that this could be her salvation. Hope was emerging.

She realized the cliché of that scenario. She hadn't orchestrated her own freedom. She was being saved! Like a typical Hallmark movie, the distressed girl had been granted a savior. At least momentarily.

However, she knew from experience that the

Hallmark movie could change to Lifetime drama in an instant. Her savior could quickly become a villain. Nothing was as it seemed.

They could have travelled a space of a few feet from her prison or a distance of miles. Her senses had been overwhelmed. Or broken. The result was the same. She had no idea of anything beyond the floating sensation of being carried and the belief that this was finally the end.

As they trespassed through the woods, she heard as his feet crunched leaves and twigs beneath him. They were disturbing nature. A disruption that had been necessary and wonderful.

She lifted her head and tried to see. Yet, the savior who carried her was dominating her focal point. A distinct chin with stubble. It appeared blond in color, but she couldn't be certain with the light. Plus her eyes were not the best after the extended periods of darkness.

The prominence of the chin was undeniable though. He glanced down briefly before readjusting his eyes to their path. She had discerned green hues in his eyes, and perhaps a flicker of kindness. He had an angular nose and square, thin face. His body was muscular and lean. It was the classic look of a Scandinavian heritage and the markings of a hero.

After some time, they seemed to reach a safe place to pause. Or rather he was tired of carrying her and was transitioning to an easier exit.

He then lifted her over a railing and laid her down on some cushions.

"A boat? Was there water nearby?" she questioned internally.

3

It was a question that was quickly answered when the roar of the engine minutes later seemed to confirm the assumption. She wondered again if she should panic, although she had resigned herself to her fate long ago. Her old life was so many miles away. There was no longer any point in fighting for it.

The air stung like a thousand needles to her skin. It was also brushing the hair from her face and reminding her to take a breath.

When she took too much, too soon, she ended up gasping on the air that her lungs had received. She steadied herself and tried once more. Luckily, she was more successful the second time.

Moments later, she finally opened her heavy-laden eyes to the blurry view of blue skies overhead. It was so beautiful that the words wouldn't come to describe it in her mind. But the tears didn't hold back. Maybe she really was escaping.

She turned her head to look at her rescuer, grateful to whoever he was.

He was at the wheel of the motor boat powering their journey. His wavy, dirty blonde hair was blowing in the wind. As if knowing her eyes were upon him, he turned to gaze at her. Briefly, she registered what she thought was a look of concern before he returned his eyes to the horizon ahead.

She drifted in and out, never fully conscious for what felt like hours. Although, she had begun thinking they should have arrived at a destination by now.

She gathered her strength and attempted sitting up when the roar of the engine finally dimmed to a hum. He turned and approached where she laid. He sat himself by her waist and looked down at her.

His eyes were definitely green, and deep set. He held her gaze as his hand lifted gently to rub her left arm. His voice was calm, strong, and steady when he relayed his command.

"Just breathe, Brianna. Everything is ok."

His words were soothing. She wanted to believe him. But she found it difficult to believe in anything anymore, even herself. Yet, she took heed of his words, and tried to breathe deeper.

The next breaths did come easier. Then the next. Their eyes never left each other. There was something reassuring about him. A kindness he displayed.

He smiled slightly. Then, she closed her eyes and faded into a peace she hadn't felt for a very long time.

2

BEFORE

B rianna's life had been considered by most to be almost perfect. Sure, she had her problems and bad days, like anyone else, but mostly, it was a golden existence.

She certainly had a loving family and some close friends. She had gone to school and had a good job as a result. There had been no tragic events to leave any permanent scars or major personal setbacks to leave her insecure. So, in the scheme of things, she was having a blessed life with very little baggage.

She wasn't a drama queen. If anything, she was drama averse. In the spirit of the "O Captain! My Captain" pledge, she had found the marrow of life and sucked it. She was a life sucker. Every chance she had gotten, she had looked for the bright side of things.

In fact, she was having what she had considered a mundane day when everything had changed.

Nothing spectacular had happened that day and she

was planning a quiet evening at home after work. She certainty had not been expecting disaster to strike.

She was walking down the street to grab lunch, half way distracted as she sorted through a work issue in her head. She was so immersed in her thoughts on how she was going to solve the problem at hand that she had failed to notice the proximity of an opposing figure.

There was a tall, muscular man in a dark suit at her 5-o'clock position. She didn't realize his closeness to her, nor did she register the emptiness of the street she was traversing. Perhaps had she not been multitasking, she might have noted the danger of her situation. Alas, she didn't see it coming.

Suddenly, Brianna's body was pulled backwards. The force of her small frame smashing against his hard body knocked the wind from her lungs. She started fighting, kicking to get free. She even tried to let out a cry for help to no avail. But it was too late. His arm had already tightened around her waist and his hand had cupped her mouth to prevent screams before the oxygen had even returned to her body. A pain radiated from her arm as he had jabbed a needle into it. She was being drugged.

More so, her struggle was rapidly becoming futile as she was being overpowered from the man's strength. She was flung like a rag doll into the back of a black town car.

"What the hell?" was all Brianna's mind processed in the moment.

Mere moments into her backseat residence, she had managed to crawl to the door handles and window buttons. Except everything was locked. Not that she had truly expected it to be that easy after the efficiency from which she was taken off the street.

"You would be wise to stop," interrupted a strong, clear voice.

She paused and looked up to meet the end of the gun barrel pointed at her. The saliva dried in her throat and her eyes widened. Her face bleached of color. It was this instant, she knew she was in real trouble. Slowly and cautiously, Brianna leaned backwards in the seat.

"That's good. You learn quickly to follow directions," said the guy with the gun, as he lowered the barrel slightly.

Her eyes scanned the interior of the car and noted that there were two men. One was in the driver's seat. The other, her capturer, was the one in the passenger seat with a weapon pointed at her. He was the one ensuring her behavior was moderated, scrutinizing her every movement for disobedience.

She was guessing that he already knew every inch of her and if she dared to breathe wrong, he wouldn't hesitate to eliminate her. Her eyes trailed back to the driver, who was pulling the car away from the curb and, thus, setting in motion her probable demise.

She had been kidnapped.

"Why?" she pondered. "I am a nobody."

She ran through the possible reasons as she also began to process her surroundings.

Black leather adorned the seats. The windows were tinted and hard to see out. Overall, the back seat was spacious and would be considered comfortable if it was experienced in a different situation.

She hadn't seen the car's make and model. But cars had never been her thing, so she doubted she would have identified it anyway. If a car had functioned, she had been happy. Right then, she had wished she had paid more attention to the car commercials that filled the TV. They could have provided valuable information to saving her future.

The one with the gun had black hair cut very short. His face was round, almost a perfect circle. And he was expressionless. In fact, his expression hadn't altered even slightly while she had evaluated him.

His eyes were dark blue and held a coldness that made her shiver. The hint of wrinkles at the edges of his eyes betrayed some signs of age. Her guess was he was in his early 40s. His thick black beard hid any indication of emotion. He was the definition of stoic. Focused on his task to keep her still and quiet.

The one driving the car did not turn around. Brianna could only gather a little about his visage from looking at the car's mirrors. She could see that his hair was longer and slicked back with some gel. It appeared dark brown but was likely lighter without all the hair product. Given the style of hair, she had already guessed he was younger.

She had begun making mental notes, hoping their descriptions would serve her justice when she got free again.

They drove along in complete silence. The one with the gun never deviated his sight from her, similar to how she rarely deviated her sight from the gun. It felt like an eternity had passed when it was likely a space of a couple of minutes.

Many thoughts had occurred to her as they rode. Mostly her mind was trying to figure out why she was taken. Who could think she was important enough to rip her from her life?

She had nothing to offer. She, nor her family, were rich. They weren't a part of high society nor did they have status. She had lived a somewhat simple life. Or so she had thought. She had travelled a bit and she was somewhat known in her profession locally. But overall, she had come from a Midwestern middle class and was completely ordinary. She had worked hard to climb the corporate ladder since college, but was nowhere near the top. She could think of no logical reason why someone would want to kidnap her.

"It must be a mistake," she realized to herself. "They grabbed the wrong girl!"

Should she let the two men know of their error? Tell them and see if they would let her go?

On the flip side, they could just kill her and dispose of her remnants versus letting her go back to her life.

After contemplating it, she decided to start resisting anyway.

"There must be a mistake. I am a nobody...and I would hate for you to get in trouble when your boss sees you show up with the wrong girl."

Neither man said anything. The one with the gun raised an eyebrow. It had been the only indication that he had heard her speak.

Since her first attempt hadn't gotten her killed yet, she decided to try again.

"My family has zero money, so there is no ransom that

could be given. It makes absolutely no sense to take me. You must have mistaken me for someone else. Someone more important."

The one with the gun now appeared amused. He was definitely smirking behind that hair. He exchanged a look with the driver, who gave a half-laugh, but gave no other sign that her words had been received. They both seemed unconcerned with the possibility that she was the wrong girl.

"We don't make mistakes," the one with the gun finally said, point blank.

Then his deadpan staring resumed.

"Shit!" her mind screamed.

It seemed they were not to be deterred. And worse, they believed they had the right girl. She was beginning to hope she would have better luck with their employer, since it was obvious she was going to meet who that was.

She averted her eyes from the gun to gaze out the window. The dark tint of the windows made it difficult to see. She didn't recognize any of the scenery she had managed to observe, but she was struggling to stay awake. She was rapidly becoming aware that her situation was dire. Mistake or not, she knew she was in serious trouble.

Brianna also reasoned that if she panicked, it would make it worse for her. She had to remain calm, keep her head. It would be the only saving grace, she assumed. It was an impossible task because she had never been so scared in life. She was frightened to her core, deeper than she had ever believed was possible.

She remembered all the horror movies she had seen

in her life and how much she had hated to watch those films because the fear made her uncomfortable. Now, she was experiencing a nightmare that went way beyond an uneasy feeling. This was a real-life horror story that wouldn't be over with a quick "gotcha" and the credits rolling. This was a reality that could be the end of her so-called uneventful life.

As much as she had thought she was a survivor, she was not prepared for this scenario. She couldn't begin to process the situation and, as much as she tried to remain calm, she had begun to hyperventilate.

The car was distancing itself from her world. She was now certain that this would not end well for her. It wasn't a dream where she could be awakened. She wouldn't laugh about it in the morning. As she struggled to breathe, the voice in her head got louder with its cries of distress. The utter chaos of her mind was incomprehensible. Panic didn't begin to describe it, because she was freaking out.

Her vision was blurring. She couldn't discern where they were any longer. It seemed to be the forest that surrounded the city, but she couldn't be certain.

She heard the one with the gun say something to the driver. Yet, she couldn't understand it because she was losing touch with reality as the drugs took effect. She struggled to remain upright in her seat. Soon, she would only see black as her body went limp.

She wasn't unconscious. Not really. She was still vaguely aware of the numbing sensation throughout her body. She could hear distinctive sounds in the background, but a fog had overcome her mind.

Moments of clarity came and went. She felt disoriented and sleepy. In those few clear moments she had, she maintained hope that it was all a vivid dream. She would wake in the morning and find she had just been drinking too much the night before. It was just a nightmare. A chilling nightmare, but one that would find her still living her usual life the next day.

As she faded even further, she knew this hope was pointless. This was no dream. This was just the beginning of the worst horror she could imagine.

3

Brianna awoke in a haze. She was lying tightly tucked into white linens on what appeared to be a queen-sized bed. She slowly turned her head in each direction to survey the surroundings. It certainly wasn't a dream like she had hoped.

The room was very spacious. It was almost twice the size of her bedroom in the city. It was also pure white. The walls and ceilings were blinding as sunlight reflected off of them. There was only one bit of color. Beside her bed there was a vase filled with red, long-stemmed roses. Their smell had given a brief sense of hope that maybe she had slept through the nightmare. Perhaps she was already awakening to discover they had made a mistake. As the fog was lifted from her mind, she became certain that this was not the case. She was still very deeply in danger

Hours passed without a sound beyond the ones she made herself. There were no people, no well-wishes, nothing to indicate that this was a sanctuary. It didn't have that feeling of safety either. The room was sterile and lacked any warmth to convey comfort. She knew that this was not a happy place, nor one of healing.

As her clarity returned, so did her senses. She felt the softness of the sheets and the weight of the blankets. Her limbs were heavy and difficult to move. Nevertheless, she started to test her mobility by pushing the covers down to her hips. Then using all the strength she could muster, she pulled herself into a sitting position. She rested her head on the wooden headboard. That one movement's effort took all the energy she had mustered. She felt exhausted. She was still feeling the effects of the drugs they had given her.

As her breathing returned to normal, she heard a crash from beyond the closed bedroom door. It stilled her heart. She listened intently to see if she could hear anything else. To her surprise, she could make out the sound of faint voices. She couldn't determine the words, but it was some indication of life.

A few moments later, it was gone. Silence dominated the room once again.

From her sitting position, she could better process her surroundings. There was very little furniture in the room. The sunlight that filled the space came from two double French doors to the right of the bed, leading out to a balcony. Across from the end of the bed was a white dresser that was flanked on the left by a simple, cushioned white chair.

Whoever had designed the room had definitely used the theory of minimization. There was no art in the room and no mirrors. It was bare. The only thing present in abundance was Brianna's sense of doom, which wasn't likely to go anywhere anytime soon.

She sat there and cried. She didn't realize the extent of her tears until she placed her hand on her chest a little while later and found it was soaking wet. Her face was numb. All her hope was fading. She had used the time alone to review her situation. As much as she had tried, she still couldn't figure out why she was here.

She soon grew tired, falling asleep not long after her eyes had dried. There had been no sense of time. What felt like hours could have been days.

The only reprieve from her solitude came much later. She was awoken when the door opened and a man walked into the room. Brianna was paralyzed with fear at the sight of him. He was a short statured man, who slithered like a snake to her bedside. She noted his movements were hindered by the slope of his back. He used a cane to aid his approach.

He was thin and had very little hair. His visage was long and horse-like. His eyes were dark and seemed almost black. The broad nose was offset by the thin lips. Still, she figured he had never been an attractive man. He did, however, convey an opposing presence within seconds of entering the space.

Her hatred of the man was immediate. She had never had such a reaction to a person, but there was a first time for everything.

He did nothing to convey any warmth. His gaze was cold and hard. It felt as if his eyes could bore a hole into her. The corners of his mouth twitched as he was

17

evaluating her. There was little doubt that he was the boss of the outfit.

Despite her fear, she didn't flinch. She raised her body to a better sitting position and pushed her chest forward. She may have been scared, but she refused to let this man see her squirm.

He stood there for a few minutes, staring. She felt like a zoo animal but she didn't falter in her courage. He said nothing. So, she returned his stare with an equally cold one of her own.

Her thoughts turned from defensive to offensive as she assessed his weaknesses. It was information that may come in handy in escaping whatever he had planned for her. She was certain that she had never seen him before this moment. He was not someone she would have been likely to forget encountering. He was also someone very difficult to read. She was having a hard time determining anything of value about him. He guarded his secrets well.

He soon turned and left the room. A smirk present on his hardened face. As he passed through the doorframe, she noted a guard was waiting for his employer to exit. He gave Brianna a "don't try anything look" before closing the door. And with that brief introduction to the mastermind, she was again left to her loneliness.

4

B rianna sometimes lost track of time in her
isolation. She became more mobile as the days
passed. However, her interaction with people
remained limited. Twice a day, a guard would deliver
food to her white prison. The meals varied little from day
to day. It usually consisted of chicken and rice or some
other bland arrangement. She grew tired of it almost
immediately, but she had to eat.

She had begun to snoop in her spare time and found
that the dresser was completely void of items, as was her
night table. The roses, however, seemed to be replaced
like magic each day. They remained the only color in the
room, a welcomed asset. Every few days, she was
delivered a new set of pajamas when her meal arrived.
The clothes always consisted of a white pajama bottom
and a button-up matching top.

On her second day in the room, she had found that
the second door of the white room led to a bathroom. Not

surprisingly, it was stark white as well. She had begun to bathe on a daily basis. It had become her only activity to anticipate. She looked forward to her sole comfort of a hot shower. The soap and toothpaste also magically appeared for her daily use. She was baffled as to how they were replaced without her awareness.

She tried to keep track of the days somehow. But, it was becoming harder as the days spanned into weeks.

The crusty old man hadn't returned. Her only indication of life beyond that room was the guards that delivered her meals and clean clothes.

She had noted that the guards rotated between two different men. One was the man with the gun who had masterfully executed her kidnapping. The other was a short and stocky man of similar age, but had less hair. The driver of the car was nowhere to be seen. She had counted four different men so far and it made her wonder how many people were on the payroll.

Such had become her existence. Boredom and silence were beginning to drive her insane until one day the pajamas were replaced with an actual outfit. Weeks had passed with no variation to the schedule until one day it was different. A day that would change the dull routine.

It started with a dress. A long, flowing empire waist dress of light pink. The cut was simple with a square neckline and long lace sleeves. It was a beautiful dress that she would have thought belonged in a wedding party.

Brianna's confusion was heightened. More than a month had passed since she had been imprisoned in the white room. She had interacted very little with other humans. She had lived in the white pajamas that were replaced on a periodic basis, and now, out of nowhere, she was given a fancy dress to wear. It didn't make any sense.

Brianna knew that the dress meant that she would be leaving the white room, at least, temporarily. What she was expected to do in the dress was the bigger question. A question, which she pondered most of the day as she stared at the garment. She played every possible scenario of it in her head, wondering again why she was here.

She was restless. There were weeks of pent up energy and too not much thinking.

"I am slowly driving myself insane," she thought.

She wasn't prepared that evening when the guard showed up to collect her. She hadn't even tried on the outfit, having decided she would resist. She planned to test the waters, to see how far she could push them.

However, she learned she couldn't push them even an inch. As soon as the guard saw that she wasn't pinked out in chiffon, all hell broke loose. He entered her room and paused. Then, without warning, he charged at her and hit her face. Hard. The punch was with such force that she crumbled to the floor. A shock radiated throughout her body. Her vision blurred. She saw spotty flashes of light and felt dizzy. The pain rebounding through her head made her nauseated. She began to whimper.

Lying on the floor, she pulled her knees up to her chest to assume the fetal position. He stood, lording over her in victory. Her arms and hands came up to guard her face as she sobbed. She was ashamed.

She didn't want to play this game. She didn't know if

he planned to injure her further. But it was a chance she didn't want to take.

"Get dressed. Now."

He didn't wait for her to acknowledge his order. He had already left the room, slamming the door behind him and making her body jolt in the process. She laid back on the floor for a few minutes, contemplating her next move. She really didn't want to get hit again. Or worse. She realized the only way to prevent that from happening tonight was to get up and put on the fancy dress. But the thought of the possibilities ahead may have been even more frightening than being punched.

What was outside that room? Being held captive and going crazy in her solitude was one thing. Her venturing into the unknown was another. Something in her psych told her that nothing good would come from putting on the dress.

She would comply though. The decision had been made for her. She would have to take her chances outside the room. And perhaps she could find a way out of this horror story.

She had played along for a month, waiting for some indication of what she was doing there. Now, she was ready to take some action. The punch to the face had awakened her from her complacency. She would get out of here or die trying.

She pulled herself from the floor and grabbed the dress. Quickly she fixed herself up, noting that the dress fit perfectly.

"Of course," she thought.

After going to the bathroom to braid her hair, she

assessed the damage to her face. It was going to leave a mark. Her left cheek was already red and slightly swollen. But now wasn't the time to fret about it. The guard would be back soon.

She returned to the white room to wait. It didn't take long. Within a couple of minutes of sitting on the edge of the bed, the guard who had hit her returned. She didn't move when he entered the room. She didn't really have time to stand before he stalked across the room and grabbed her forcibly by the arm. He dragged her to her feet and pulled her after him. They were still treating her as if she were a disobedient 8-year-old child.

He moved her quickly down a bare hallway that had less distinction than her room. A short distance later, she was being pulled down a wide wooden staircase. From what little she had seen in the last twenty seconds, she already knew that this was a house of grandeur. But she didn't have long to ponder its size before she found herself being thrust into a dining room.

The room was of moderate size, the long twelve seat table set prominently in the center. Dark wood paneling adorned the room and the furniture was of a matching finish. The table was set for two with a full ensemble of wine glasses and multiple forks. The abusive guard assumed a position in front of that door. His stance foreboding, she had no intention of trying something. And as she assessed him, it didn't look like he was planning to budge or let her pass anytime soon.

Cautiously, she moved farther into the room. She had assumed that the crusty old man would be her dining companion. It seemed an obvious choice and her mind raced with the possibilities of what he would reveal, if anything. She was praying that she would finally get some insight into why she was brought there.

The crusty old man entered the dining hall a few minutes later. She was nervous when she saw him, wondering if she would find herself at the end of a fist again. He crossed the room and sat himself at the table without glancing at her. Once seated, he lifted his head to where she still stood. It didn't take a genius to interpret the look he gave her. His expression indicated she needed to sit and do exactly as she was told, immediately.

Slowly, she seated herself at the table and found the courage to look directly into his eyes. He didn't' blink or show any sign of weakness. In fact, he appeared amused by her. The left side of his mouth crinkled and he shrugged with a grunt. It was a game and he was the master at playing it.

He turned his attention to the kitchen staff, who had manifested from nowhere. With a nod of his head, the first course of soup was served. He ate in silence, sipping the broth. She watched until he motioned for her to begin. This was the first non-bland food she had had since her kidnapping. She had to admit to herself that it tasted delicious. She would have been able to somewhat enjoy it, but her jaw hurt to move from the blow she had taken earlier.

They dined in silence at first. He didn't even look at her. However, the arrival of the second course ushered the crusty old man to finally speak.

"You are comfortable, I trust," he asked.

Brianna was flabbergasted. He was asking if she was

comfortable. How would that be remotely possible? She was being held against her will.

"Actually, no," she wanted to replay, but she assumed he wasn't truly asking.

She was pretty sure the crusty old man was off his rocker, which made her more afraid of him. She kept her eyes on her food and took the safe route. She silently nodded. She didn't dare meet his eyes. She stayed focused on the food and cowered before him throughout the dinner.

He didn't say much else. He just periodically watched her, making her feel like a lab rat.

When the last course was taken away, she didn't dare move away from the table. She had hardly eaten any of the food. The knots in her stomach had prevented it. The crusty old man hadn't indicated he had noticed or cared. He merely grunted and nodded each time he finished his food to indicate the next course was to be served. The entire dinner consisted of grunts and head nods with very few words.

Brianna didn't raise her head once the dishes had been cleared. Her eye line stayed focused straight ahead. She felt the crusty old man's eyes boring into her. Yet, she refused to meet his gaze. It was the one bit of control she had had in more than a month. It was another act of defiance despite the fear that had motivated it.

A few moments later, she felt a tap on her left shoulder.

"Get up," the guard said sternly.

Slowly she began to push herself to her feet, never taking her eyes from the table. She moved with precision to command. This was, after all, the same guard that had hit her earlier and gave her what was sure to be her first black eye.

As she stood, the guard pulled her chair back and grabbed her by the back of her left arm. His grip was firm but not punishing. He guided her back to the white room.

She did not know if the crusty old man watched her leave. She suspected that he had.

5

AFTER

She had been asleep for a day. At least, it felt like it. She had slipped in and out of consciousness several times. But each time she opened her eyes, she felt like a bus had hit her. It had been incentive to go back to sleep.

When she finally managed to keep her eyes open, she was lost. She didn't know where she was anymore.

She knew she was in a bed. A soft bed with soft sheets, in a room that was filled with personal items. She wasn't at the house in the forest anymore, or worse, left to die in a rickety old shed.

One thing she did know was this room was the complete opposite to the white room. It was warm and inviting because of the clutter. There were books and magazines stacked on the bedside end tables. There were framed photos of landscapes on the walls. There were clothes on the sitting chair that appeared to be cast off, awaiting their destination in the dresser that flanked the chair. And then the dresser had more stacked books, a digital camera, some folded shirts, and other items that she couldn't determine from her position.

It looked like a home.

However, it wasn't the absence of sterile white walls or even the evidence of what appeared to be a life being lived. Rather it was the dog that had curled itself at the corner of the bed. A dog that had rarely left its spot during the duration of her slumber. Or during her half-slumber when she laid in the bed and wondered if she was going to die from the aftershock of pain her body was experiencing.

The dog was a comfort. She wasn't familiar with many dog breeds, but she was fairly certain this dog was a spaniel because she had watched Lady and the Tramp many times as a child. However, this spaniel was different from Lady because it was white with red-brown spots. It even had red freckles dotting its nose. The dog's eyes were big, dark, and sad. The classic "doggy eyes," which had conveyed a comfort and safety she hadn't been sure still existed. She had felt instant relief at its presence and devoted perch of guard.

The guy who had carried her from the forest was there too, off and on. He would come into the room to check on her. He left her water on the bedside table, he watched her silently as he petted the dog. He never seemed to linger long. However, she imagined he viewed her while she slept too.

His gaze was kind and unassuming. He had rarely spoken when he stepped in for his status checks, careful not to disturb her.

It wasn't until the fourth or fifth time he visited that he finally said something.

"How are you feeling?" he inquired.

His voice was as soft as she had remembered from when he had reassured her on the boat.

She didn't trust him though. She wasn't sure she would trust anyone ever again.

"I'm...fine," she struggled. Her voice felt raspy from nonuse.

He nodded slowly, disappearing for a few minutes to get her some more water. She sat up in the bed to drink it, slowly realizing how dry her throat was.

He shrugged his shoulders.

"I don't believe you, you know," he replied flatly.

His face showed compassion as he continued, "but for now...are you hurting anywhere, physically?"

She had been in pain so often over the last few months, she wondered if she had anywhere on her body that wasn't currently hurting. Pain had become a part of her life and she bore it. As she took stock now, she realized that physically her ankle throbbed and her shoulders burned.

"Yes. My right ankle for one. It hurts at little," she managed meekly.

Without hesitation, he reached toward her leg. Brianna revolted and scrambled up into a seated fetal position. Like a scared animal, this had become her normal state. Fear.

Seemingly realizing his error of moving too quickly, he held up his hands in the surrender.

"I am sorry. I should have warned you. And moved more slowly," he told her.

He quietly lowered his hands and eased one knee unto the bed.

"May I take a look at your ankle? I know you have no reason to trust me. I don't expect it. But...if your ankle hurts, maybe I can help you," he offered.

She considered what he had to say as he got closer. For some reason, her eyes darted toward the dog still resting on the corner of the bed. As if looking for some indication from an animal that this guy was good. She knew it seemed silly to look to his dog for reassurance. If anything, the dog was going to be loyal. To him. Yet, she found that the dog's calm demeanor was the thing to reassure her in that moment.

She met his gaze and slowly extended her right leg towards him. He, in turn, slowly eased his weight onto the bed and rested there, waiting. He kept eye contact with her the entire time and waited a little more to make sure it was okay for him to ease forward, to touch her.

Slowly, he nodded his head.

"I am going to feel of your ankle now," he warned.

And then he touched her. She flinched slightly, despite knowing what he intended to do. However, he didn't show signs of being offended. He simply began to evaluate her ankle, looking it over at different angles.

She could tell it was swollen by looking at it herself. The throbbing she felt was another indication of what she suspected. She had guessed it was sprained when it had happened and she knew exactly what had caused it.

She had done it to herself in a fool hearted attempt to escape the shed.

"When was the last time you walked on it?" he asked.

"I am not sure," she answered. "I know what I did to hurt it. But it could have been days ago or over a week. I lost track of reality in that shed. I am not sure how long I was there, so I am guessing. And truthfully, I wasn't really walking much in the end. There was nowhere to go and no energy to try. They stopped feeding me in there. I imagine that if you hadn't come when you did, I would have died eventually."

"Hmmm."

He continued assessing her without openly reacting to her statement. She wasn't positive he had heard her, or perhaps, he hadn't cared how close to death she had been.

"Well, I can't be sure without moving it. Would you be okay with me doing that?"

She considered it for a few seconds.

"I don't know... Who are you?"

He looked surprised at the timing of this question, as if he had deemed it unimportant anymore. He paused before responding.

"I'm John."

She gave him a skeptical expression, but she didn't remove her ankle from his grasp.

"Just John?" she asked firmly.

"What else would you like to know? I mean, do you need to know my life story before you let me help you?" he retorted.

She didn't have a response for him. What she did have were more questions, tons of them.

Who was he? Where was she? Was she truly as safe as he had said? Could he be trusted?

She wanted to ask these things. Instead she hesitated. She knew he could easily lie. Just as his name didn't have to be John. He could tell her anything and she wouldn't know if it was the truth.

Her mind was reeling. She needed to have some answers. She was determined to find out why this had happened to her. She had already planned to uncover the truth behind what she had seen in that house. He may not have all the information, but he obviously had some of it. He had found her, after all.

She decided she didn't have to know all the answers at that exact moment. She did, however, need to be cautious. After the things she had seen, the things she had experienced, she knew that vigilance could be the difference between life and death. And if he wasn't going to be forthcoming, then she couldn't trust this man until he had earned it.

He was still staring at her. Her permission to check out her injuries still pending. Yet, she said nothing else. Lowering her head, she nodded to indicate it was okay for him to proceed with his analysis.

He inched forward and began testing her flexibility and pain points by bending her ankle in different directions.

Finally, he spoke.

"I will explain everything in time. For now, you should know you are safe. I will help you."

She raised her head at that statement, meeting his gaze.

"And my name really is John," he repeated.

She was caught off guard. It was as if he had read her mind or had heard her internal dialogue that had questioned everything he had told her.

She nodded slowly to acknowledge his assertion, wearier now than before at his supposed mind reading abilities.

He merely returned to assessing her ankle briefly, before standing and abruptly leaving the room. When he returned a few moments later he had an elastic wrap with him.

"It does seem sprained. I am going to wrap it. Okay?" he explained.

"Okay," she uttered.

"You know, you can look at me. I promise that I won't hurt you."

"No. I don't know that," she accused.

They stared at each other for a moment, held in a deadlock that neither wanted to break. He swallowed hard and lowered his eyes first, giving her the victory for that moment.

He simply worked on his task of wrapping her joint without further words. It wasn't until he had the bandage firmly in place that he looked at her once again.

"Does anywhere else hurt?" he asked.

"Yes, there are several places...my right side. Every time I breathe, there is a pain. Why don't you just take me to the hospital?" she demanded.

He tried to hide his flinch, but she had immediately

noticed it.

"Well," he started.

"Well, what?" she countered, her defenses beginning to rise.

"I don't know if that is the best idea, given the circumstances," John replied.

He slowly got up from the bed and stood by the footboard, staring at her. "I will get you some food and think it over. And if I can figure something out, I will." he replied.

Brianna didn't have a chance to respond before he turned and left the room, closing the door behind him. She sat dumbfounded as fear began to creep in again.

"Why wouldn't he want to take me to the hospital? Unless...he has something to hide," she reasoned, silently to herself.

Her heart sank. It made perfect sense. How else could he have found her?

The house had been remote, buried in the forest. She imagined the shed in the woods had been the same, if not even more isolated. It seemed logical that this John wouldn't have known about the group by happenstance. Plus, they had kept her a secret for almost seven months.

Kidnapped. Restrained. Isolated. And then there were all the unexplained, weird things she had seen in that house. The portrait gallery she had found, by itself, was enough to haunt her for her entire life.

As she sat in the bed, it had just dawned on her that her rescue wasn't likely a rescue at all. He wasn't there to help her. She had merely been traded from one prison to another.

6

The dinner had been the beginning of Brianna's loosened constraints. After that night, she began to have limited freedoms.

Every day a new outfit arrived. It almost always seemed to be circa 1950s, but they were beautiful evening gowns. The strangeness of the dresses did not escape her notice. She had seen that the suits the guards wore and even the crusty old man's apparel was more modern.

She was being escorted to the dining room each evening where she was treated to a nice meal. And each morning and afternoon she received a small portion of food. Typically, it was some fruit and a muffin for breakfast and a cheese for a snack. It was stark difference to the bland food she had received when she was first there. She had wished it was a little more substantial, but she knew better than to complain.

She wasn't sure what to think of these changes. She

assumed they were trying to acclimate her to the environment.

Soon, she was surprised by one more small liberty. She had been sitting in the white room, bored when a guard abruptly entered. She jumped up from her spot on the floor so quickly that she struggled to gain her balance. The guard just stood in the doorway until she composed herself.

Once settled, he simply stated, "Follow me," and exited the room.

Dumbfounded, she obeyed and made her way out of the white room. Down the long corridor to the stairs, she followed the guard without speaking a word. He didn't speak either, reminding her that words didn't seem to be a currency in this place.

As they reached the stairway landing, the guard turned to lead down another hallway. She was finally getting a glimpse of how massive her prison really was. They passed several doors in the long hallway before they stopped at the fourth one on right. He opened the door and brought her into a study.

There were books everywhere. Encased in dark wood framed bookshelves, the walls were lined with texts. The books themselves were all hardcover and many seemed very old. There were two identical brown leather couches facing one another on the left side of the room, a coffee table located between them. On the right side of the room, was a large dark stained desk where the crusty old man was working.

Brianna didn't bask in the opportunity to spend more time with him. She secretly hoped it was just a summoning to inform her of something before she was quickly dismissed. She had rather been bored and alone in her white room prison than spend another moment with this man. She had found his company tedious, at best.

She looked to the guard and he motioned for her to be seated on one of the couches. With a prolonged sigh, she made her way to her leathered seat. As soon as she had settled, the guard was gone from the room.

"Lucky him," she thought with resignation.

Brianna didn't want to look at the crusty old man, but she found that it was very hard to avoid it, given the circumstances. She dared a glance to see that he was still sitting at his desk. He was focused on some papers in front of him without the slightest notice that she was in the room. After watching him for a few minutes, he reluctantly looked up at her with disdain.

"Yes?" he asked.

She was startled. Despite having enticed his speaking to her, she didn't have anything she wanted to say to him.

"Uh, is there something I should be doing?" she asked stupidly.

He motioned to the books on the shelves.

"Help yourself," he replied before he swiftly turned his attention back to his papers.

She raised up from her position on the couch and began perusing the choices. There were medical and anatomy books, and then science fiction, history, and philosophy. She saw a large selection of psychology texts.

The whole collection was to her, quite odd. She was baffled to no end. There had to be more than five thousand books in this study, but very few fiction or pieces that someone could read for enjoyment.

The medical and anatomy books were the most perplexing. She couldn't figure out why the crusty old man would have them. The reasons that occurred to her were chilling to the core. She knew these were not the books that normal people had, even educated. It was disconcerting and her mind began to wonder why and how they were referenced.

She had been standing there for several minutes, contemplating. She had felt the crusty old man's stare on her back the entire time. She turned to see that he was, indeed, watching her.

He said nothing, just gave her a stoic glare. So Brianna quickly grabbed a book without looking and sat back on the couch.

She had picked an analysis of the human psyche and the effects that manipulation had on the mind.

"How appropriate. I can learn what being held captive here is going to do to me in the long term," she thought, sarcastically.

She looked again at the crusty old man and it didn't seem that he had any intentions for her other than witnessing him work. She didn't dare to attempt a conversation or interrupt. She also figured that finding a different book would be met with contempt. Thus, she found herself turning the pages of the text, trying to read some of the passages without avail.

She had begun to wonder the point of bringing her to the study. Not that she was complaining anymore since it gave her more objects to analyze. She guessed that this trip to the study would stem the boredom she felt on a daily basis, at least for a day or two.

After what seemed an eternity, the guard re-entered the room. She anticipated this was her cue to leave. She stood, but was motioned back down. The crusty old man walked over to sit on the couch opposite of her. He stared at her for a very long minute before finally speaking.

"This was a test, my dear," he rasped. "You have passed. This obedience will allow you some additional freedoms."

As he spoke, he motioned to the guard to come forward. On command, he crossed the room to a position that was hovering over her. If she hadn't already been intimidated by his presence from her previous experiences, she would have been now.

"If you abuse these freedoms, they will be taken away without hesitation," the crusty old man continued.

He motioned to the guard and her attention was drawn to the object he was holding in his hands. Unexpectedly, the guard kneeled to the floor and grasped her right ankle firmly. She felt a slight weight as a band was strapped around her leg.

The guard stood and stepped backward as she began to examine the device. It was a black strap with a small box attached. It appeared to be an ankle monitor like what was used on criminals in house arrests. She was certain there wasn't going to be a way to remove it.

"My dear, if you venture beyond your parameters, this will dislodge a painful shock. It can be quite debilitating. I have seen grown men cry. I don't recommend you test it. And if by some stroke of luck, you are still able to move your body past that shock, you should know that it is also GPS enabled. We will come after you," the crusty old man informed her.

Brianna wasn't surprised that they would have an ankle monitor with GPS enabled. She was more shocked that she was being given this supposed increase in freedom.

If her count was correct, she had been in this nightmare for approximately six weeks. For the first month, there had been no contact at all. And now, she was being given freedom to roam.

She assumed it had to be a trap. Even as the guard was strapping the device to her, she had been waiting for the carpet to be ripped out from under her feet. She also knew that she would test the limits of this monitor the first chance she got. Shock or no shock, despite all that she had endured, she hadn't even begun to give up hope of escape. This development just solidified her plan to get out or die trying.

With the crusty old man's nod, the guard gestured for her to follow him out. It was clear that if she was going to be given access to roam, it didn't start immediately. The guard herded her back to her room where a new dress for the evening was already waiting.

"You have thirty minutes. Be downstairs on time," he said before abruptly exiting.

So she was responsible for getting herself to the dining room. If she was receiving some leeway, it didn't include skipping her nightly meals with the boss.

Either way, she was anxious to start testing the limits. She dressed in a hurry, making herself presentable within ten minutes. If she were truly on point with her timing, she expected to have a good twenty minutes to explore uninhibited.

"You just can't get lost!" she reminded herself.

Cautiously she turned the knob to the white room door and peered into the hallway. It was completely empty and quiet. As she eased out of the room, she started looking to the ceiling for cameras. She didn't see any evidence of them, or at least they weren't visible to her.

She crept down the hallway. She moved so slowly, she had begun to worry that she had spent five of her twenty minutes to go thirty feet. She told herself to just make haste and get down those stairs to explore while she still had the opportunity. Knowledge of this house was the only way she would make a formable escape. Her life depended on it.

Once she as at the stairway landing, she had to decide as to which direction to go. She knew that if she continued straight, she would head towards the dining room and what she believed was the front of the house. If she turned to the right, she would be back in the long hallway with infinite doors, one of which led to the book-filled study. The only other option was a singular door on her left.

She realized that she needed as many chances as she could get to map out the floor plan. She would need more than the twelve minutes she had left. She desperately wanted to explore, but it was a better decision if she paced herself. Otherwise, she might get caught, effectively ruining her plan.

She chose the door to the left because of proximity, praying that this first choice wouldn't cost her. Her hand shook as she turned the knob to the door.

"Pull off the Band-Aid, Brianna!" she reprimanded herself.

She fumbled for a light switch in the darkened room. Quickly flipping it upon discovery, the light was so bright that she saw colors distorting her vision. For a full minute, she was disoriented about what the illumination was revealing.

A bathroom.

"Damn!" she cursed before realizing that was audible

She knew she may have just given her position away. Although it had occurred to her that they were monitoring her every move anyway. Like a mouse in a maze, she was betting that the GPS technology on the ankle monitor had already been switched on.

Regardless, she did a quick scan of the bathroom to see if there was anything of interest. It looked to be a non-significant washroom, so she quickly exited.

As she made her way back to the main hallway, she debated the options. She could keep exploring to find a more interesting room or she could go on to the dining hall. If she were late to the dinner, she could blame her tardiness on being unguided. But she would probably end up with a guard again with that excuse. It was a gamble.

She decided to not risk getting assigned a guide. It was the best bet.

When she entered the dining room, it was empty. The table was set and she seated herself in her usual chair.

"My usual chair?" she caught herself.

She didn't want anything to become habitual.

"This will not be my life!" she resounded in her head.

Patiently, she sat and waited. The time didn't pass any faster without the presence of looming guards, she realized.

When the crusty old man finally appeared, she noted that he was acting almost jolly. It scared her. He had never expressed any emotion besides the occasional contempt. She wasn't sure what she should make of this new attitude, other than it was truly terrifying. She was also determined she wasn't going to ask.

But the dinner passed as it had before, very little talking and a lot of staring. She was relieved when he gave her permission to excuse herself. Except this time, she was shadowed upon her trip back to the white room. Given the escort, she was paranoid that they were aware of her little detour before dinner.

It made her anxious, but she knew she had to keep trying to find a way out. She would just have to be smarter about it. As she laid in bed, she formulated a plan. She would continue to test the boundaries and collect information. At night, as the house was asleep, she would expand her search.

There was a way out of this place. She was sure of it. Just as she was certain that she would find it.

7

Brianna had been reviewing her current situation when John returned to the room a few hours later. He startled her when he barged in and, without pause, sat beside her on the bed. She wasn't comfortable with that level of familiarity, particularly when she believed he may not be as trustworthy as he had claimed to be.

It kept replaying her mind. Why hadn't he taken her to a hospital? Or notified the authorities? Why was he hiding her?

She was still tired and very confused. He had carried her out of the forest, rescuing her from the crusty old man and his band of goons. Only to hide her away in a dingy little apartment? It didn't add up.

"I will take you to the doctor's clinic in a few minutes. First, I want to explain myself," he started.

Once again, he was anticipating her doubts. Or she

had become transparent in her thinking. Either way, it was setting off her alarm bells.

"I realize it probably appeared cryptic that I was tending to you myself and not taking you to the hospital," he continued.

"You think?" she thought.

However, she remained quiet. She had learned that you find out more if you wait and don't respond too quickly. It was better to let a person lead than react prematurely and change what they had planned to say.

"I was hesitating for two reasons... First, we aren't in America and the quality of healthcare is a little sporadic here, at best. Second and more importantly, I don't know if they are looking for you. I suspect they are," he said.

This information had her sitting up straighter in the bed. The idea that the crusty old man was still after her made her eyes water and her body shake.

She nodded slowly and chose her response carefully. She wanted to ask the right questions, ones that would appear innocent enough to garner an answer. The type of questions that would get him to believe she was naïve and weak. It was a ploy, but she hoped he might reveal more to her than he intended if she got his guard down.

"Where exactly are we?" she simply asked.

"Right, sorry. You wouldn't have known. Right now, we are in the Hale Islands. I am hoping to get us to Australia soon. It is safer there. But it is also difficult to arrange our escape at the moment. They have people watching everywhere here, so we have to be careful," he replied.

"The Hale Islands?" she probed.

"Yes, what about them?"

"I have never heard of them. Australia, sure. But exactly how far away from Australia or larger civilizations are we?" she inquired.

"Brisbane is just a few hours flight away. These islands don't have many inhabitants, but they do get some tourists now, at the resorts. The very rich come here to play. There are a handful of indigenous peoples, mostly Polynesian descent. And no offense, but you would stand out."

"Like I said, I am not sure who is watching. The people who took you have a lot of influence here. It is what a lot of money can buy you these days. You get all the privacy and security you want. No one asks questions about your motives. Money allows you to do whatever nefarious things your heart desires," he described.

She debated then if she should ask what she really wanted to know. He had seemed open so far about where they were, so maybe he would tell her more.

"Who is he exactly?" she blurted.

"Who?"

His confusion apparent from his bewildered expression.

"The man who kidnapped me."

"Christ, you don't know! What exactly do you know about where you have been the last seven months?" he inquired.

"Not much," she confessed.

She had been so focused on survival, she hadn't yet begun to process everything that had happened to her. It wasn't that she couldn't remember. Despite wanting to block out the majority of the events of the past year, it was seared into her brain forever. It was just that the crusty old man had guarded information well. Even though she had repeatedly tried, she had found out very little of their operation at the house.

She was aware she would need to sort it all out, eventually. But now wasn't the time for it. She wasn't ready to think about it. She also wasn't ready to give him what little information she did have, even if he could help her make sense of it.

He interrupted her thoughts with an audible sigh.

"Right. Well, let's get you to the doctor. I was going to carry you...or you can hobble, if you prefer. You looked ready to jump out of your skin the last time I sat down so...it is cool if you want to walk on your own," he said.

"Yeah, I can manage alone," she stated defiantly.

"I figured you would say that," he smiled.

He stood and stepped back from the bed. Still gazing at her, he motioned to indicate he would follow after her.

She gathered her strength and scooted to the edge of the bed. Pausing only briefly to take a deep breath for strength, she made quick work of standing on her own two feet. The pressure from her body weight made her ankle throb harder, making her wince at the first touch with the ground.

Ignoring the pain, she hobbled to the door frame. She didn't look at him as she passed, although she knew he was scrutinizing her every movement. She put all her attention into moving her body. But she didn't bother to hide the grimacing she felt as pain radiated up her leg.

Even with the wrap, it hurt like hell with the slightest step.

He said nothing as they made their way out of the bedroom and into an open living space.

She did a quick look of the place, making snap judgements about how sparsely it was decorated. There wasn't the minimalist feeling to the decor. It was the lack of personal effects and the type of furniture used which gave her the impression this place wasn't often lived in or visited.

"This way," he directed as he opened the door to the apartment's hallway.

They entered a dimly lit hallway that was reminiscent of "old timey" hotels. It reminded her of old horror movies with its flickering, low lighting and the dark, dirtied walls, which hadn't seen paint in decades. She gazed at the floor and saw old shag carpeting that was at a minimum of two decades past needing to be replaced.

She just then realized she was barefoot. It occurred to her that hopping to the car may not be the best at avoiding any glass or any sharp objects on the ground. Given the looks of this rundown building, she was likely to encounter issues.

"Could you carry me to the car?" she asked him, embarrassed.

"If you look at me when you ask," he said curtly.

She raised her head and looked directly into his eyes. She was struck by the fact that these were the same kind eyes that she had thought she had dreamed up when they had met a few days ago. A day she recalled him carrying her away from her actual living nightmare. She may not be able to completely trust him, but he had been her hero. So, she had to at least try.

"Will you carry me to the car?" she asked again.

"Of course."

He closed and locked the door behind them. Then without fanfare, he swept her up into his arms. As if she weighed nothing, he began the trek down the hallway.

When they emerged to an almost vacant parking lot, she noticed his demeanor had changed. He instantly became more guarded as they made their way to his car. Still cradled in his arms, he pulled her closer to his chest as he moved towards the parked vehicles. She saw his eyes darting in every direction, surveying the area for danger. His focus was razor sharp, yet there wasn't a soul in sight.

He drove an old sedan that matched the hotel's décor. It was extremely outdated and looked like it was from the 1950s. As she looked around the lot, she noted that there were a lot of these older cars. Given the scenery, she thought this place may be like Cuba where things haven't changed in decades because of the restrictions on growth. It was a time warp.

He quickly dropped her into the front passenger seat and ran around to the driver's seat. They had pulled out of the parking lot and were making their way down the road before she could blink. The increased sense of urgency was making her nervous.

She soon rebuked the thought of Cuba when they passed more modern facilities and cars. In fact, it seemed the opposite as they got further away from John's place.

It was dusk and the views as they drove along the

coast were breathtaking. The surf crashed onto the sand in a hypnotic rhythm. The sky was painted with lilac and pink hues. The tree leaves were rustling in the soft breeze. If it had not been for her situation of being kidnapped or not being sure whether she could trust her current companion, she would have considered this paradise.

They arrived at a clinic a few minutes later. The parking lot was sparse of cars here too. They entered through a side door and were ushered down a hallway to an exam room by a man in a white lab coat. There didn't seem to be any other staff in the building, so she figured it must be after hours.

John confirmed her suspicions when he said, "We couldn't take the chance of coming here during normal hours. I called in a favor. This doctor can be trusted."

"But can you?" she continued to wonder to herself.

They waited silently in an exam room for a few minutes, occasionally exchanging looks between them. The awkwardness was growing with each passing second. It was a relief when the man in the lab coat finally entered the room, greeting John with a half hug. She had already assumed they were friends.

"Hey mate! Good to see you," he addressed John.

He was a friendly looking fellow with a bright smile. He was tall with dark skin, dark hair, and dark eyes. She assumed he was of Polynesian descent given his coloring.

"How is it going?" he directed his question to John.

"It is as you see," John responded and motioned toward Brianna.

She sat silently on the patient table. Staring down at

her feet, she realized she still wore the white pajamas from her captivity. Although they were more brownish from all the dirt. It was awkward and embarrassing to her, but she wasn't sure why it bothered her.

The doctor approached her and waited for her to raise her head to look at him.

She had been doing this a lot recently. She didn't look people in the eye anymore. She was gun shy and, at the moment, slightly mortified at her appearance. She wasn't sure why it mattered. The man was a doctor, he was there to help her. He didn't care what she was wearing or how horrid she must appear. After all the horrible things she had experienced, all the pain, her hygiene didn't matter.

When she did look back at him, he smiled.

"We are going to get you looked after. Is it okay for me to examine you now?"

"Yes," she mustered.

With her consent, he began his exam of her. Directing her with his hands when he needed her to do something. He checked her heart rate and pulse first, followed by checking her blood pressure and listening to her lungs. Then he unwrapped her ankle and repeated many of the flexibility checks that John had performed.

"Would you mind undressing so I can check you for additional injuries?" he asked.

Still bashful, she nodded her head. She didn't move an inch. She just stared at John the entire time, ignoring what the physician was doing.

"I will excuse myself then. I will be just outside," John stated before abruptly exiting mid-exam.

Left alone, the doctor continued his exam without

interruption. He sighed frequently as he assessed the cuts and bruises on her chest and abdomen that had previously been hidden by the pajamas. Yet, he made no comment and asked zero questions about how she got them. After he had finished a minute later, he instructed her to dress and then stepped out of the room without giving her another glance.

He was gone for a solid ten minutes before he returned to the room with John. A move that made Brianna's anxiety sky rocket. She was immediately suspicious.

"Brianna?" the doctor addressed her.

"Yes," she responded.

"I don't know the particulars of the situation you found yourself in, but there has been significant abuse to your body. It appears that not only were you malnourished but you had...well, some recent trauma to your body. There are definite signs of abuse," he paused, waiting for her reaction.

She stared at him, not confirming or denying anything.

"Is that correct?" he quietly asked.

She nodded, but she didn't feel the need to elaborate further. At least, not with him.

He looked at John.

"It is like I said. Her body is covered in cuts and bruises. She likely has broken ribs and other fractures." He turned his attention to Brianna. "I can't be sure without x-rays, obviously. You should go to the hospital."

John shrugged.

"Well, I am not sure that is possible right now. Is there

anything that you think that will keep her from healing or, maybe could prohibit her from flying?" he interjected.

That statement piqued her interest for several reasons. There was a mix of fear and hope.

The idea of getting off the island had its appeal. The only hesitation was whether he would take her to someplace better, somewhere she could start to get her life back.

"I wouldn't recommend a long flight," the doctor stated.

"How about to Brisbane or Sydney? I would prefer to take her to the hospital there." John suggested.

"That should be fine, but I would recommend that she go sooner than later. Just make sure she gets some x-rays," the doctor responded.

"Great, thanks! We will leave in a few days when things cool down a bit," John said.

She was about to ask questions when John held up his hand to silence her, like quieting an unruly child.

The doctor nodded.

"As long as you don't wait too long. Take care of yourself, young lady."

After the doctor had left, she started to protest when he silenced her again with his hand. A gesture that she definitely didn't like.

"We are leaving tonight. I didn't want the doctor to know on the off chance that they are looking for us and that information accidentally got shared. It is a risk either way, but the sooner we get out of these islands, the better. For you," he added.

"You think your friend will tell them?"

"He isn't really what I would call a friend. And, no. I don't think he will say anything," he told her.

The idea of getting to Australia excited her to no end. It was a majorly developed country and there would be a chance she could be truly free from the horrors she wished to forget. It also meant the opportunity to report the people who took her. It was a step in the right direction.

She still didn't know if she should trust John. If anything, she had more doubts after the doctor's visit than she did before it. He treated the doctor as a friend but claimed they weren't. They had disappeared for ten minutes. He was postponing her going to real hospital and interacting with more people. She had no idea what the doctor and him had discussed behind her back. And he had shushed her. There were some things that were too suspect.

On the other hand, she couldn't dismiss the fact that he was actively working to get her away from the islands, to save her.

Time would tell if he turned out to be who he said he was. If not, then she would need to be prepared to make a break for it. Alone. But for now, he was her best bet.

She decided just then she would remain stoic and focused on her survival at whatever means were necessary.

"The sooner, the better," she smiled slightly at him and replied. "I'm ready now."

8

BEFORE

The days passed more quickly once she was plotting. She had decided her best chance was to take her exploration slowly. Unless, of course, something occurred to threaten her new limited freedom, she would do it in stages.

She spent the next few days in the white room, running through possible scenarios and escape plans. The only problem was that until she explored, it was all speculation. She needed real intel.

On the first morning after her ankle monitor was attached, she started small. She traveled the hallways by her room, looking for guards. She didn't dare venture downstairs at first. In fact, she didn't travel greater than 100 feet from the white room door.

Every time she investigated, she was met with nothingness. Even as she journeyed farther into the house, she never saw any guards. The only time she met with another human being was around meal times. It was the sole occasion she had encountered people.

Each morning, she was awakened to the delivery of a small breakfast. At noon, a guard would still bring a lunch tray and then disappear. At five o'clock, the guard would now come to the white room to give her a dress and the thirty-minute warning. She would descend to the dining room and the dinner would start at 5:30 p.m. on the dot.

Her schedule ran like clockwork.

For several days, she learned the patterns of the house. Once the food had arrived, she would immediately peek into the hallway to see if the guards lingered. Delightfully, they didn't.

On her journeys to the dining room, she searched every corner and never saw evidence of surveillance. She knew there were people in this house, but she also never saw them going about their business. When she did see the staff, they were always quick about their work and showed no emotion, at least not for her or her situation.

After she witnessed a week of no deviations from their routines, she decided today would be when she tested the waters. She was going to take a risk to head downstairs.

She eased out of her room about ten minutes after the lunch tray was delivered. She had decided to wait for the longer time window so she could explore a little longer.

The upstairs hallways had been predictably quiet. She walked slowly and as silently as possible, listening for any possible indication that someone was coming. She heard none.

Within a minute, she had already reached the stairs and was making her way down them. She grimaced as the floorboards creaked beneath her bare feet. But she would not be deterred. When she finally reached the landing, she exhaled the breath she had been holding as she descended from upstairs.

Now, she had the decision of which way to turn.

She opted for the hallway of doors, toward the study. She knew it was a gamble. She was more likely to run into the guards, or worse, the crusty old man. But it had more possibilities and something had compelled her towards that hallway. It felt more forbidden.

As she gazed down at the row of closed, wooden doors, it felt like a game somehow.

"See what is behind Door Number Two, Brianna!" she announced in her head.

"Stop being so ridiculous," she whispered to herself as she crept forward.

She wandered slowly down the corridor, not sure where to begin. She grabbed the first knob she saw and turned it. Slowly the door slid open and she stepped inside. Darkness engulfed her.

Entering a dark, strange room wasn't something she felt overly comfortable doing given her circumstances. She had watched enough horror movies to know it was a stupid move. In this case, however, she felt it was prudent.

She didn't want to draw attention to herself. If she could help it, she didn't plan to turn on the light. She inched her body forward and prayed her eyes adjusted.

Luckily, they did within a few minutes and she could see where she was.

It was a bedroom. She made out the outlines of the furniture, including two beds. What was strange is there didn't seem to be any visible windows. A bedroom without light seemed even more like a prison than her own upstairs. She counted her blessings that she had not been placed in this room instead of the white one.

Although, maybe having a view of the scenery was worse. It was a reminder of what she couldn't have. The ultimate tease.

She took a step further into the room and noted how small it was. The furniture was Unitarian. There weren't any dressers for clothes either. She was concluding that this room was for "on the job" sleeping. It was functional and wasn't intended to be a space anyone lived in. She imagined this was where the guards or servants could nap. In which case, she was damn lucky she didn't wake any of the staff when she stumbled in.

As soon as the thought had dawned on her, she made a beeline back to the door. If this was the place for napping, she was betting the odds of getting caught had multiplied exponentially every second since she had crossed the threshold.

She made a quick exit from the room and headed further down the hallway, stopping just one short of the study door on the right.

Although there was nothing special about it. She had a gut feeling that she should choose this door. She eased toward it and listened for movement. Nothing. Complete silence.

"Or the doors are thick enough to block sound," she thought.

Just as before, she hesitated slightly before turning the knob. But it was now or never. She slipped inside quickly and closed the door behind her.

This room wasn't pitch black because there were four floor to ceiling windows letting light in. It was long and narrow, easily the size of a football field. She noticed that she had entered on the far-left side and there was another door mirroring it on the far-right. The room was filled with paintings and appeared to be some sort of an art gallery. Intrigued, she approached one of the paintings closest to her to take a closer look.

She blanched at the sight of it.

"It's me!" she exclaimed, horrified.

It was an old oil on canvas, circa another century. And it depicted the portrait of a woman who matched her likeness in every way. The only caveat was the wardrobe appeared to be from the mid 1800s.

She didn't understand. She stared, dumbfounded. She was paralyzed for what felt like an eternity. How was it possible they had a painting of a woman who could have easily been her twin?

She moved to the next painting, hoping it might provide some insight.

At the first look at this one, she simultaneously felt numb and nauseated. It also was a depiction of her likeness, only this woman was in an outfit that looked to be from the 1600s.

"What the hell is this?" she said aloud.

She was becoming frantic. She rapidly walked to each

of the paintings in the room. To her horror, she
discovered they were all women who looked exactly like
her. Each from a different period. The most recent one
seemed to be a framed photograph from the 1950s.

She wasn't sure what the oldest one was, but it
seemed to be from a time period before the United States
had existed. There were at least twenty portraits in total.

She had stumbled into a gallery of Doppelgängers.

Now, more than ever, she was confused and scared.

On the bright side, she had guessed this was likely the
reason she had been taken in the first place. Her
resemblance to these women was the why.

She had thought that knowing the reason she was
here would have comforted her. Plus, she had believed if
she could figure it out, perhaps it could help her escape.
Her realization did the opposite to her hopes. She knew
without doubt that she was in over her head. She knew it
was not a mistake she was here and that getting out was
going to be a formidable challenge.

A panic began to rise within her. It felt as if her skin
could not contain her. Her heart was palpitating, her
head was faint, and her breath was shallow. She ran from
the room as fast as she could. She didn't think of anything
except for one thought.

"Get out now!" she recited in her head

She reached the landing of the stairs, but she didn't
run up them to return to the white room. Instead she
turned and headed towards the dining room, believing it
was near the front of the house. An assumption that
turned out to be correct when she found the front door a
few seconds later.

She fumbled with the doorknob, a task made more difficult from the tears streaming down her face. She kept pulling and turning at the knob before realizing that the door was locked. Quickly finding the deadbolt, she snapped the level in the opposite direction and tried the knob again. The door swung open and she was flooded by fading daylight and the smell of fresh air.

"You don't have time for this! Just get out!" she said to herself as she hurled herself across the front porch and down the stairs leading to the front drive.

Stopping only for a moment to gather her bearings about her surroundings, she hurriedly decided to run for the woods that surrounded the house. Her hope was that she could get lost in the forest. She prayed for the trees to give her protection long enough to determine a game plan.

She took off in a sprint, not bothering to waste time looking behind her.

She didn't see the guards on her heels. She didn't know that they were close enough in proximity to tackle her. She didn't know that her attempts had been thwarted, by herself. She just felt the pain rushing through her body as it was pounded into the ground a few moments later.

9

AFTER

The ride from the doctor's office was quiet. John seemed to be deep in thought, hopefully planning their departure for Australia. The thought of escaping to a modernized country or just a place she had heard of before, was greatly appealing. She dared to hope that she could find help because the recent series of events had her questioning John's motives. She thought that, just maybe, he was one of the good guys and he was truly there to help her. It was too early to tell. She had to keep her defenses up until she could be certain.

Her highest priority was to get to a more populated area. After that, she planned to ask him a lot of questions, starting with how he had found her in the woods. She may have been delirious at the time, but she had still been aware that her location was very remote. It wasn't plausible that he had just happened upon her in the middle of nowhere. He had to have known about it. Or he had somehow discovered it upon investigating her disappearance from society. He unquestionably knew more than he was saying.

She gazed at him as he drove back to his apartment. He was impossible to read. Despite the appearance of openness, she had already deemed him to be secretive. He had an easiness about him that suggested she could ask him anything. The only issue was she couldn't be sure the response would be honest and forthcoming.

He could also teach a class on how to be stoic. He had the best poker face she had ever seen. His face revealed absolutely nothing about what he was thinking. The few times their eyes had met, he hadn't betrayed his feelings that way either. Those green irises were not the windows to his soul.

He was guarded. A sentiment that she could understand, but one that made her even more cautious and slow to warm up to him. But for now, he remained the best possibility for freedom. After all, he had kept her safe for at least 48 hours.

It was a start.

She shook her head. Her life had been reduced to an hourly rate for survival, which was an actual improvement in her situation. She didn't dare to dream too much of the future yet. Her hopes rested in escaping the reaches of the people who had kidnapped her. That had to be her only focus going forward.

She turned her attention to the road in front of them. The peaceful scenery increasing her mind's tendency to wander. Within minutes, it became easier to push any creeping uncertainties aside. She believed that was the effects of being surrounded by a beautiful landscape.

She was so distracted she didn't immediately notice they were pulling into the apartment's parking lot.

"Stay here. I won't be more than a few minutes. I just need to grab a few things. If you see anyone, and I mean anyone, duck down... Actually, maybe you should duck down anyway. I won't be long," he said.

He didn't give her a chance to dispute his instructions. He jumped out the car and took off at a sprint for the complex's entrance.

"Sure. No problem. I love being ordered around," she said sarcastically to herself.

Nonetheless, she ducked down into the seat as he had suggested and listened to the silence that was engulfing the car. As she waited, his warning had increased her awareness, or her paranoia, tenfold. She heard the beating of her heart, the shallowness of her breathing, the ticking of the engine as it cooled, and the wind of the cars passing on the nearby street.

It felt like four hundred forevers before the pounding of the car trunk slamming shut forced her to jump out of her skin. She perked up from her hiding spot to investigate, like a prey sticking its head into the waiting mouth of its predator. When John hopped into the front seat a few seconds later, she nearly wet herself. He paused to look at her awkwardly cowered in the floorboard, almost trembling with fear.

"It is okay now, you know? I told you. I will keep you safe," he soothed.

He didn't wait for her to agree. He already had the car

rolling before she could even crawl back into the
front seat.

After they were moving steady again, he started to fill
her in on his plan.

"So, here is what I am thinking," he began. "I think
our best option is to pretend we were tourists who were
here on holiday... But to pull that off, we will need some
new clothes, especially you. You can't exactly parade
around in dirty pajamas and avoid notice. So, we will go
to the market and pick up some beach looking attire. We
don't want to arouse any suspension, so we must be
careful to try to blend into the crowds. After we are
finished at the store, I will get us setup for a flight out. I
think we will be off the islands in no time."

"What about the dog?" she asked, remembering her
bed companion over the last few days.

"What about him? He isn't mine," he informed her.

She was exceedingly confused.

"Who does he belong to then?"

He looked at her, raising an eyebrow.

"The neighbors. Why?" he responded, acting
somewhat dumbfounded at her question.

"No reason," she indicated as she turned her attention
back to their route, effectively ending the discussion.

She has assumed the dog was his. It seemed a little
odd to have a dog spending so much time at your place
when it wasn't yours, especially if you weren't around
very often.

She had gotten the impression that the apartment
was transient. The dog had acted as if it was at home and
John was its master.

How did he know the neighbors well enough that their dog logged several hours of mattress time at his place? And why did the pup obey his commands and act attached to him?

It was also curious that a dog belonged to the supposed neighbors. She hadn't seen or heard any signs of life at that apartment building. It had seemed as if they were all alone there.

It didn't quite add up.

However, her perplexity over the matter was interrupted because the trip to get clothes turned out to be a short one. They had pulled into a nondescript parking lot across from an open-air market. It was packed with people, many who appeared to be tourists taking advantage of the shopping.

"It is probably best if we stay together and make this as quick as possible," he indicated.

He had extracted her from the car, grabbed her hand, and pulled her across the road and into a sea of carts filled with produce before she could process what was happening.

The brightness of the fruit and vegetables was overwhelmingly beautiful. The business of the market drowned out any of her worries as people came and went. Everyone was immersed in their own world and didn't give them a first glance.

He began to weave quickly between the people, literally dragging her behind him. She winced loudly from her hurt ankle. Her body wasn't ready to move so quickly. Upon hearing her pain, he stopped and realized that she couldn't maneuver as fast as he had wanted.

Eyes wide at his error, he leaned in and whispered in her ear.

"I am so sorry. I forgot. Are you good to keep going?"

The new proximity of him had created an intimacy that was making her self-conscious. She wasn't comfortable with him being that close. His hot breath on her neck had made her shutter.

"Not at that speed. But I am okay to continue if you go slower," she whispered back.

He smiled briefly and nodded. He led her farther into the open market. His ease at dodging people mulling around was impressive. He was in complete control.

They soon arrived at a store with racks of beach wear, mostly flowery dresses and big, floppy hats. It was amazing that the "beach" style seemed to be universal or at least common to the tourists' spots around the world.

He began flipping through hangers and smirking every so often. She thought had he been her boyfriend, this would have been an amusing sight. The attention he gave to a rack of dresses was comical. Especially since she had determined very little differences between them besides their color. He, however, genuinely seemed disgusted one minute and bemused the next.

He looked back at her watching him and asked, "What size do you wear?"

"It doesn't matter," she answered.

"Of course it does! We have to get you something that fits," he defended.

"They will all fit. They are one-size fits all. Wrap dresses," she told him, smiling for the first time.

"Oh," he said, slightly deflated. "What do you like then? How about this one?"

He held up a purple flowering dress with black spaghetti straps. It seemed to be the sort of dress that no matter how you tied it, it would be revealing.

She wasn't too keen on the open back and plunging neckline that the dress he picked would entail. So, she pointed to a different one with a little more fabric.

"That green one will do," she said.

He shrugged before he grabbed the green patterned dress and started looking around the store at other items.

"We should get you a hat and sunglasses too," he said, nonchalantly.

He walked over to the sunglasses rack and began perusing the shades.

Brianna followed him and watched as he tried different shades on himself and browsing like any other tourist. She had to admit he looked good in all of them.

She looked at him then, truly seeing him for the first time. She had noticed that he was good looking before, a striking figure that wouldn't be ignored. Now she began to focus on the bone structure that would lend itself well to be a male model. He was a sight that could take her breath away had they met under different circumstances.

He settled on a pair of brown tinted aviator shades and handed her a similar pair to try. With a nod of his head, he turned and started looking through a rack of men's shirts that were equally as flowery as the patterned dresses.

She never understood why men wore these shirts, but

for some reason she thought that John would change her mind. She had a feeling he would make even those shirts look good.

She noted then he wasn't watching her. She could slip out of the store and find her own freedom at any time. However, the fact that he was not eyeing her spoke to his confidence that she would stay. He believed they had coupled up to him for the duration of his plan.

He wasn't wrong. Although she had decided that she should begin formulating a contingency plan. She needed to have an out ready, just in case. She was beginning to see more of who John was, but she was very weary. There was also the fact that if they got caught by the crusty old man and his army of goons, John may not be capable of protecting her. She needed to think of all the possibilities and be prepared for them.

Resolved, she picked out a pair of glasses and quickly found a sunhat as well. She brought them over to John who was mulling over a hideous pink patterned shirt. He appeared to be indecisive when it came to selecting his own clothing as well. She considered him one of those people who looked good in everything, so she wasn't sure what he was fretting over. As she handed him the sunglasses and hat, she motioned to the cashier to indicate they should go.

"Yeah, you're right," he said with a sigh and made his way over to the counter to pay for their items.

They exited the store moments later. As they made their way down the row of carts, he grabbed her hand and held firm. Without asking, he intertwined his fingers into hers and then gave her palm a squeeze. She didn't fight him on it despite the fact her heart was racing.

He led her further out of the market and they were on their way back to the car within minutes. There would be no idling today.

As they made their way back, he never once let go of her hand. Every few seconds, he gazed over his shoulder to assess how she was making it. It was these little moments of concern that was building her faith that John was the good guy she had hoped.

"How about you change in the car and I will change behind it," John said before he popped the trunk open and went to do just that.

Anxious to get out of the pajamas, she eagerly complied with his request. She quickly changed behind the passenger side door, wrapping the dress in a classic halter top tie. She slapped on the sunglasses and hat to finish the ensemble. Noticing herself in the side mirror, she checked to make sure her cut and bruises weren't visible. Luckily, she had chosen a dress style that hid the majority of her injuries unless you were looking closely for them.

She had to admit that the dress looked somewhat good on her despite her decreased weight. She actually did appear like she had been on vacation and was at leisure with her boyfriend. The effect of the new attire was so convincing that she almost believed it herself, momentarily.

After changing, she hopped into the car where John sat waiting. When she got back into the car, their eyes met.

He smiled.

"You look good in that," he said.

"Thank you," she said and held his gaze.

His smile widened and he nodded his chivalrous head. He pulled out his phone and began typing away, looking for available flights to Brisbane, she assumed. She sat and waited, the anxiety starting to subside a little. It took a few minutes before he said anything about his search results.

"We have a flight in a few hours. It is all set," he informed her.

She felt a glimmer of hope that she would soon be free of this island and in a country she could navigate better. Yet, she reminded herself to not get too excited because she had been disappointed in the past. This attempt, however, was becoming the closest she had gotten to her restored independence.

"Success!" he exclaimed and smiled brightly at her. She smiled back.

"Do we go to the airport now?" she asked.

"Yes, I think we do. It is a risk. Someone may spot us but that is a possibility of just sitting here too," he replied.

"Ah okay," she commented.

They drove past the town on their way to the airport. She gazed out the window and took the opportunity to get a good view of it. The streets were lined with small square buildings painted in assorted bright colors. It gave the place a coastal feeling that matched with the landscape. She guessed it had been exaggerated for the tourists, much the same way that other tropical paradises had been. It was quaint, having a charm she hated to admit was there. She wanted to hate the place.

It only took ten minutes to arrive at the airport, which was unbelievably small. It wasn't what she had expected, appearing to be merely a single airplane hangar. The parking was the size of one football field and was close enough to the door that patrons could walk to the airport entrance instead of needing shuttles. In fact, there were only a handful of cars in the parking lot and, once again, no other people in sight.

She could see two small planes waiting on the tarmac. They couldn't have had more than a ten-person capacity for each of them. She squinted to get a better look and soon assessed that these were all charter planes.

She threw her dirty pajamas in the backseat before following John to the entrance. She noticed he had pulled a luggage bag from the trunk. She figured he must have grabbed a few items when they had stopped at his apartment building.

Once inside, it was apparent it wasn't an official airport. The place was a large, one-room hanger with high ceilings. The roof was tin and the floor was concrete. It was a simple and functional place that housed about half a dozen small planes and one medium-sized private jet.

She had already guessed who owned that private plane, a thought that made her stomach turn.

They walked up to a small wooden desk in the front of the hanger that was manned by an old man with a full beard. John and him quickly began conversing in a manner that suggested they too were old friends. Both were laughing and virtually patting each other on the back. She wasn't sure when, but at some point, John related the information about their scheduled flight.

She was amazed at how easy it all was. Within twenty minutes they were all checked in and directed to an open waiting room to wait for the pilot's arrival.

John didn't seem to have any concerns and had strolled along with the swagger of a confident man. She was surprised at his ease. She watched him in both awe and fear.

Was this a performance? If it was, she was impressed with his talent for acting. She had always worn her heart on her sleeve and didn't know how to disguise the fear she felt at being caught or her inherent distrust of someone who seemed so calm. She was jittery as hell. She couldn't help but constantly look over her shoulder and in every other direction too.

It didn't take long for John to notice her fidgeting and grab her hand. He gave it a reassuring squeeze and smiled over at her. Then he winked and continued about his business of chatting up anyone who was around and pretending to read a newspaper he had found on the side table.

She just sat there, alternating between shaking and being stiff as a board. John again noticed her behavior. He leaned over and began whispering in her ear.

"It will be okay, but you have to relax."

She turned her head to look at him, eyes pleading for more reassurance. He leaned even closer and put his forehead to hers. It was a move that was incredibly intimate and her body wanted to revolt at the proximity of his face. She wasn't ready for someone to be this close, especially someone she wasn't sure she could trust.

Surprisingly, she didn't pull back from him this time either. She raised her eyes and looked back into his, straining her pupils at the closeness.

She felt his warm breath on her face and heard the rhythm of it, slow and steady. It was soothing in a way she had never anticipated. She began to exhale slowly, matching his rhythm, breath for breath. She felt her muscles relaxing, her heartbeat slowing as he kept his forehead pressed to hers.

"We will make it out of here. I promise," he said.

She gave him a faint smile in agreement before pulling back from the intimacy of the moment. She leaned back in her seat, determined to be more hopeful than she had been in more than half a year.

He handed her the paper and turned his attention to the people watching with an amused scrutiny.

"Nervous flyer," he joked.

As she gazed over the paper, it hit her that she hadn't done something as freeing as reading a newspaper in a long time. The simple tasks that she had once taken for granted seemed so wonderfully new to her now. She could make choices about how she spent her time again.

It was an Australian national paper. Brianna found that she didn't follow the stories very well because she was unfamiliar with the laws, the players, the geography, and pretty much anything about Australia other than its existence. However, the stories didn't really matter to her, it was the mere act of doing something normal that she relished.

The time passed slowly waiting for their flight. They exchanged very little conversation and it seemed as if that made it worse. When the pilot showed up, however, they both found themselves grinning. It wasn't long before they were loaded up and in their seats.

They were almost there.

She found she was holding her breath again, waiting for the push back that would signal they were on their way. John grabbed her hand and held it in his lap. She stared at their joined hands as he began to trace and caress her palm. He didn't look at her. His eyes were focused on his massage.

The plane began to move and they were taxiing to the runway. The motion of his fingers circling on her skin was making her faint. She couldn't deny it felt good. Damn good.

She looked once again at his profile as the plane turned to face its departure route. He finally took his gaze from their hands and looked deeply into her eyes. With a rapid sigh, he lifted both his hands and cupped her face. In a blink, he pulled her face to his. She closed her eyes and felt the waves flowing down her spine as his lips collided with hers.

His lips were so soft and sensual that her thighs felt like they had burst into flames. What started as steady embrace quickly escalated as she opened her mouth to meet his tongue.

Within seconds, they were both engulfed. She lost any sense of anything in that moment but John's mouth on her own. She didn't notice the plane leave the ground or hear the thumping sound of the wheels going up. She just felt the comfort of this man who had pulled her from her nightmare. The man whose kiss was so overwhelming that she forgot for a moment that the nightmare had ever happened.

10

Her entire body hurt. She was laying in the bed, back in the white room. Her face was streaked with tears, bruises freshly forming. She was in complete agony. Her mind was tormented with images from the gallery of Doppelgängers and haunted by the site of fists crashing into her body with a force that was crippling.

She hadn't witnessed the first punch. She had been tackled to the ground when she felt its effects ricocheting throughout her body. The first blow had been to her left side, just below her ribs. She had nearly vomited from the impact that felt like a thousand-pound weight striking her spleen. It had been instantly debilitating.

The second punch she had seen coming directly at her face. The anticipation of its impact hadn't dulled the pain. It had felt as if her head would explode. Her vision had blurred and a white fog had overtaken her view. The pain had been unbearable and radiated to every part of her face. She had instinctively reached her hand to feel the wound and found her skin had already been warm to the touch.

Just as she had been pressing her fingers to her eye to assess the damage, a kick came to the right side of her chest that had left her gasping for breath. She had rolled over onto her side and curled up into the fetal position. Her throat dry, she had been unable to cry out.

Bracing herself for more, she had closed her eyes and waited for the pain to come. But it truly amazed her that she hadn't seemed to feel the rest of the blows before her body had given up and she had passed out.

Now, laying in bed, she wished she could block out everything from that day. The fear she had felt before didn't compare to the horror that vibrated in every inch of her battered body. She was broken.

It was obvious that whoever these people were and how badly they wanted her there, they weren't afraid to inflict punishment. After the events of the afternoon, she wasn't sure they wouldn't resort to murdering her if she tried to step out of line again.

She spent the rest of the night crying, lamenting over her situation. They didn't bring her food that night or insist she come down to the dining room. She was left alone. All alone.

The solitude proved to be a very good thing that night. If any of them had interacted with her, her resolve might have weakened from fear. She might have accepted that this was her fate and she would have walked the line from that point on. As it were, she spent the night seething in anger and growing more determined.

By the morning's light, her pain had lessened. The guards showed up with her breakfast but they didn't look at her. They dropped it off and left, refusing to make eye contact. It didn't' matter though. She had no desire to interact with the men who had beaten her or the ones that had watched.

Happily, the pain they inflicted hadn't had the effect they had intended. They had hoped to subdue her, to teach her a lesson and make sure she behaved. They had failed.

She was would try again. She would get out, even if she died in the process. It would take more than a beating to stop her now.

That rest of the day proceeded like normal. She didn't see or hear from anyone until they delivered her dinner outfit. Another 1950s garb that made her want to throw up.

It was floral A-line that looked like something a Stepford wife would wear. She didn't quite understand what was going on with these people, but she now suspected that the crusty old man was trying to recreate her into one of the Doppelgängers. She made a mental note to go back to the gallery and take a closer look at the photograph from the 1950s for clues.

For now, she dressed for dinner and followed the routine that had been set for her. When she descended the stairs that night, she was weary but not scared. She proceeded straight to the dining room and sat in the same chair she always did. She kept her head high as she waited for the crusty old man to enter. She planned to put on a brave face and show him that he didn't break her.

He entered the room a few minutes later, hobbling along as he always did. When he seated himself, she felt his eyes upon her. But she didn't make eye contact with him at first. It took a couple of minutes of silence and his eyes boring into her before she turned her head to face him.

His brow was furrowed, his eyes were narrowed. His nostrils were flaring a bit and his lips were a thin line. He was most definitely pissed. The question was, at whom.

Suddenly, he screamed out for one of the guards.

"Patrick!" he said so forcedly and quickly that Brianna literally jumped.

One of the guards entered the room and stood at command. The crusty old man rose from his seat and approached her side.

She was becoming afraid and she was certain it showed in her face. The proximity of him standing beside her gave her chills. Without warning, her worst fear came true. He touched her. He grabbed her chin and turned it to face the guard, holding it up to ensure that Patrick saw the damage to it. Steering her jaw from side to side, the crusty old man said nothing at first. It was as if he was letting her swollen and bruised injuries speak for themselves.

He was not happy with their work.

"Do not strike her face again," the crusty old man said matter-of-factorily.

It was not lost on her that he didn't tell his guards to not beat her, only to not hit her face again.

"How chivalrous!" she thought sarcastically. "Such a noble gesture."

She gently turned her head back to stare straight ahead. But the crusty old man didn't fight to retain his grasp on her chin anyway. He let go of her and continued to stare at her for a full minute. Then he seated himself back at the table and continued to look at her. She refused to return his stare and kept her eyes on the wall in front of her.

"They won't punch you again. But if you try to run away again, they will catch you. You have to remain and follow the rules or it won't end well for you," he said.

His voice was positively chilling. She didn't care. She had decided they wouldn't defeat her spirit. Feeling defiant, she found herself speaking to him.

"What? They will kill me? Well, go ahead," she said in contempt.

He pursed his lips. But he remained stoic to her first verbal protest.

Slowly, he turned his head to the guard and nodded a dismissal. He then looked in the opposite direction to where a server stood waiting with plates in hand. She hadn't noticed before this moment and was reminded again how authoritarian the whole operation was.

No one questioned the crusty old man, they just waited for his command and did what was demanded. She began to wonder how such a decrepit person could reign so completely in this modern age. His employees seemed more like servants, bowing to his whims. It was another mystery she intended to solve.

The rest of dinner passed much like the ones before it, quiet and otherwise uneventful. Except this night when she was released to go back to her room, she was resolved to sneak out after hours to see what she could find. It was about time that she pushed the limits of the parameters they had at night. It was also time that she figured out who these people were and what they truly wanted with her, if she could.

Once she got back to the white room, she quickly changed into the white pajamas that had become the staple of her wardrobe. Then, she waited.

It seemed like an eternity of waiting. She listened for sounds that the house was going to sleep and was surprised to realize that she had already learned the indicators that the house was at rest.

When she heard the signs that it was clear, she peeked into the hallway. It was as empty as she had suspected it would be. She eased her way downstairs and made her way to the long hallway that led to the gallery of Doppelgängers. It was dark but her eyes had already adjusted to the night. She was careful with each step to proceed silently and be hyper aware of any sounds. Yet, there was silence in all directions.

She started at the gallery. Since she now knew what was behind the door, she could approach it with an objectivity. She slipped into the gallery and found it pitch black. Slowly, she made her way to the windows and threw open the curtains. There wasn't much moonlight to help lighten the room, but there was enough that she could make her way around.

She began at the far right corner of the room and systematically worked her way around to each of the portraits. There were twenty-four women in total, going back to what appeared to be the Renaissance era. After studying them one by one, she began to discern minute differences amongst the women.

She wondered if any of the ladies had been related to each other and it had accounted for some of their similarities. She had heard of a Doppelgänger and knew it was supposed to be two people who looked exactly alike but bore no relation. However, it didn't seem logical. There were too many women over an extended period of time. It was too much a coincidence for one family line of females to have that much alike. Plus, she wasn't related to them.

Her gut told her that some of these women had been taken against their wills, some of them had been prisoners for no other reason than the misfortune of looking the way they did. She had no proof of this theory, of course. It was just the feeling that her situation was not unique.

Once she had scoped out the paintings, she paused to see if there was anything else of interest in the room. However, there were no clues to be found and it seemed this was just a gallery. A petrifying collection, for sure. But there wasn't any real information about who these women were and how they ended up being the art of a sick and demented man.

Brianna wanted answers. Standing in this room, she

knew this was just the tip of the iceberg. There was something sinister happening and these women's faces were hiding it. She would find out how it was all connected, what this alternative reality was. Once she did, she was certain she would find her way out of it.

11

AFTER

Their kiss had ended soon after takeoff. They had exchanged a heated look between them, and then they didn't make eye contact again for the duration of the flight. She spent the remainder of their time airborne looking out the window at the ocean below.

Her mind was reeling. She couldn't process what had just happened between them. She had to admit that she found him attractive. It would be difficult to find a female who didn't find him appealing. But she didn't know if she could trust him. It all hindered on that one fact.

She didn't really know anything about him. Yes, he had pulled her out of a nightmare. Yes, he had been attentive and caring since the moment she had met him. Yes, he had organized and paid for their escape to Brisbane. Yes, that kiss made her feel alive in a way that she didn't think she ever would again.

Yet, she was still leery. She couldn't imagine that

anyone who had been where she had been would blame her for it. It would be irrational to not be scared after all she had gone through. It was perfectly normal to question his motives, to question everyone's motives.

He didn't say a word to her either. He also didn't touch her after their lips had parted. He kept his head back and his eyes closed, although she had doubted he was actually asleep. She had sneaked a few looks at him to see if, or how, he was reacting to their kiss. She saw nothing beyond his closed eyes or, at least, his pretense so he wouldn't have to discuss it.

When the plane's wheels touched down in Australia, he opened his eyes and gave her a long, reassuring look. He grabbed her hand, squeezed it, and gave her a sheepish smile. She guessed it meant he wasn't completely avoiding her.

"Almost there," he said.

Garnering her confidence, she asked, "Almost where exactly? Where do we go from the airport?"

"I have some friends in Brisbane. They have a house. I thought we could go there. It would be good for you to be around other people too. But if you have any anxiety about that, I can get us a hotel room."

She raised an eyebrow at that last statement.

"I would get you a hotel room alone," he backpedaled.

"What would you like to do?" he asked then.

"I don't know. Why not go straight to the police station?" she suggested.

He looked surprised for a moment before shaking his head.

"Yes, we can go to the police station. I intended to do so...I just thought you may like to clean up first. If you want to go straight to the police station, then we will do that," he agreed.

He nodded his head in the direction of the plane exit.

"C'mon. Let's get going," he directed her.

She followed him off the plane and waited as the pilot got his bag for him. They made their way to the transportation area where John called for a ride. It didn't take long before a taxi showed up and they were on their way.

As promised, he told the driver to drive straight to the Brisbane police station.

It was a quiet ride with a deafening silence between them. He seemed preoccupied with something. There was something in his body language because she got the impression he didn't want to go to the police. He wouldn't look at her, only stared out the window with a hardened look on his face. His expressions gave her the idea that he was working something out in his mind. Although she still couldn't read him well enough to have a clue what he was thinking.

The route the driver took from the airport sent them through suburban areas before turning along the river. A detour that Brianna was happy to take. She was excited to see more civilization than she had seen all year.

Brisbane was a beautiful city. The buildings were tall and modern as they got closer to downtown and to the city police station. It was a stark contrast to the Hale Islands. She found that her relief grew in proportion to the height of the buildings that characterized downtown Brisbane.

However, her relief seemed to rival John's anxiety. He was fidgeting, tapping his foot incessantly. He had avoided making eye contact with her and now, his demeanor was decreasing her solace.

"Are you okay?" she finally tried.

He looked at her with a raised eyebrow.

"Yes, of course," he assured. "Why?"

She motioned to his jittery foot.

He sighed.

"I can't go in with you at that police station," he finally admitted.

"Wait. What?" she demanded just as the taxi was pulling to the curb.

They had arrived. The timing was impeccable.

He didn't respond at first. He told the taxi driver to idle for a few minutes and ushered them both out of the cab. He placed his hand on her elbow as he led her to the sidewalk.

"The police station is that building straight across there," he pointed. "I can't be seen there because I can't be implicated with what you are about to tell them. I can't really explain right now, but here."

He handed her a piece of paper.

"That is my mobile number. When you get done telling them everything you need to...or if you need my help again, then give me a call. If not, then I wish you luck, Brianna," he continued.

His grip on her elbow tightened as he leaned down to

lightly kiss her cheek. As he pulled back, he hovered with their faces breaths apart.

"I hope to hear from you."

Then, he turned and jumped back into the cab. As the car disappeared down the street she was left stunned.

He was gone.

She stood there for a minute, flabbergasted. Looking over at the police station, she realized that she had prepared herself mentally for recounting her tale with John by her side. In the last 48 hours, she had begun to rely on him. He had brought her to the police so that justice may be served on the crusty old man and his crew. But she didn't want to do this alone anymore. She wanted him there with her.

Now, she stood mere feet away from the police station but she found herself hesitating. Instead of going into the building, she was staring down the empty street hoping that he would reappear.

He didn't.

She mustered her strength and crossed the road to the entrance.

"Here goes nothing," she said to herself.

She marched herself to the front desk and told the receptionist she needed to see someone about a kidnapping.

After an agonizing twenty-minute wait, she was escorted back to a detective's desk. He was an old man with the lines of wisdom showing in his face. His remaining white hair was thinning and he was 50 pounds overweight. He wore a suit that had seen better days; she imagined he had too.

She didn't waste any time before she began telling her story. She described how she was taken and kept against her will for seven months. A fact that didn't register a reaction from him. He listened as she told him about her recovery and how she and John had made their way to Brisbane. He was patient and kind with her, touching her arm each time she got choked up.

He jotted down notes on a notepad as she spoke. She felt certain that she was coming across as a crazy person. She had stopped herself several times as she recalled the events over the last year, doubting whether she should continue. The detective, however, always reassured her and waited for her to keeping going.

The whole tale took 45 minutes.

As she had heard her own story, she realized she was likely to be dismissed. She knew that she would send herself home if she was in his shoes.

From the outside, she was an American who showed up to an Australian police station claiming she had been kidnapped. She had no evidence to support her claims. What was more, she suggested she was taken by a cult because she was a Doppelgänger to some unknown woman. The whole thing sounded like the ramblings of a lunatic or, worse yet, a conspiracy theorist.

She felt the anger build in her as she waited for the police to respond to her claims. She was beyond pissed now that John had left her to do this alone. He must have known how it would sound. Maybe he had counted on it.

Although his words were echoing in her head. The "can't be implicated" was already haunting her and she wondered what he had meant.

The detective finally stopped writing

"Thank you miss. We will need to do an investigation into your claims and get back to you if we find anything."

"You don't believe me, do you?" she accused.

"Miss, you made a lot of serious accusations. I am not saying that these are falsehoods. I am saying that we need to see if there is cause to investigate. We need to see if there is evidence or even witnesses to substantiate your claims."

"You don't believe me," she concluded.

The detective looked at her and shrugged his shoulders.

"It does seem to me an unlikely scenario. But I will make a few calls and see if there is anything that checks out."

"Well, I suggest you start with contacting my family to tell them I am okay!" she yelled.

"Miss, please calm down. We will contact your family to let them know you are here. You may want to go to the United States Embassy as well," he suggested.

"I plan to do just that!" she said before she stormed away from his desk.

Internally, she was yelling at herself more than anyone else. She hadn't thought this move through. She was so determined that her captors paid for imprisoning her, she had shot off her mouth. She had appeared to be insane. She had been lucky they didn't call the mental facility to come get her.

This was not good.

She made a quick exit from the police station, still peeved at the outcome. Despite her understanding of how her account came across, she had hoped the detective would have recognized the truth. She didn't blame him. It was a wild tale. It was just a disappointment she had failed again.

She wandered aimlessly down the street, not sure what she should do or where she should go. She didn't have any money, so her options were limited. She could try to find the USA Embassy to report her reappearance and ask for their help. Or she could try to get ahold of John.

The thought of John in that moment brought mixed emotions. On one hand, she was furious that he had left her at the police station and had basically abandoned her without any means. It was late in the afternoon now and she would need a place to stay for the night. And food.

She knew that she had already taken for granted all the kindness John had shown her.

She had rationalized that she didn't know his reasons for not accompanying her into the police station. He had just said he couldn't be involved. He had left her his number and told her to call him if she needed help. Well, right now, she needed his help. And the answers to a few questions.

She stopped and looked around, noticing that she had no idea which direction she had walked. Luckily, she had wandered in the direction of a coffee shop. It seemed to be a good a place to see if she could locate a phone to call John.

Her hunch turned out to be correct as she found a kind patron who agreed to let her use their mobile phone. When he answered on the first ring, Brianna felt a little panicked. She didn't know what to say to him. But after the third "hello" from him, she figured she had to say something before he hung up.

"John? Hi. It is Brianna," she started.

"Oh, hey!" he replied. "How did it go?"

Somewhat relieved at the tone of his voice, she answered honestly.

"Not so great. They thought I was crazy... I don't know what to do now."

There was an awkward pause where neither of them said anything. She discerned quickly that this was a moment where she needed to find some humility and ask for his help.

"John. I know you have done a lot for me over the last few days and I haven't really said thank you... And I hate to ask but could you help me tonight. Then I won't bother you again," she pleaded.

"Brianna, I told you to call if you needed me. I meant it. Just tell me where you are and I will come get you," he responded.

Thirty minutes or so later, she noticed John outside the coffee shop as he passed the window. He was carrying the same confidence that she had come to identify with him. Seeing him again, her feelings were once again conflicted. She was grateful he had showed up when she called for help, but there was a twinge of anger over being left earlier to look like a fool with the police.

He entered the shop and scanned the seating area until he found her. After their eyes met, he seemed to hesitate before he began his approach. It was almost as if he sensed her contradictory feelings and was weary of her. If he had been truly confident before he entered the coffee shop, he was somewhat shy now as he made his way to her.

She started to stand but he motioned for her to stay put as he grabbed the chair across from her to sit down.

"I wanted to talk to you before we go," he started. "I shouldn't have left you at the police station."

Once again, he had anticipated her reservations. She was amazed at his continued ability to know what she was thinking. She raised her eyebrow to demonstrate her interest in his next confession.

"I felt bad after I left you and wanted to explain...why I did what I did. If you don't want to go anywhere with me after I tell you this, I will understand," he continued.

Her anxiety level had skyrocketed. She was worried as to what he was about to reveal to her. What would make her question not leaving with him?

"Okay," she slowly replied, drawing out the word to show her dread.

"I guess I should just come out with it. It was also the reason that I knew where to find you in the shed. I used to work for them."

She felt the lump in her throat forming within seconds of his confession. Her eyes widened and she felt a cold sweat forming. She was certain she was the deer in the headlights because he immediately leaned forward, placing his hand on hers.

"It isn't what you are thinking. It was a long time ago. I didn't know what was going on at first. When I found out what they were doing, I got out."

She was speechless but her mind was racing with

remarks. Her skin was tingling and the nausea had returned. She started to pull her hand back from the table when he gripped it tighter and leaned even closer.

"Brianna. I got out years ago. Just calm down and listen to me for a second. And when I am finished, you are welcome to go. If you want. I won't stop you or try to hurt you. I want to help you. If I were planning to hurt you, I would have done it already," he whispered.

She looked at him pointedly with that last comment.

He shrugged.

"Logically, you know that is true. If I was going to hurt you, I would have left you in that shed. Or worse. I wouldn't have done any of the things I have done to get you away from there. I certainly wouldn't have taken you to the front step of the police station!"

He paused to see if she was still listening.

"Brianna, think. Would I do those things if I wanted to hurt you?"

She thought about it for a moment before shaking her head.

"No, I don't think so," she managed calmly. Although she still felt shaky. "Okay. Tell me the rest of it."

He leaned back in his chair and released her hand. He took a deep breath before beginning.

"A few years back, I was getting out of college and didn't know what I wanted to do with my life. I had thoughts of joining the FBI, but I ended up taking a bodyguard position," he began.

As he recalled his past, she leaned back and crossed her arms. She wasn't sure what she thought about him yet. But as she studied him, there was an honesty in his account. He was humbled and reflective. There were also rips in his veil of confidence. For the first time, she believed he was seeing the full picture of who he was and not just the façade of a man who had everything controlled.

"I don't want to make this story too long, plus I try to not think of those times. I found myself in a bad place. But soon, I realized that the job wasn't what I was told."

He paused and then looked directly at her.

"You weren't the first girl they took," he revealed.

"What?"

She acted surprised. But she wasn't truly shocked because of the things she had learned from exploring the house during her captivity. She already knew there were others. She just didn't want to show her hand yet.

"Years ago, I was working in the house where they held you. And one day, a girl appeared."

He gave her the once over before continuing, "She looked very much like you."

Brianna shrugged now. This revelation wasn't something new to her. She was chosen for her face. Like Helen of Troy, the face that started a war. However, she didn't tell John this fact. Her tentative trust in him was already on shaking ground.

"I didn't know it was happening and when she showed up, it made me sick. So, I got out," he finished.

They sat in silence for a bit, staring at each other.

"Is that it?" she eventually asked.

"What else do you want to know?" he retorted.

"What happened to the girl, for starters?" she rebuked.

His eyes got big and his face displayed his panic.

"I don't really know," he replied.

"So you just left her there?" she discerned.

He didn't respond immediately. He lowered his eyes

"Yes, but I got you out of there," he quietly stated.

They sat in silence again, this time neither daring to look at the other. She noted when he began tapping his foot, fidgeting the way he had in the cab from the airport. She, however, was processing this new information and wondering what it all meant.

To his credit, he wasn't rushing her to comment or react about what he had told her. She had noticed that he hadn't apologized for being a part of the group that had taken her. On the other hand, if he was telling the truth then he would have information about the inner workings of that organization.

She contemplated that for a few minutes. She had made a vow to herself during her time in captivity. She promised herself when she escaped she would do what she needed to do to bring this group down.

She wasn't surprised that there were others before her, even as recently as a few years ago. She had spent many nights wondering how many girls there had been. The gallery she had found had more than two dozen portraits. None of them had looked recent, so the question remained about the fate of the girl who John had mentioned.

"What now?" she finally said.

He raised his eyes to meet hers.

"Well, that is up to you," he cleared his throat. "My offer still stands for you to come with me and let me

continue to help you. But if you don't want to be...
associated with me, given my past, then I will direct you
where to go. I am not here to hurt you. Truly. I
meant that."

She had already made up her mind about her
next move.

"I will go with you, but I have a few conditions first,"
she indicated.

He nodded his head.

"Okay, what are your terms?"

"Well, I want to contact my family. For starters."

"Of course, that is understandable," he responded.

"I also have questions. I want them answered," she
demanded.

"That is doable. Is that it?" he asked.

"For now," she said

"Okay, let's get going then."

12

Brianna had spent every night exploring the house for the last week. Systematically, she had snuck into room after room to see what she could learn. After six nights of investigation, she was no closer to figuring out who these people were or the seedy history behind all the Doppelgängers.

Her nightly journeys had uncovered a couple of bedrooms, a storage closet, and, as of late last night, a return to the study.

She had thought she may find answers there, but she soon discovered the desk drawers were locked. She scanned the books again but found nothing enlightening. She even tested for fake shelves or books that were levers for secret doors. Yet, the search for hidden passageways was fruitless.

Most of her daytimes had been spent theorizing and concocting bizarre scenarios to the backstory. There was also a fair bit of analyzing her ankle band, trying to find a way out of it.

The one constant of her routine was the dinner every night in an outfit straight from the 1950s. The conversation with the crusty old man was non-existent, not that she minded. She was truly amazed that he was perfectly content to sit in silence, night after night. Then again, she also imagined this is what he had intended. She was meant to be an ornament, a relic to a time when men dominated. Garbed in her dresses, she was the ultimate living trophy.

The more time passed, the more certain she became of that one fact. She was there to be looked at and admired for her appearance alone. And that realization made it clear to her what she should do. If the crusty old man wanted a decoration, she would make him believe that is what he had. She would not stand still and look pretty for nothing. She had a brain. It was time that she used it.

She also realized that this plan could majorly backfire. It had to be well thought out before being executed.

The more she contemplated, the more she reflected on the woman's movement. It was a curious association, but one that resonated in her mind. Change didn't occur overnight. It took time before women were heard and believed to be more than part of the furniture. And time happened to be the one thing she had in abundance at the moment.

She remembered all the books and articles she had

read about how women fought for their place in the world, particularly the workplace. Brianna had been fascinated with the fight they had faced as a woman who was working in the corporate arena. She had also found herself in these situations before and it was good to remember how she had worked her way up the ladder to the position she had held. She recalled the days when she would walk into a room and there would be surprise that a woman was going to handle the issues at hand.

She had worked through those times, one by one, and had somewhat proven herself. She had been more than just a pretty face when she had been taken. A thought she resented now.

That evening, she started slowly. At the appearance of the guards, who made way for her to enter a room, she bowed her head and said, "thank you." A gesture that was astutely planned.

It did not go unnoticed. She noted the slight raising of eyebrows and the scrutiny those two little words caused.

As she made her way to the dinner table, she visually smiled a little. Her goal was to be happy and polite because it wasn't what they were expecting. She would also become chatty and vocal in time.

She had realized the last few months she had been playing the part they had expected from her. She had been sullen and then, resistant. She had remained quiet, depressed, defeated. She imagined that was the response they had been anticipating. They certainly had been prepared for that reaction.

It was the end game that she was playing. She could

see two positive results to her plan. The first was she would miraculously gain their understanding and not be seen as a prize anymore. And just maybe they would release her. It was the longest long shot in history of long shots.

The more likely scenario would be that she would catch them off guard when she tried to make another escape. She hoped that in time they would start to trust her, believe she had accepted the fate they had given to her.

She was relying on the element of surprise to make her way out of this place. A classic use of misdirection.

When she heard the crusty old man entering the room, she turned to look at him directly for the first time. He was about halfway to the table before he even noticed her gaze. He paused briefly but continued his path without fail. She didn't look at him again that evening.

She knew she would have to make small moves that built over time, otherwise it wouldn't be believed. So each day she would give the crusty old man more eye contact and politely thank the staff whenever she saw them.

She was keeping up her nightly investigations of the house. The last few nights had led to the discovery of a massive kitchen, a sitting room that overlooked the front yard, and another bedroom. However, it was the kitchen that was the most exciting for her. She immediately began looking for knives that could cut her ankle strap or be used as a weapon. Except all the drawers were locked.

"Figures," she muttered.

She had found the same thing in every room she had

entered. Everything was locked. Nothing was left lying around.

"Where was the trust?" she questioned.

There were a few cabinets open and she found them stocked with food and dining ware. She decided to take one of the wine glasses with the thought she could try to turn it into a makeshift knife. She figured she could hide the glass in her room until the time came that she would break the glass. It was worth a try. After all, she did grow up watching MacGyver do much more with lesser tools.

The other rooms were uneventful. She had learned nothing new and there weren't any other useful objects like she had found in the kitchen. She imagined MacGyver would have fared better.

Returning to her room the night after the kitchen excursion, she fretted over where to hide the wine glass. She thought at first that she would just place it under the bed. Even without a bed skirt, it was the only place that was out of plain sight.

She changed her mind about fifteen minutes later. She told herself she was being paranoid, but it didn't matter. After some trial and error, she ended up situating the glass between the bed frame and the wall. This way it wasn't visible if one of the guards happened to look under the bed. The base of the glass was wedged between the mattress and the frame. She hoped that anchoring it would keep it from falling or that any movements of the mattress wouldn't put too much pressure on it.

Now, she just had to be careful and wait for the right moment to use it.

Every day she was getting closer to that moment. The

subtle changes to her demeanor were being noticed. With a bit of luck and time, she should be able to convince them that she had stopped trying to fight it.

In the interim, she would try to get some answers to who they were. She had decided that she would go to the source and ask the crusty old man. It was a ballsy move.

She knew she couldn't just ask them who they were and what they were doing here. She would have to use some finesse. She would have to be charming.

She languished at that thought, but there was not time to wait. That evening at dinner, she opted to finally attempt polite, small talk. She would focus on the meal first. If it went well, maybe she would move to the weather, despite not knowing the weather from being kept indoors.

"Excuse me, sir. But if I may ask...what is this dish called?" she asked with the meekness of a child.

He looked back at her with an amused disdain.

"It's fish" he stated.

She had to bite her tongue to not give him a snarky remark in return.

"Yes, I was wondering about the bread. It is different than anything that I can remember having before I got here," she explained.

She lowered her eyes, deliberately. She wanted to appear weak and demure. And it worked.

"It is ulu," the crusty old man said after studying her a bit. "It is a fruit bread similar to fruit cake."

"Ah okay," she replied.

"I can't say that I have ever had fruit cake. My family was always giving it away if we received any as gifts at Christmas. So I never got to try it," she lightheartedly joked a minute, tryin to ease the tension she felt.

He didn't smile.

"Thank you," she said

He nodded his head and grunted a bit. He didn't look at her. It wasn't the best response but, then again, it was progress. She decided that she would press her luck to try a different tact.

"I was wondering something else..." she trailed off.

He raised his eyes in skepticism again and stared at her with complete disdain.

When she didn't immediately continue, he grumpily asked, "What?"

"Would it be possible for me to go outside sometime? I would stay on the grounds. It is just to get some air and sun," she said rapidly.

Then she waited, making sure her head was bowed in submission.

He didn't respond at first. But she knew he was analyzing her facial expression before he answered. She made sure to keep her eyes downcast and any emotions she was feeling in check.

"Matthew," the crusty old man summoned one of the guards to the table.

"Yes, sir?"

"Tomorrow morning. I want you to get Brianna from her room and show her the parameter that she may walk outside."

"Yes, sir."

The crusty old man looked back at Brianna,

anticipating some gratitude. She played the part and graciously thanked him.

With that arrangement settled, the crusty old man excused himself from the room. She soon followed him and kept in the white room that night. She didn't want to risk getting caught out of her room. She feared that her request for access to the grounds had aroused suspicion of her or late night activities.

Sunlight was pouring into the room the next morning when the guard, Matthew, arrived. He led her down the stairs and down the long hallway to the right of the stairs. At the end of it, they exited through a door into a fenced yard.

Brianna was overwhelmed at the beauty of the land that surrounded the house, especially in the early morning light. She had spent hours gazing out her balcony doors to the grounds below. The doors had always been locked, so she had never gotten the full view.

The house was atop a hill that was surrounded by dense forest. She knew it must be a tropical environment based on the foliage she saw. The trees seemed endless. Despite her situation, she was truly overwhelmed at the prettiness of it all. It was both inviting and foreboding.

As the guard led her into the yard, she turned and looked back at the house. It was as massive as she had suspected. It towered at three stories and was covered from top to bottom with natural brown siding. The architecture reminded her of the American Pacific Northwest style that adorned the waterfront of Seattle. The lawn was a perfectly manicured landscape that extended in a 50 yard radius around the house. Then the forest wilderness took over.

"You have range to walk within fifteen yards of the house. Any farther and it will set off the alarms and send shocks through your body. I don't suggest testing the limits this time. We have instructions to keep you here at all costs," the guard informed her before stepping back to monitor her at a distance.

"Thanks," she muttered.

She wandered around the house, the guard constantly tailing her like he was part of the Secret Service. Except he wasn't there to protect her at all.

She made it appear that she was wandering aimlessly. She would look off into the distance, then at the ground, but she always returned her sight to the house.

If the guard was asked, he would say that she was innocently strolling the yard for exercise and the vitamin D consumption. He wouldn't report back that she was casing the place, which was what she was actually doing.

She was permitted to walk the grounds for about an hour before Matthew told her they would be returning to the indoors. She had reveled in the last hour and it gave her more hope than anyone could have tried to suppress.

The sunlight had rejuvenated her spirits a little, a likely a sign that depression may have been setting in from the lack of exposure to the sunlight. She realized that she would need to be outside as much as possible, if only to keep her Vitamin D levels up. She couldn't afford to become apathetic now.

She would make sure to thank the crusty old man. She honestly felt gratitude to have gotten outdoors.

And she would continue to be as pleasant as possible. Her efforts over the past week to play the part of a meek, obeying female had garnered some more limited freedom All she had to do was continue her acting because one day the opportunity would present itself for her to flee into those woods. She was determined she would be ready when that day came.

13

J ohn took her directly to his friend's house. Within half an hour of leaving the coffee shop, they were pulling up in front of a modern home on the river. It was a series of grey boxes stacked on top of each other with floor to ceiling windows to overlook the water. She was imagining that the décor would be futuristic and cold as the exterior suggested. She was mistaken.

As they walked through the back door, she was taken aback at the homey feeling that the interior conveyed. It was an open floor plan with rooms blending together in harmony. The home was decorated with warm colors and lots of layering of the light. There were knick-knacks everywhere and vibrant art on every available wall. The full-sized windows permitted the glow of the river to seep into the design and add to the aesthetic. It all combined to make it one of the loveliest and most welcoming places she had ever seen in her life.

She was so busy marveling at the beauty of the place that she didn't notice the other people in the room with them. They approached her for an introduction.

It was a man and woman, who seemed to be in their mid-30s. He was tall and athletic with brown hair and honey colored eyes. His skin was a smooth caramel color that matched his eyes. He moved with the same confident gait that John had and smiled so brightly it lit the room more than all the lamps combined. His contentment with life was easy to see.

The woman was truly gorgeous, with the look of a porcelain doll. Her skin was smooth and flawless. Her oval face was offset by long blonde hair that ran the length of her back. She had a button nose and striking, blue eyes that were only second to John's in their beauty. She immediately wondered if they were related given some of the similarities between their features.

If the man was all friendliness, she was all polite reserve. It was not surprising that he was the first to speak.

"Welcome to our home, Brianna. We are so glad you decided to join us," he said.

"Thank you," she replied. "From what little I can see, it is a lovely home."

"I am Ethan. This is my wife Annabelle. John, you obviously already know."

He gestured to each of them as he rattled off the information.

"There are more of our friends that you will meet tomorrow. For now, I understand you wanted to make a phone call to your family in the States?"

She was overwhelmed, but managed to reply.

"Yes, please. That would be appreciated."

"Come with me, dear. We will get you situated and then see if we can get ahold of your family," Annabelle directed.

Brianna looked at John and he nodded in agreement before following Annabelle upstairs to a bedroom. Compared to the white room and shed where she had spent seven months of her life, this place was cluttered.

In a similar style as the house, the room was filled with dark brown wooden furniture. The linens were a dark blue with grey accent pillows and throws to add to the feeling of comfort. This room's art was black and white photos of Ethan and Annabelle acting goofy in various worldly locations. It gave the room a personal touch but also made her wonder if she was entering their personal bedroom.

"Is this your bedroom with Ethan?" she asked to be certain.

"Oh no. This is one of the guest rooms. If you don't think you will be comfortable, we can see if someone wants to switch...I bet someone would trade with you," she responded.

"No, this room is fine. I just wasn't sure with the photos of you and Ethan," Brianna explained.

Annabelle turned to look at the photos and shrugged her shoulders.

"Nope, these are just the ones we chose for this room. I have never thought about it before."

"Uh, thanks. This room is great, really. It is pretty. I

just didn't want to impose if it was yours," she backpedaled.

Annabelle smiled.

"Brianna, relax. You didn't offend me. So, I figured you would want some clothes," she said as she gave her the once over.

Brianna was still wearing the topical dress that she had gotten before they had left the island. She suddenly realized that she must have looked ridiculous to the Brisbane police. This could be part of the reason they hadn't believed her, she thought. She had shown up dressed like she had just returned from vacation and she had spun a tale of being kidnapped for seven months. She probably wouldn't have taken herself seriously either.

"Yeah, some cleaner clothes would be great," she told her.

"Okay, great. I will go grab a few things from my closet and be back in a few minutes. If you want a shower while I am getting some things, the bathroom is in there. I shouldn't be more than ten to fifteen minutes," she indicated as she left the room.

"Well, I might as well," Brianna said to no one.

She headed into the bathroom and took a shower. She meant for it to be quick, but she found that the hot water felt good. She stood under the water until it turned cold. She had to have been in there longer than ten minutes. Annabelle was likely to be waiting on her.

She was wrong. When she exited the bathroom, she found a pile of clothes laying on the bed. There was an assortment of choices but she opted to try the jeans and t-shirts for the comfort. The rest she would try in the morning.

She made her way back downstairs and found the three of them sitting in the living room talking.

"Hey, how was your shower?" John asked as she entered the room.

"Really good. Thank you. And the clothes, thanks for those too," she responded.

"No worries. Maybe tomorrow we can go shopping for a few things for you," Annabelle told her.

"Would you like a beer or something?" Ethan asked.

"Yeah, that would be great too," she replied.

John motioned for her to come sit on the couch by him as Ethan went to the kitchen to grab her a beer. They sat awkwardly sipping their beers for a few minutes with no one saying a word or looking at each other.

Brianna finally broke the silence when she asked, "What now?"

"We were just discussing that before you came down," John indicated.

"What did you come up with?" she asked.

"Obviously, we have to make sure that they don't come after you," John answered as Ethan and Annabelle nodded their heads.

"Is that a possibility?" she fretted.

"Yes, it is. I suspect they aren't far behind us already," John indicated as he nursed his beer.

It all seemed surreal. A few days ago she had been languishing on a dirt floor in the forest, waiting to die of exposure or hunger or finally finished off by the people who had taken her. Now, she was sitting around with strangers, drinking a beer, and discussing the fact that her kidnappers were likely following them, as if it was small talk.

"I have some questions," Brianna told John.

"I am sure you do. Go ahead. Ask."

She thought about it for a minute. She had more questions than she could process, but she didn't necessarily want to ask everything at that moment. Particularly with two new strangers listening. She felt weird and self-conscious. She didn't want to relive the experience again and risk being judged by these people she didn't know.

John was different. He had been there and, as he had told her, he was once a part of the group. He had to have some ideas already about what she had encountered. She hoped to couple his knowledge with what she had gathered on her own during her captivity. The information could be useful to bring them down.

She also had to think about what her plan would be. What was she going to do about her life and getting back on track? How was she going to ensure justice to her kidnappers, especially if she couldn't get the Brisbane police to believe her. When would she return to the States? And how would her family and friends react to her being home?

For now, she decided to start with a few simple questions.

"How long did you work for the people who took me?"

"About a year," he replied while he continued drinking his beer, unfazed by her question.

"Who are they?" she cut straight to the point.

He looked at her pointedly before leaning forward. He placed his beer on the coffee table, effectively getting everyone's attention. This wasn't a casual conversation anymore.

"I am not sure how you expect me to answer that," he replied. "They don't really have an official name that I know. It is all secretive. They tell the new guys the bare minimum. I will say that they are an organization, a well-funded one."

"Yes, but why do they take girls that look like me?" she interrupted.

"I don't know the 'why' of it, honestly. I didn't ask too many questions. I just got out."

He sighed and then shook his head to himself.

"Brianna, I thought of myself as a good guy. And before I knew what happened, I was involved in illegal activities. When I looked to get out, I found out how much power they had. They made my life hell and I had to go underground to escape their reach. If they find out it was me that helped you, I am likely a dead man."

He seemed upset now. He rested his elbows on his knees and his head in his hands. He didn't look at her or his friends. She turned her gaze to Ethan and Annabelle She found both of them despondent. The room had grown very quiet.

Ethan was the first to speak again.

"Brianna, we have been trying to find a way to expose the organization and stop what they are doing for a while now. It is kind of a grassroots effort. When we found out about you, we knew we had to be the ones to get you out."

"We figured John was the best one to get you out because he was the most familiar with the island where they were keeping you. And he knew how they operated, so he could anticipate their moves better than us," Annabelle continued.

"Wait, how are you two involved in all this?" Brianna inquired.

"We have known John a long time. When he was able to get away from those people, he came to us. He told us the whole story. And, well, we believed him," Annabelle provided.

"For a bit, we didn't do anything. We just went about our lives," Ethan said.

"But then my conscience got the best of me and I knew that I had to do something. I called Ethan and Annabelle. We all hooked up with some others, a few you will meet tomorrow. We have been working on finding out more about them. And trying to figure out how far their power reaches," John finished.

"We think it goes fairly high. We have found they have connections all over southeast Asia and here in Australia. We know there are ties in the United States and we suspect there are connections in Europe." Annabelle interjected.

"We also know that they go after girls that look like you do. It is like a Doppelgänger thing. We aren't exactly sure how many they have taken, but we suspect you are at least the fourth. We also aren't sure what happens to the girls...we think that they eventually kill them," Ethan supplied.

The silence that overtook the room after that

information was deafening. Brianna was certainly shaken. She stared at the walls and contemplated what they had said.

John had leaned back into the couch and took long drags on his beer. After a bit, Ethan got up and brought him another one. Annabelle was toying with some fringe on the bottom of her jeans, absentmindedly. Periodically, she would also take a drink of her beer. Ethan got up several times, many times without a reason. The whole mood was somber.

It was Ethan who once again broke the silence.

"So Brianna, have you ever been to Australia before now?" he asked.

She was surprised at the question. It seemed assured and innocent. When she looked at him in disbelief, she could tell he was trying to lighten the mood. Maybe a lighter mood was a must at the moment. She was tired of the dreary and could use some fluff.

"No, this is my first time. I can tell you two are Americans too. How long have you been here?"

"Almost two years," Annabelle answered.

"We were from the East Coast. Connecticut to be exact," Ethan added.

"So, if I may ask...what do you do? This house makes it seem like you do well for yourselves."

"Well, we both had some family money. But I am also a computer programmer. So, I am able to work remotely, pretty much anywhere in the world. And that affords a good living," Ethan said.

"And I do some freelance writing, but I don't really make that much," Annabelle relayed.

"I guess I am a kept woman," Annabelle winked at Ethan.

"Well, your home is stunning," she complimented.

John remained quiet as they made some small talk, mostly the couple telling her about the differences of living in the US versus Australia.

Brianna would glance at John from time to time, but he continued to act disinterested in their conversation. After a bit, he excused himself and went outside to a deck overlooking the river. Ethan soon joined him as she and Annabelle talked about her writing assignments.

She pretended to be interested in Annabelle's work as a lifestyle writer and her desire to start a website like Gwyneth Paltrow. In reality, she could care less. It was likely a means to an end to prevent any more awkwardness.

She kept looking over her shoulder to see whether John was still outside chatting with Ethan. They stayed on the deck for a long time, apparently in an intense conversation. Brianna's curiosity was piqued as to what was being discussed so passionately. Annabelle also picked up on the body language from the deck and attempted to reassure her.

"I bet that John is worked up again about not doing enough," she said as she shrugged her shoulders. "He does that sometimes. He feels really guilty about leaving that other girl behind and not knowing what became of her."

"That is understandable. I would feel guilty as well," Brianna related.

"Yeah, I guess. Do you want anything else to drink?"

Annabelle asked before she stood and walked toward the kitchen.

"No, I am good. I think I may excuse myself and get some sleep for the evening," she told her.

"Sure thing. Goodnight!" Annabelle wished.

As she made her way to the stairs, she remembered that she hadn't called her family yet. She figured it was probably better that she had forgotten because she had much more to process now.

"Hey Annabelle, do you think I can call my family tomorrow when I have a clearer head?" she asked.

"Of course. It is probably better that you get some real sleep first anyway. We are here if you need anything," she replied.

"Thanks. Goodnight."

"Goodnight. And Brianna, we are very glad you are here with us."

"Me too," she said before she walked up the stairs and went to bed.

It had been a very long day, but she knew as she laid her head on her pillow that it was a good day. All the normal had rubbed off. It was the first day she had begun to feel truly free again. A feeling she intended to keep.

She woke in a slightly disoriented state a couple of times during the night. But there was no fear. She laid in the bed, staring at the ceiling, and listening to the silence. She had grown accustomed to the quiet but in the place, it was comforting. She was cozy in this bed and felt at ease in Annabelle and Ethan's home.

She knew she was amongst friends. She felt safe again.

She worried at how quickly she was starting to trust these people. Perhaps it was too soon. Maybe she would have trusted anyone that got her out of her nightmare or showed her some kindness. She promised herself that she would remain cautious, but she was optimistic after tonight.

When daylight came, she remembered that she had wanted to call her family. She was ready to reclaim her life on her terms.

She pulled herself out of bed and found a pair of jeans and t-shirt amongst the stack of Annabelle's clothes. Somewhat presentable, she made her way downstairs. As she approached the base of the stairs, she heard their voices. They seemed to be in an animated discussion, but she couldn't make out what they were saying.

She inched closer to discern what they were saying without being noticed. She managed to get a little closer, but she couldn't make out much about the conversation. Figuring she wouldn't get anywhere this way, she decided to join them.

Except when she cruised into the kitchen, a silence overtook them as soon as she was spotted. A curious reaction, they all began to busy themselves with kitchen chores. John began making more coffee, despite the full pot that was sitting on the counter. Annabelle began perusing a cookbook and writing on a grocery list. Ethan just awkwardly began looking at the ceiling and his feet, completely absent of a kitchen activity to make him appear distracted.

She decided that this time, at least, she would speak up and ask what was being discussed.

"So, what has got you all clammed up? What is it you don't want to me know?" she asked.

The incredulous looks were shared by all three of them, as if they were going to deny they had been talking at all.

Finally, it was John who spoke.

"We were discussing our plan. We didn't figure you would want to hear about it. We all assumed you would begin your journey back to your life and want to forget any of this ever happened."

Brianna was a bit surprised. They all believed that she would just go home and act as if the past months had never occurred.

"As if I could ever forget what they did to me. I am a bit shocked that you actually believe I could just let it all go. I want to make them pay for what they did," she retorted.

The three of them exchanged a look before John asked her.

"Does this mean you want to join us?"

She paused for a moment before answering.

"Well, yeah. I guess I had intended to join you and help expose them. I don't want it to happen to another girl. But do I have to decide, definitely, this exact moment?"

"No, of course not. But we also can't afford for you to know what we are planning," he paused before continuing. "We have been working on this a long time. We think we have what we need to bring them down."

She looked over at Ethan and Annabelle, who remained quiet.

"I don't want to stand in your way..." she trailed off again.

"But I did want to help. And I want to go home too. And I want to see them go down for what they did... I am really confused," she honestly revealed.

"I'm sorry. I didn't mean to imply that you couldn't be trusted earlier. It is just..." he started.

"It is just that we have so much invested and can't afford for anything to be derailed," Annabelle interrupted.

"We just need someone who is all in and completely focused on what we are doing. We don't blame you if you can't commit to that right now. That is all we were trying to say, unsuccessfully," Ethan finished.

"We don't want to hurt you. You have been through a lot. What we are planning may be too much for you right now," John added.

She wasn't sure how to respond to what they had said.

Rationally, she understood their concerns about her messing up their plans. They didn't know her or what she was capable of. She was a wildcard.

On the other hand, she felt rejected. Insulted, really. She had earned her place to fight back.

John was right about one thing, she had been through a lot. She was entitled more than any of them to be at the forefront of bringing those guys down, starting with the crusty old man.

She didn't say anything at first, but her facial expression must have shown her feelings about it. At a minimum, John had noted that she was upset because he moved closer to her and laid his hand on the her small of her back.

"I'm sorry. We didn't want to offend you. And you are obviously angry," he began.

She was angry, so much that she didn't look him in the eyes as he was trying to calm her. She didn't move away either. She just stood there like a brick wall.

"Please look at me, Brianna," he said.

After a forceful exhale, she complied to find the kind eyes that she had become dependent upon over the last few days.

"How about you go call your family? And then, we can start getting you ready to go to the embassy and get the necessary paperwork for you to go home," he suggested.

She was unbelievably frustrated now. The whole situation irked her and she felt as if they were deliberately trying to exclude her.

"Actually that is exactly what they are doing," she thought to herself.

It was a thought that pissed her off, but she wasn't sure what she could do about it right now. She had no clue how to proceed. Did she voice her frustrations? Did she accept it and just plan to go home?

She could cry and play the victim, a thought that usually didn't occur to her because that hadn't been something she did. And if she did speak up for herself, insist that she be included in what they were planning, which of them did she approach?

John would the logical choice. He had spent the most

time with her. He had seen firsthand what she had been through and would understand. She hoped.

She took a breath to calm herself from her frenzied state.

"John, can I talk to you outside?" she asked.

He looked up, surprised.

"Yes, of course," he replied and led her to the deck overlooking the river.

She waited a moment before she began to make her case, mostly because she wasn't sure where to begin. At first, she said nothing but just stared at the water passing in the river. She looked over at him and noted he was doing the same. She needed to figure out what she wanted to say.

She turned to face him.

"John, how did you feel when you found out what these people were doing? When you realized that you had been lied to and were part of everything they were doing, or possibly worse than even you knew?"

"I felt like shit. You know that already," he said tersely as he continued to look at the river.

"So you can maybe imagine a tenth of what I am feeling," she retorted, pointedly.

He turned to face her then, his face unamused. She couldn't tell if that last remark had angered him, but she didn't care at that moment.

She continued, "You may think you get it because you worked for them for a bit. But I lived it. A nightmare for more than seven months of my life. They did things to me that I can't begin to process. I am not even ready to think about it yet. But it is not a question of just wanting to help. It is that I need to help."

He looked at her, a grimace on his face. His eyes were downcast now and he seemed to be thinking over something before he responded. She turned back to the railing and looked out over the water once again, waiting.

He finally lifted his gaze to focus on her.

"Okay. You can be included in what we are planning."

She looked at him then as he continued.

"There will be some conditions. For starters, you would need to wait to let anyone, including your family, know you are alive."

"Wait. What?" she asked, concerned.

"Brianna, what we are planning... We cannot risk any media attention or worse, government interference."

"What? What exactly are you planning?"

"I can't tell you. Unless you are with us. In this case, unfortunately, you would have to decide to join us or not, blindly. This is the reason we assumed that you would not be part of our plan. It requires you to trust us. To trust strangers. And it means that your family and friends and the whole world will not know what happened to you, yet," he explained.

"So, let me get this correct. I am only allowed to know what the plan is if I agree to help? And that involves not connecting with anyone I love to let them know that I am alive and safe again? I won't know what I am signing up for until after I sign up? I have to do that blindly," she questioned.

"Yes," he said flatly.

"That isn't much of a pitch," she somewhat joked.

He looked at her in surprise at her attempt at light hearted humor and half smiled.

"Well, it is a good thing that I didn't major in business," he quipped back, immediately realizing that his joke fell flat.

She didn't know what she was going to do. She absolutely didn't like the idea of mindlessly agreeing to a plan to bring down the men who took her. She knew firsthand how prepared the crusty old man's people were. She didn't have a clue how ready John's people would be to fight them.

She hated the not knowing with the fire of a thousand burning lakes, as her grandmother would have said.

"I need to think about it. How long do I have?" she asked.

"Well, not long. We hoped to move forward in the next few days, after we got everything with you settled. But the thing is you can't call your family until you let us know. I'm sorry. Are you going to be okay with that stipulation?"

"I guess I have to be," she responded.

They stood for a while staring at the water, side-by-side, without talking. He was leaned forward with his forearms resting on the railing. His stance indicating that he felt he had the weight of the world on his shoulders.

After a bit, Brianna broke the silence and surprised him with a random question.

"So, I was wondering...no matter what I decide to do, I am going to need some clothes. Would that be possible?"

"Don't you have Annabelle's old stuff?" he inquired.

"Well, yeah. Kinda. It is just...well, I don't have any underwear. I feel would feel weird," she told him.

"Oh. Yeah. Sure. I get that," he muttered.

For the first time, she noticed he was blushing. And she saw that her innocent question had lightened the mood dramatically.

He grinned.

"So, you are telling me that you are commando right now?"

She nodded, "I don't remember the last time that I had underwear. That was something that was neglected from my daily wardrobe. I certainly wasn't going to ask for it."

He laughed then. A full, hearty laugh that she didn't fully understand.

"Why didn't you say something?" he asked.

She genuinely smiled then too. She thought of the ridiculousness of not having underwear for almost a year. It was going to feel heavenly to have a bra and panties again, she thought.

"Well, I am saying something now," she replied.

"I think that can be arranged," he said as he motioned for her to come back into the house.

14

She had made progress during the last couple of weeks. Her strategy of pretending to be the Stepford wife was working out brilliantly. She had garnered outdoor time every day except for a few days when it had been raining.

Her hopes were high from that fact alone. If you added that she now had a general idea of the size of the house and some insight into their security details, it wasn't likely her spirits would break anytime soon. It was progress. And the intel was going to pay off in a big way.

She had also gained ground with the staff and the crusty old man. She had somehow managed to make small talk more and more each day. Like a "well-bred" female, she had started by talking of the weather and made her way from there. Now she would have actual polite conversations each evening at dinner.

She was the picture of pleasantness. She had even started to sneak in questions aimed at figuring out who these people were or any weaknesses she could exploit for her freedom. It had proven to be the more difficult aspect of her plan.

She had contemplated what the next steps would be. But she hadn't liked the conclusion she had reached. She assumed she would have to get on a personal level, somehow make friends in the house. She reasoned that the guards would be the most likely choice since she spent most of her time around them. She also knew that the crusty old man would not be easily befriended. He would see through her manipulations.

The wisdom that came with age would be her downfall in this regard. The younger male guards were the best candidates. Specifically, she figured the guard who typically accompanied her on her outdoor outings would be the best option.

She would start simply. She would begin with getting his name. It was amazing how much friendlier people felt when someone called their name to address them. It was a trick she had used in her career. There was no reason to think it wouldn't work here too.

That day when she was making her rounds of the grounds, she had lingered closer to the young man than she did normally. She was looking for an opportunity to casually ask his name. At the end of her hour as she was approaching the house, she saw her chance.

"Excuse me," she said to get his attention.

For the first time, he looked directly at her. Although she wasn't convinced he actually saw a human being when he did. But it was time to change that perspective, if she could.

"I thought I should know your name by now," she stated.

He didn't seem convinced to give it, but he surprised her when he responded.

"Mark."

"Thank you, Mark," she noted.

He just nodded and motioned for her to enter the house as directed.

It wasn't a huge reaction, but it was enough to be encouraging. It was enough to give her the courage the next day to say his name and politely ask if he had noted a bird flying between the trees. He acted disinterested at first but called her attention to more birds flying around a few minutes later.

She genuinely smiled because it was a sign that this Mark guy was not immune to her civility. It had given her reassurance that there was hope of befriending the staff. Every day she found a way to talk to Mark about little, insignificant things. It didn't take long until they were chatting on a daily basis and she found herself listening to him regale tales of his life.

She listened intently and pretended to be intrigued. She asked questions to show she had remembered his stories. She made him think she was taking an interest in his life. In reality, it was a way to keep him talking. She had also learned early in her professional life that people tended to enjoy talking about themselves. They were apt to like people who encouraged them to talk about themselves. It was a well-thought tactic that appeared to be working.

It was only a couple of weeks before he started

visiting her room in the late afternoons to continue talking to her. She honestly didn't like him being in her room. It made her feel very uneasy. If the truth be told, she didn't care for Mark as a person. He was one dimensional and chauvinistic. Yet, she didn't feel she had a choice in the matter. She needed an ally. So, she sat on her bed's edge and listened as Mark droned on about nonsense every day. It was getting more difficult to act interested, but she reminded herself why she was doing it.

The others hadn't seemed to notice the increased contact between her and the guard. At least, no one said anything that she had overheard or acted any differently toward her. She imagined if there was knowledge of it, then the crusty old man would at a minimum indicate his displeasure in some fashion. Things seemed to be going swimmingly though. She even found herself in polite conversation with the crusty old man on occasion.

If she had known how quickly it would all change and how misguided her decision to chat up this particular guard would be, she would have relented sooner. Alas, she didn't anticipate Mark's growing attachment. She hadn't sensed his particular level of crazy.

She found out one afternoon when he came to her room to "continue their talk" as he had indicated.

She felt uneasy from the moment he had entered the room. He was fidgeting and acting erratic. He would sit down and then immediately stand to pace before sitting again. She wasn't sure how to react to his current behavior. She decided for the moment to remain quiet and not make any sudden movements. Similar to the what you do if you had run upon a snake in the grass, she thought. She waited to see if he planned to pounce.

He eventually did. After a few minutes, he had settled on the edge of the bed, only a few feet away from where she was positioned.

She thought there was enough distance between them. She was wrong. She had been so wrong about all of it.

She hadn't seen his first movements. She hadn't sensed he was attacking. It hadn't fully registered before he was on top of her.

He lunged at her like a cougar who was finally making its move after thoroughly stalking its prey. His chest pinned her body to the bed. It was at this moment that she fully noticed how long his torso was, which was not surprising given his height. He had obstructed her entire frame including her legs. His hands had already secured both of her arms above her head. She was completely immobilized within seconds. His face was hovering about hers, eyes daring her to try to get loose.

She looked at how his body was weighing her down and assessed how much trouble she was in. It wasn't good. She didn't have a clue how she was going to fight free.

She took a deep breath, looking him directly in his eyes. He didn't speak. He just licked his lips and smiled in a purely wicked way. It was as if he was signifying he had already won. He also didn't make another move. He just laid there on top of her, asserting his control.

Brianna didn't move either. She wasn't sure what her

reaction should be. Her uncertainty was becoming second nature. She wanted him off of her and feared what he would do. He had the power right now. She was completely restricted.

Her mind had already begun running through all the terrifying possibilities when he suddenly rolled off her. He stood and left the room without a word or backward glance.

The sudden exit hadn't given her comfort. She didn't believe he was done with her or that he wouldn't exert his control over her again. This was the beginning of a game. It had been as clear as day in his smile. He would try again. The next time, she needed to be prepared.

She was shaken by how vulnerable she had made herself. She had permitted this to happen by engaging with him in the first place. She was weak. That fact was clearer now because a simple guard was able to dominate her with very little effort. And he would do it again. She was certain of it.

"How am I going to defend myself?" she pondered.

She couldn't ask the crusty old man because he would question the guards and discover that she had been encouraging the conversations. He was likely to blame her anyway. Or worse, he may even figure out that her behavior of late was all a manipulation to find a way out of this place.

She wouldn't allow the guard to violate her again either. She knew with absolute certainty he would try again to do far more than just pin her down next time. She had to think of a way to defend herself. If, or when, he tried to assault her again, she would be prepared.

That evening she wracked her brain to think of what she could do to make sure he kept his distance. She needed a plan quickly because there wasn't any way to tell how long he would wait before he made another move.

She sat distracted throughout dinner, trying to figure out a way to sneak one of her utensils to her room. She had assumed they keep a tight inventory of those items. She had noticed the kitchen staff, who had cleared the table each night, seemed to be scrutinizing the silverware to ensure everything was collected. She guessed they would notice if a knife was missing. Perhaps she could keep one of the forks since there were several of them. Even that would be risky.

The whole thing was stressing her out more than she already was. She was scared. She was finally admitting it to herself.

"Well, what else is new?" she asked herself.

She had been kidnapped, neglected, manipulated, virtually starved, and physically beaten. And now she was in danger of being raped. She had to do something. No matter the consequences. She would fight Mark somehow.

It would just have to be with a weapon from somewhere other than the dining room because she never saw an opening to take one of the utensils.

She fretted about what she would do if Mark showed up in the night. It dominated her mind to a point that she lay awake that night. She jumped at every sound, tossed and turned, and even found herself shaking from the thought of what he wanted to do to her.

She would add sleep deprivation to the list of offenses, she thought.

It had been a colossal mistake to think she could have found someone there who would feel sympathy for her. Reflecting on it now, it seemed like it had been a stupid idea from the beginning. These people saw her every day. She was a hostage and they did nothing. At best, they were turning a blind eye and it wasn't okay.

It was a struggle, but she finally managed to fall asleep. The night passed without incident and the next day was much like the one before it. She decided that she wouldn't make a tour of the grounds that day, just so she could avoid Mark. She spent the day in her room, sitting in the floor, staring off into space, and lamenting about her previous life.

However, she didn't sit quiet at dinner. She maintained the polite demeanor she had been projecting the last few weeks. As far as the crusty old man was concerned, she had happily adjusted to her life and role.

For the next several days, she kept the same routine of staying indoors, avoiding Mark. She saw him in passing, but she didn't interact with him. He appeared calm and disinterested in her. His expressions were the definition of blank each time she saw him. He didn't give any indication of being threatening.

She needed to get back outside to continue formulating an escape plan. She decided she would test it out and request to go outside the next day. If Mark acted erratic, she would come up with a plan to get rid of him as her guard.

When it came time the following day, he didn't give

any indication that anything had happened between them. He was completely professional, whatever that meant for a man employed to guard a hostage. He kept a watchful distance and didn't demonstrate the slightest interest in her or what she was doing.

It was as if it had never happened. As if she hadn't ever asked his name or starting chatting with him. She didn't know what to think of it. Perhaps someone had found out what he had done to her. Or maybe he had gotten in trouble, just as the other guards had when she was beaten.

She wasn't going to complain if that was the case. It would allow her to get back to her plans. Better yet, it was time to construct a new one since befriending the staff was not a good idea. Except she would remain cautious of this particular employee, make sure to stay clear of him no matter how it affected her plan.

Her routine returned to the status quo over the next few days. Mark remained stoic and never breathed a word of their encounter. She began to relax again.

Then she was awoken forcibly a few nights later. The room was pitch black and she was being jostled by something. The terror that overcame her was without comprehension. She was disoriented, but she could tell that someone was on top of her, restraining her. She didn't need her eyes to adjust to know who it was.

The smell of his cologne was repulsive. She was gagging on it as she began to squirm and thrash under his weight. He brought his face closer and she could feel his hot breath on her cheeks.

"Don't fight it," he whispered, raspy.

"Like hell," she retorted.

She turned her shoulder to be perpendicular to his chest and managed to get herself partially free. He desperately tried to grab her arms to pin them down. She, however, began kicking with her legs. She used the distraction and momentum to crawl out from under him. She quickly kept moving, landing on the floor with a thud.

He didn't waste any time coming after her. She hadn't scrambled to her feet before he dove from the bed and tackled her again. Luckily, he had misjudged in the dark. He landed short. He rapidly tried to climb his way up her legs to pin her chest down again, but was failing miserably as she kicked harder and harder.

She knew that she wouldn't be able to get past him to get to the door on the other side of the bed. Screaming didn't seem to be an option as she already struggled for breath. It had only been a couple of minutes, but she was already exhausted. She made a snap decision that crawling under the bed was the only escape.

She was halfway under it when he finally succeeded with restraining her legs. He was pulling her out from the bed as she used all her upper body strength to scratch her way back under it. In the struggle, she noticed that the wine glass she had stolen over a month ago had fallen in the commotion from its hiding place. In a desperate move, she grabbed it as he dragged the rest of her body towards him.

Everything stopped for a moment. He stood straddling her, breathing hard from the struggle.

Once again thinking he had gotten the best of her, he

reached down to flip her onto her back. As he leaned down, she used the moment he was close to make a last ditch effort. She swung her arm with the wine glass in her hand as hard as she could. By some miracle, it made contact.

It didn't knock him out like she had seen in the movies. But she had hit him with enough force to break the glass. Even more lucky for her, she had made contract near the left temple and it appeared that some of the glass had broken the skin, gotten into his eyes.

Blood was gushing down his face and dripping on her. He almost immediately fell backwards onto his butt and covered the wound with his hand. She was almost certain she had done some damage as he began saying "my eye, my eye," over and over again. There was so much blood.

"But not nearly enough for what he deserved," she thought.

She used this time to climb over the bed and get to the door. She didn't hesitate before running into the hall and began screaming "help." She ran down the stairs to the main floor, pleading for assistance.

The irony of her situation was not lost on her. She was asking her capturers for help. She would be surprised if they even cared that she had been attacked.

She ran straight into the arms of another guard. To him, she was sure she seemed hysterical.

He began attempting to calm her, except she would have none of it. All at once, it came crashing down on her. All the emotions she had been holding back came at her at once. She crumbled to the floor in a crying mess. She truly was hysterical.

She was so enthralled in her emotional break that she didn't notice when the crusty old man had appeared. She didn't hear him inquiring as to what had happened. She was too overwrought to know that the guards and crusty old man went into her room and found Mark sitting in the floor bleeding.

He didn't bother to come after her. He just sat there and waited. Brianna didn't hear the gunshot that would kill Mark. She didn't witness the bloody mess in the white room. She was given a sedative shot by one of the staff, but she couldn't tell who had given it. She knew nothing except her anguish as her view went to black once again.

Sadly, she didn't believe she would awaken to better conditions this time either.

15

John was true to his word. He took her to a department store and told her to go get the items she needed. He didn't accompany her. In fact, he acted much like a bored husband waiting for his wife to finish her tedious shopping. It felt so, normal.

At first, she went about the task with a purpose. Soon, however, she found that she was going through the motions. Her mind was definitely elsewhere. She had a decision to make.

It was an impossible choice for her. For months, she had dreamed of going home and now she had a chance to do it. She could leave it all behind and go back to her life. She wouldn't ever be able to pretend it hadn't happened, but she could get as far away from it as possible.

Or she could put blind faith in strangers, who claimed they had a plan to take down the people who had ruined her life. She felt an obligation, for sure. She didn't want a future Doppelgänger to suffer the way she had. She also wanted justice, for herself.

She was afraid, more scared than she had been in the entire seven months of captivity. She was petrified to get close to that environment again. She knew what they were, what they were capable of. She feared she would be taken again and there would be no way out this time.

It was paralyzing to think about it.

It was a justified fear too. The only people who would know she was alive were three strangers who were attempting to outsmart an organized group of crazy people. She wouldn't be allowed to let anyone know that she had been found. This part of the equation worried her the most. She wondered what would keep her from slipping into the abyss.

She also wondered what help she would be to them. She hadn't been able to escape on her own despite many attempts. She thought of all her failed plans and the bloodshed it had created.

She guessed she had succeeded in somewhat escaping, if you counted them throwing her out as if she was yesterday's trash. She had managed to anger the crusty old man enough that he had just given up on her, put her in a shed in the woods.

It was a small accomplishment. She proved herself unworthy of being held by them anymore. She had been left to die. They would move on the next girl, if they hadn't located one already. A thought that filled her with rage. A thought that made her choice clear.

She abruptly went to find John. He was sitting in a chair with his eyes closed. He looked like he had been sleeping peacefully, but his eyes opened abruptly when she got close. His sudden movement made her jump.

"Sorry, I thought you were sleeping," she said.

"Just resting my eyes a bit," he replied with a wink. "I didn't get much sleep last night. Ethan and I were up early too."

"Oh okay. I actually wanted to talk to you some more about that," she began. "I'm in."

He didn't really react. He simply nodded his head in understanding as if what she had just declared was like announcing she would wash the dishes after dinner.

He slowly stood.

"Is that all you needed?" he asked, nodding his head at the garments she held.

She looked down at her hands with several bras and panties in them. She also had a pair of spandex workout pants and a plain blue t-shirt.

"Yeah, it is just a few things. Annabelle loaned me the rest," she explained as she released the clothes to his grasp.

She was confused as to why he was changing the subject and acting as if he didn't hear her desire to participate in the upcoming takedown. She had thought it would be a bigger deal.

"You know you can get more than these things. You don't have to rely on Annabelle's clothes," he told her.

She shrugged her shoulders in reply and he gave her a scornful look.

"C'mon," he said as he started towards the women's section of the store.

She followed him and watched as he grabbed pants

and shirts. He didn't speak to her, just silently completed his task. He finally passed the stack of clothing back to her. He motioned towards the dressing room and went in its direction without checking to see if she followed.

A few hours later they returned to his friend's house. He hadn't spoken a word about her announcement that she would join them in their quest. His lack of response wasn't just disappointing, it was downright unnerving.

They had bought her several options for clothes, mostly black workout clothes. She wasn't sure why he grabbed so many of these items from the racks. The only logical assumption was he was assembling what she needed to join them. She couldn't think of a plausible explanation as to why John hadn't reacted or said anything to confirm her involvement.

If she was correct, she speculated what they were about to do was something very physical. An assumption that made her even more nervous at not knowing the plan. In classic Brianna style, she had been overanalyzing for the past hour. She knew on some level she was being ridiculous, but she kept doing it nonetheless.

John had carried her shopping bags inside and threw them on the couch before heading straight to the kitchen.

"You hungry?" he asked over his shoulder as he made a beeline for the fridge.

"Yeah, I am. Where are Ethan and Annabelle?" she replied.

"I am not sure. They were supposed to run some errands this morning," he answered.

He didn't make small talk as he pulled out the

148

sandwich ingredients. In fact, he avoided looking at her too as he set about the chore of making them lunch.

"Do you like meat? They have turkey and ham both," he indicated absentmindedly as he prepared the bread with mayo and veggies.

"I can make one for myself. I am not a complete invalid," she told him as she moved into the kitchen to do her sandwich herself.

He moved aside to share the counter space and continued to make his food without acknowledgement.

"Your silence is unnerving me," Brianna finally told him.

"Hmmm...how so?" he said.

He appeared unfazed by her worry. He even had a slight smirk on his face as he began eating his sandwich.

"Well, I told you I was in on the plan... But you said nothing. Actually you have been really quiet all morning," she explained.

He didn't speak immediately, just slightly nodded his head. He looked at her and studied her before he spoke. He had tilted his head to the side and furrowed his brow. She, on the other hand, was becoming more frustrated.

"Why are you just staring at me?" she voiced angrily. "Stop! I have had enough of people staring at me like I am a lab rat. The crusty old man did that!"

Suddenly, he started laughing. A hearty, deep laugh which baffled her to no end. After a minute, he composed himself enough to ask.

"You call him the 'crusty old man'?"

"Yeah."

He smiled widely.

"That is hilarious. And accurate."

He paused for a minute before continuing.

"I am not trying to unnerve you. I am skeptical that you have actually thought it all the way through in only a couple of hours. I haven't addressed it because I expect you don't mean it. Or you will change your mind. And we can't afford for me to give you the information until we do know you are on board. As I have said. I am not meaning to be a jerk here. My concerns are very valid."

"So you don't believe me?" she asked.

"Honestly, no. I don't," he held up his palm to indicate for her to wait for him to finish. "Just listen to me for a second."

She suddenly felt tired and defeated. She was overcome with a rush of negative energy that felt like it had nowhere to go. Her shoulders slumped.

He walked toward her and placed his hand on one of her shoulders.

"Please just listen. I will explain why I am hesitant," he calmed her.

"Since I found you, you have been going non-stop. I haven't seen you really react to everything you went through in the compound. And that worries me."

He paused to see if she was listening. She looked up into his eyes and silently nodded.

"At some point, it will come crashing down for you. When it does... Well, you are a risk. A big one. I am not trying to exclude you. I want you to be involved. But we have been working on this for a couple of years now and I have to proceed with caution," he continued.

They stood there staring at each other, neither one

speaking. He had his hands on each of her shoulders now, bracing her stance. She was apathetic, similar to how she had been when he had rescued her.

He was right. She had been operating on an autopilot since he carried her out of the woods. She had been so focused on survival for so long, she hadn't stopped to process everything she had experienced. She hadn't let the emotions of it all bubble up. She was still shut off, almost void of feelings.

"I think I may go for a walk. I need to think. If that is alright?" she responded.

"Yes, of course. Should I go with you so that you don't lose your way," he asked.

"No. I need to be alone for a little while. I need to think about everything," she answered.

He sighed and released her arms. He turned and retrieved a cell phone from the kitchen counter.

"Alright. At least take this so you can get help if you need it."

She smirked.

"Or if you get lost," he corrected with a shrug.

"Thanks," she said.

As she made her way out of the house, she stopped. Turning back to him, she simply stated, "You're right."

She left then. She found an entrance to a boardwalk along the river. She wandered for a bit, looking back at the city or out over the water. She thought a lot about what John had said. She had known immediately he was right. Despite being free again, she hadn't given herself the liberty to consider how she was feeling. She was trying to get from one step to another and just keep breathing. She hadn't allowed herself to fall apart.

She understood why John was worried. If she was to join them and, then crack under pressure when they were in the midst of their takedown, it could destroy everything they had worked to achieve. He had said the three of them had spent years putting it all together. It was obvious they had a lot riding on it. She would be weary of her messing it up too.

She didn't know what to do to convince them. She truly wanted to help. She stood by her decision that returning to her life could wait. She also wanted revenge. She didn't have shame in admitting it. But the real question was whether that was enough motivation for her to keep it together.

She had begun to reflect on her time in the house. She had been through so much there. Yet, she was still intact. She had never given up, even when she got thrown into the shed to "rot."

The thought of that place gave her shivers to think of it, but it also filled her with rage. An anger that perhaps she should show John and the others. It wasn't that she was void of feelings. She had just gotten accustomed to suppressing her emotions. She had played the game too well. She had refused to let them get her down. She hadn't given them the satisfaction.

Now, it seemed it was the time to let her guard down a little. She needed to show John that she could be trusted to handle herself. She would give them the confidence to believe in her and, maybe, she would actually find it within herself as well.

She walked back to the house and saw Ethan had returned. Annabelle was still out. However, this time there were some new people to meet.

In the kitchen, she found John and Ethan engaged in a casual conversation with two other men. The newcomers were sitting on the bar stools drinking beers while John and Ethan leaned against the counters doing the same.

At first they didn't hear her come into the house. They were laughing and very animated. She stopped to watch for a minute before they discovered she was there. It was comforting to happen upon a group of guys discussing sports. Once again, it felt very normal. A feeling she was quickly getting used to.

Despite feeling timid, she decided she would approach them with a confidence she was hoping she could fake. She wanted to begin reassuring her new friends that she was up to whatever they had planned.

It was one of the new guys who noticed her first. He looked over his shoulder and then did a double take when she saw her. Both men immediately got to their feet when she entered the room.

"It is okay guys. At ease," she joked.

"How was your walk?" John asked without delay.

"It was really good. I figured some things out. But I can tell you about it later. What game are you guys discussing?" she inquired.

"American football. I'm Robert. This is Chris. You must be the Brianna that I have heard so much about?" he started.

Robert was average height with dark skin and dark

hair. His eyes were a bright green that would make a cat jealous, though they weren't as striking as John's. She guessed it was because John had longer lashes that augmented his eyes. Robert was so broad shouldered it made her wonder if he ever played any of the football he was watching. He looked like a linebacker.

Chris was the opposite. He was pale and lanky. His light brown hair was dull and cut short. His features were neither odd nor distinctive. He was as average as she had ever seen. It had been her experience that these guys were the nicest because they had to be. They usually weren't attractive enough to be cocky dicks unless, of course, they were overly charismatic. Chris wasn't either of those things.

"Yeah, I am Brianna. Should I be frightened about what you have heard?" she said with a smile.

She looked over at John. It was as she had suspected. He had a curious look on his face. He was scrutinizing her every move and didn't know what to think of this charming creature before them.

The men all exchanged a look between them that made it clear these guys knew about her. The one called Robert replied for all of them.

"No. We haven't heard anything bad about you."

She looked pointedly at John, her eyes pleading for explanation of what they knew. The silence in the room was truly uncomfortable. She didn't want to ask the depth of their knowledge. It occurred to her she didn't know how much any of them knew. She hadn't been forthcoming.

She looked around the room at each of them, none daring to make eye contact except John.

"I think it is time that we had a chat about what you think you know about me and my past. And more specifically, I want to know how you knew about me before we met," she demanded.

They exchanged looks amongst themselves. Except, once again, John. His focus was solely on her. They all started clamoring to say something but only one voice came through loud and clear.

"I have known about you for two years," John said.

Everyone got quiet. Brianna was shocked. It was a bombshell that had the power to shake her to her core. But instead, she stayed calm. She waited. She wanted to hear more before she reacted. She knew he was about to reveal something.

"John, do you think this is wise to talk about now?" Ethan interrupted the silence before John could continue.

John just waved Ethan off, his demeanor was completely relaxed.

"I knew about you two years ago because that is how long ago they started a plan to take you. And your replacement has already been chosen. Though I doubt they have grabbed her yet. You aren't the first, I told you that. The last few didn't fair very well. I am not sure where they are buried, but it is almost certain they are dead. Because they didn't fit the mold they needed. They didn't obey. It was where you were headed."

With that bit of information revealed, all three of the other guys left the room with their eyes lowered and grimaces on their faces. However, she wasn't going anywhere until she got the rest of the story. A rage had overcome her. The implications of what he had said was resounding in her head.

"You are going to have to explain further...like a lot," she said.

"What exactly do you want to know?" John asked.

"Well, for starters how you could know what they were going to do to me for two years and wait until after they did it to intervene!" she screamed.

"It isn't that easy," he began. "Yes, I knew about you but I didn't know the specifics. I knew your first name but not your last. I didn't know where you lived. I didn't get that much information... And even if I did, I am not sure I could have intervened..."

"What? Why not?" she demanded.

"They are really connected, Brianna. If I had stopped them from grabbing you then they would have just taken the next girl. And we wouldn't have known where they were located," he explained.

"Wait! How could you not know where they were located? You said you worked for them! You rescued me from there. That doesn't make any sense," she retorted.

"Actually, it does. There is more than one compound. When we got information that they were setup in the Hale Islands, we planned your extraction. It had to be timed right," he continued.

She felt sick to her stomach. She wasn't sure she wanted to hear anymore. They had let her go through hell for seven months and did nothing.

"Look, I know it sounds shitty. And yeah, maybe we

could have figured out who you were and stopped it sooner. We did the best we could. Once we found out where you were, we did everything we could to get you out of there. And we are all very sorry for it... I am sorry for it," he finished, finally looking defeated.

They stood there for what seemed like forever. She was speechless. She didn't know how she should take this information. One part of her was angry. The logical side of her understood on some level.

"I want to reiterate that you are free to leave here anytime. We understand if you can't stand the sight of us. If you blame us. Blame me," he added. "I promise you that if you want to go, we will get you home."

She wasn't sure how she was going to respond when suddenly Ethan burst into the room. He was out of breath, pale, and looked panicked.

"Ethan, what the hell?" John asked, obviously concerned about what had gone wrong.

"They have Annabelle!" he yelled.

"What?" John demanded.

"They have Annabelle. They grabbed her when she was out running errands. I just got the call. John, we have to go get her!"

John immediately began comforting his friend.

"We will get her back if that's true. Just calm down and tell me what happened," he reassured.

He looked up to Robert and Chris, who she just noticed were in the room as well.

"Someone needs to fill me in," John demanded since Ethan was struggling for breath.

"We were out front hanging out when Ethan got a call

on his cell phone. He looked like he had seen a ghost. Then he ran into the house and we followed. That is all we know," Chris recanted.

"Ethan?" John asked, looking to his friend for more information.

Ethan took a deep breath, trying to regain his senses and calm himself from his worry.

"I got a call from them," he started. "When I answered, they asked if I knew where my wife was. And then they said I really should keep an eye on her because she just might...disappear. And they hung up."

"So they didn't say they had her or make any demands?" John questioned.

"You know they have her!" Ethan screamed again. "What else do you want? A fucking billboard sign? Or maybe you'd prefer her body delivered to us as proof?"

To her, Ethan seemed to be acting reasonably. She understood why John wasn't jumping to conclusions, but she would have reacted the same as Ethan.

She was beginning to see, even more so, that John was always cool under pressure. He got all the information before he reacted. It was something she admired about him, especially in this situation.

Maybe she could understand why he had waited to extract her. She may not be able to forgive it yet, but she was beginning to comprehend it.

"Ethan, just calm down for a minute. I am not disagreeing with you. I am just trying to understand what is happening."

He walked to the cabinet and grabbed a glass that he

proceeded to fill with water. He handed it to Ethan as he began giving instructions to Robert and Chris.

"Robert, please get the California guys on the phone. Have them start tracking Annabelle, starting with her cell phone and the necklace. Even if they just trace her last movements, it will be important information if the Doppelgangmen have, in fact, grabbed her," he instructed.

"Chris, get ahold of all our contacts who track the Doppelgangmen and see if there has been movement. Tell them to look particularly close at the Hale Islands compound."

"Doppelgangmen?" she interrupted, confused.

"The men who took you. That's what we call them." John clarified.

He the continued with his directions, clearly taking the lead in handling things.

"Brianna, we are going to have to table our discussion of what I did and didn't do wrong in dealing with your kidnapping and subsequent rescue. As you see, we have more pressing matters," he told her.

She bowed her head.

"Of course," she managed. "Is there anything that I can do to help?"

"No, we have everything covered for now. There isn't really much any of us can do until we get some more information," John reassured.

"Okay, I will stay out of the way," she said.

"Thanks. I appreciate it," John responded.

The hours passed slowly. All of the men were busy on the computer or phone, searching for Annabelle. Brianna aimlessly wandered the house. She felt useless. Then again, she agreed with John. There wasn't much she could do to help.

It didn't take long for them to confirm that Annabelle was indeed missing. They tracked her cell phone using GPS to an outdoor recreational store not far from her and Ethan's house. Luckily, she also had a necklace that had a GPS tracker installed in it. They had finally accessed her location and discovered it was, in fact, on one of the Hale Islands.

Chris was still waiting for intel about what the motive for taking Annabelle was, besides the obvious. They hadn't heard anything more since the call that Ethan had received. However, it was clear that the Doppelgangmen were up to something.

John had started planning with Ethan and Robert while Chris was working on finding out the group's movements. She was surprised when Ethan brought out a stack of papers from his office and laid them out on the dining room table. There were maps, banking and credit card statements, and pages upon pages of notes and transcripts.

She desperately wanted to know what was being planned. Afraid of being rebuked, she slowly approached the table and stood quietly listening. John looked up at her for a second, but nodded before returning his focus to the map in front of him. Ethan was combing through a notebook and seemingly finding the information he needed as he jotted down additional notes. None of them paid any attention to her. They were too busy.

"Robert, we are going to need the most recent security

logs. Can you start on getting those for me?" Ethan asked.

"Yeah, sure," Robert responded before heading to his laptop and getting to work.

Brianna peered at the maps that John was intently studying. She quickly noted they were full of pencils markings. Someone had outlined access points to specific islands and placed "x's" at what she assumed were significant places. There seemed to be several small islands that were important.

Meanwhile, she saw that Ethan had just pulled out a house floor plan. A house for which she immediately recognized the blueprint. It was also covered in pencil markings and had notes jotted by asterisks.

"What are the asterisks?" she interrupted.

Ethan gazed up at her and sighed.

"They are the compound's access points or weak spots," he said, sounding agitated.

She didn't hold his attitude against him. He was worried and trying to focus. She leaned over and took a better look at the blueprint. It didn't take her long to get herself oriented to the layout. She knew the majority of that house well.

She was quick to locate her room and many rooms on the first floor, having had thoroughly explored them. However, it surprised her there was a massive basement and attic that were also divided into rooms. Although she never saw them come and go, she guessed this is where the staff lived. It made sense as she contemplated it. They had always been available and now she knew they had been holding her on an island.

Looking at their intel, she didn't know what the

information the guys were gathering meant. It was all out of context for her because she didn't know their plans. But she figured they knew what they were doing. She was the actual evidence of that.

"We are going to have to go tomorrow," John finally indicated to Ethan.

"We won't be ready yet," Robert interjected.

"Yes, but we don't really have a choice now," he retorted and looked at Ethan. "You know what they will do to her. She isn't a Doppel. There is no need to keep her alive."

He had placed his hand on Ethan's shoulder. She couldn't imagine what was going through his friend's mind. But all of them knew what Ethan was feeling. He was wearing one of the grimmest expressions she had ever seen.

"What do we need to be ready?" Robert asked.

"Not much, I don't think," John replied. "We will have to change it though."

John looked up at her.

"You still willing to be part of this?" he asked.

She looked around the room and they were all staring at her, waiting for her reply.

"Yes. I am still in. I told you that I was. What can I do to help?" she demanded.

"I am not sure yet. I will have to figure that out tonight," John indicated. "But it is good to know that we have another person. I think I have an idea how this can work out."

"I truly hope you do too," Ethan agreed.

"Chris? Do you have any data on the security detail

yet?" John probed.

"Not yet. I need a few more minutes, at least," Chris responded.

"Okay. While we wait on that information, the rest of you come here. This is what I am thinking," John stated.

They all gathered around the table except for Chris, who continued hammering away on his computer. John pointed to a remote island that was marked with only two x's.

"I think this is the most likely place they would take Annabelle."

"You don't think they will take her to main house?" Ethan asked.

"She isn't a Doppel. We have to reorient our thinking," John explained. "They reserve the main house for the Doppels. No. I don't think they will take Annabelle there."

"What makes you think they will take her to that particular island?" Robert asked.

"We will use Chris' information to verify, but this island had a security post set up. They are going to want to guard her until they are sure she has served her purpose, I think," John answered.

"And just what do you think their purpose for her is?" Ethan demanded.

John bowed his head when he responded, "To get us to come there."

The group was quiet. Brianna began wondering if taking Annabelle was a trap. From the moment John had rescued her, he had been looking over his shoulder. He had told her that they were still a threat. It was amazing how quickly she had forgotten that once they were back in the business of a city.

Then she remembered, she had been taken from a city in broad daylight. It was a reminder that nowhere was truly safe. It was likely this was a trap because it would be stupid to lure someone without a plan to catch them. These Doppelgangmen were not even remotely dumb. They would have a plan.

"Until we have the intel that Chris is working to get, this is all circumspect. Either way, I think we need to use Brianna as bait for them," he explained as he looked at her for a reaction.

She didn't like the idea, but she had been suspecting as much. It was the most logical strategy. She was something they wanted. They had thought they had disposed of her and left her to die in the shed. Now, she was not only free but, in a position to expose them. She was actually surprised it took them this many days to retaliate.

She nodded her head in agreement. She knew what was expected of her. Surprisingly, she was okay with it. The last few hours had had her wondering what purpose she would serve. How was she to be of any help? Despite living at the house for almost seven months, she didn't know all the weak spots before seeing them on the blueprint.

It wasn't from a lack of trying, but she didn't have the insider knowledge that could help them. She certainly didn't have the muscles to take on the guards. And in her current physical state she doubted that she could even win a catfight.

Her mind apparently wasn't a match for the Doppelgangmen either or she would have been able to escape without help from John.

She hated feeling down on herself but after seven months of failing, there were certain facts she had to face. She had to realize that her Houdini skills were limited. Her role was to use her face to draw the Doppelgangmen back to her.

"What did you have in mind?" she asked.

"Well, there are just the four of us since we are going tomorrow. We will have to split up, two and two," John started.

He pointed to one of the x's.

"This is where I think Annabelle will be held. Over here is the security station, of sorts. Although I imagine the guards won't be at the station. They will be keeping a close eye on her."

"Got it!" Chris interrupted.

He joined them at the table, bringing his laptop.

"So they are keeping her on this island. Here," Chris indicated, pointing to the same one that John had said it would be.

"Are you sure?" John asked.

Chris smirked at him before continuing.

"I pinpointed the location based on the devices the guards are using. I also confirmed it with Annabelle's necklace. Given the number of pings that I am getting, there seems to be around six guards stationed there. That is the best guess anyway. There is no way to be absolutely sure. There could be guards who aren't connected, but I don't think so given the setup of their organization," he related.

"Right. We will access the island at this cove," John began. "It may be surveyed, but if we go in at night then it should provide some cover."

"Coming in at night is really risky. We won't be able to see very well. And they have the home court advantage," Ethan pointed out.

His tone conveyed the defeatism he obviously felt.

"It is the best option," John replied. "There is no element of surprise here. They know we are coming. The most we can hope for is to make landfall without detection. Even though it is a long shot."

"We should do what is smart," Robert interjected. "If there is such an option."

"What is the rest of the plan?" Brianna jumped in.

"Shouldn't we hear all of it before we decide if it needs to be modified?"

John nodded his head in appreciation and finished explaining his plan. There were a few more interruptions for clarification, but it was a decent plan given the circumstances. There were a few things they would need to play by ear, but overall it had potential.

Once they went through it once more, Ethan excused himself to take a shower. She imagined that was just an excuse to be alone. Either way, she was hoping it would help him relax a little bit.

The other three guys went back to reading notes and familiarizing themselves with the information for tomorrow's mission.

"Mission?" she thought to herself.

She was in over her head. There was only one thing that would make her feel better about what she was walking into tomorrow. Not going.

She grabbed a map and started to study the geography of the island where Annabelle was being held. She thought she might as well be prepared before going into the fire.

It was a small island and seemed to be covered in forests, if the topography was accurate. However, the bright side was if one of them got left behind there would be plenty of hiding places. As she looked it over, she grew curious as to the island where she had been all those months.

"John?" she got his attention. "Where is the house? Which island?"

He came over behind where she was seated at the table. He leaned over her, casting a shadow of the map laid out in front her. His presence made her feel safe and nervous at the same time. A reaction that she had every time she was close to him.

She was sure he had no idea what he was doing to her emotions. He appeared unaffected by their proximity. He simply pointed out an island that had more x's than the others and walked away. She studied it, thinking to herself how different the island was from what she had imagined. It was amazing how perspective changes things. And memories.

When she looked at the blueprints to the house next, she found that it was harder to remain detached. She was chilled from the shivers running through her body. Her mind was on overload from all the bad images replaying in her mind. But she forced herself to focus and learn every detail of the house that she hadn't discovered firsthand.

She wasn't sure why she was committing it to memory. She trusted John's judgement. He had been analyzing the Doppelgangmen for years. He knew their patterns. It was probable that Annabelle was exactly where John had said. But in case they had her in the compound, she wanted to be able to assist the guys. Or maybe she didn't want to wind up trapped herself. She didn't plan to be caught off guard ever again.

It wasn't long before she needed some air. Without a word, she got up and went outside. She leaned against the railing and stared up at the night sky. The stars were so visible that she started retracing the lines of the constellations. She had done it so many times as a child. Growing up in the country, there weren't a lot of activities to keep you occupied. It wasn't lost on her that it was the first time in over a year that she had stopped to look at the stars. Another sign that normal was returning, at least momentarily.

Even as she was marveling at the beauty, she was alert enough to hear John approach. He handed her a beer and then mirrored her position of star gazing. There was an awkwardly comfortable silence between them as they sipped their beers.

"I used to stare at the stars when I was a kid," he remembered aloud. "I grew up on this farm in the middle of nowhere."

"Me too," she related, surprised.

"The plight of country kids, I guess," he smiled.

It was a smile that was different from the others. It was more natural, his eyes lighting up. She felt that familiar nervousness again as her body grew flushed.

No man had had this affect on her before. She admitted to herself. She liked him. He had a charm to him that made it easy to be around him. His confidence was sexy as hell.

He turned and returned her stare. After a breath, he moved closer and cupped her face in his hands. She closed her eyes and leaned into his hands. His thumb moved in a semicircular motion that was arousing. Her heart felt heavy in her chest and she forgot how to breathe.

She opened her eyes again. His eyes were on fire, glistening in the dim light. His body had inched closer so that there was no space between them. He slipped his hand from her cheek to her neck. Without hesitation, he slowly pulled her the remaining space between them and guided his lips to grip hers. Over and over his lips pulled at hers, his tongue repeatedly slipping into her mouth.

The man seriously knew how to kiss. He teased her just enough to have every inch of her begging for more. She lost herself for a while. The bodies merged together in an embrace that erased the individuality of each of them. Every part of her body was hot to the touch. She was overcome by the sensuality of the moment.

Abruptly, he pulled away from her. His breathing quick and rasped.

"You sure about this?" he implored.

She only managed to nod before his lips once again claimed hers and she gasped at their victory.

16

S he awoke in a dark room again. It was becoming a familiar occurrence. She was groggy and realized that they must have given her a large dose of that sedative.

Then she remembered why.

She wondered why she didn't feel numb after all that she had experienced. She truly wished she didn't feel emotions anymore. It would make things easier to accept it. But she did still feel. The anger, the rage, the defeat. They were all stirring inside of her at the thought of what Mark had tried to do.

Flashes of the attack went through her head in a blur. She had made it out but what had happened to Mark? She vaguely remembered hearing a gunshot after the crusty old man went upstairs. Did they kill him? Was she imagining what she secretly hoped, that Mark was dead? Would they really shoot one of their own?

The thought that he was dead gave her mixed

feelings. On one hand, she wanted him to be gone. She didn't want to have to see his face again after what he had done. On the other hand, she didn't want to feel responsible for a man's death.

She grudgingly had to admit that she had instigated the contact between them. She had encouraged him to talk to her. If what she had heard was accurate, she had taken part in his death.

She needed to find out what happened. She sat up in bed and quickly realized that this was the white room, her room. She immediately turned her head to the right to look at where their fight had concluded.

Bile started to rise in her throat. The outline of Mark's dead body visualized. He was slumped against the wall in the corner of the room. As her eyes adjusted, she could see more details of his corpse, causally left in the room to rot beside her bed.

His skin was blanched and beginning to grey. A stream of blood had dried down the side of his left cheek from where she had struck him. Dark brown blood was slowly dripping from his agape mouth and collecting on his chest. She noticed that his chest had a single hole that was highlighted by the darkened stains surrounding it.

His eyes were the most haunting. They were wide open and glossed over in permanent fixation. They seemed to be judging her from the grave, saying "you did this to me."

She began to dry heave and double over from the cramping that came with not being able to vomit. Her skin was cold and clammy, her eyes burned in her skull. She wanted so desperately to have not seen this image.

She couldn't wrap her brain around why he had been left there. She had been drugged to calm her from her frantic state. Then they had placed her in the bed next to a corpse. He had been shot and then left as if nothing had occurred.

For everything she knew about these people, she hadn't expected this outcome. She had thought he would have been reprimanded for attacking her, the way the other guards were for beating her upon her escape attempt. She didn't believe that they would just kill one of their own and leave him to hauntingly welcome her from her slumber. She was convinced more than ever that these people didn't have souls.

Suddenly, light flooded the room. Her vision blurred in colors as she struggled to see who had turned on the lamps.

There was a guard standing by the switch. But he wasn't the only one in the room. The crusty old man was sitting casually in the chair across the room.

She was shocked that she hadn't noticed that he was in the room with her. He hadn't spoken. He hadn't moved. He had just watched her as she had awoken to more horror. He had waited for her response. His face revealed no emotions. He sat with his legs and arms both crossed, inspecting her the way he had from the very beginning. He was the epitome of creepy.

She decided to speak. The body beside her convincing her she had very little to lose now

"Why did you leave him here?" she demanded.

"You needed to see it," he paused. "This is your doing.

You thought you could manipulate us and this poor fellow lost his life as a result of your games."

She was petrified. She didn't move or dare to breathe. He sat there calmly then, saying nothing else. He just watched her with scornful eyes. She felt like a child being scolded, except it was on a more dangerous level. She wasn't sure how she should react to his assertion, despite it being true. Her inner voice said to not admit guilt. He could be fishing for confirmation that she was trying to play them. She didn't want to give it to him.

"What do you mean?" she managed as innocently as she could.

"Don't play coy with me, my dear. You aren't that stupid. What you are is finished here," he deadpanned in a tone that was terrifying.

"I don't know what you think that I did. He attacked me. He came in here while I was asleep and jumped me. I was merely defending myself," she claimed.

The crusty old man began to smile. A truly sadistic expression if she had ever seen one.

"You have been encouraging him. You were leading him on for weeks, my dear. Did you think I hadn't noticed? Did you not think you are constantly monitored? Did you believe that I haven't been watching what you were up to every night?"

He questioned her as he motioned his head in the direction of the ceiling.

She looked but she didn't see anything. Yet, she was pretty sure he was alluding to hidden cameras.

Or he was bluffing. She still wasn't sure whether it was some sort of game. Either way, she reasoned she would gain nothing from admitting responsibility. She knew with absolutely certainty that the crusty old man would do what he wanted to do anyway.

"I don't know what you are talking about," she defiantly stated.

Again, the smile crossed his face.

"I had better hopes for you, my dear. I thought you would come around. I figured you stopped your sneaking around and snooping at night. You had stopped trying to escape. I guess I thought you were smart enough to have figured out it was futile. I even allowed you the little friendship with poor ole Marcus there. I will give you credit though. It was impressive use of that wine glass as a weapon. I would have thought that would have failed," he explained.

She paled at his words. He had known every move she had made. He had been watching.

In retrospect, she should have guessed it. It was naïve to think that they weren't monitoring her every move. She bowed her head because she knew she would have to take whatever punishment was coming her way. She shrieked at the ideas of what that would be.

"So, my dear. As I was saying, your time here is complete," he finished saying.

He motioned to the guards to come forward. She was suddenly surrounded by four large men with ropes in their hands. She was debating how to defend herself when they simultaneously began their jobs. They held her legs and chest down as one administered another sedative. Then quickly, they bound her ankles and wrists.

The only avenue left for her was her voice while she

still had one. She made good use of it to protest their actions. Soon they placed duct tape over her mouth to silence her last defense.

They hoisted her up over one of the guard's shoulders and all four marched out of the room and down the stairs. She tried to wiggle free, but found that her struggles were met without opposition. She was simply thrown onto the ground like a lump of potatoes. The impact of the fall hurting as she was unable to brace herself.

They waited for her to quit fighting before they picked her up again. She was escorted via the guard's shoulder out of the house. As they neared the parameter, an overwhelming pain spasmed throughout her body from the ankle monitor being activated. Her body twitched and became stiff. Her vision blurred and everything went black.

She awoke sometime later in a darkened shed. There was a bit of dim light coming in from a high, dirty window. She looked around the shed and found it mostly sparse. The floor was dirt and the walls were wood. There appeared to be small mounds of sticks in one of the corners, but otherwise it was empty. It smelled like a musty basement, likely from the humid air that it encased.

She discovered her feet and arms weren't bound anymore. She promptly got to her feet and tried the door. Not surprisingly it was barred shut from the outside. She approached the window and found it too high to reach from her height. But there were some sticks in the corner that she might be able to arrange to get the extra feet needed to reach the window base.

As she got closer to the pile, she noted that this was not sticks, but a small mound of bones. This time, however, she didn't feel nauseated at the sight of death. This time her rage began to overtake her. She picked up what looked like a femur and threw it across the room. As she did, she let out a blood curdling scream that was long overdue.

"Who the fuck are these people?" she yelled, conscious that no one could hear her.

They intended for her to stay there until she starved to death or worse. Then they would pile her body into the corner to decay with the other people who had met their fate in that shed. She had to fight back. She couldn't give up yet.

Returning to her original idea, she began stacking the bones beneath the window. In a morbid thought, she realized these were sturdier than the sticks would have been. She carefully stacked them to build the best support with the most height she could arrange. Finally satisfied, she climbed up the pile and found that she had built her stool well. She could reach the bottom of the window to see out and try to push it open.

It wouldn't budge. She pushed and pushed, but to no avail. It wasn't moving.

She thought next to break the window using one of the bones. She climbed down from her perch and found a small rib bone to use as a hammer. It bothered her a little that she was using someone's old bones to break free. Then again, they probably would have done the same if the situation had been reversed.

She climbed back up and began pounding on the glass. After a couple of good hits, it began to splinter. It didn't take long to hollow the glass from the frame with her tool. Now, she just had to hoist herself up and out. That was all that was standing between her and freedom.

The only issue was it wasn't as easy as it seemed in her head. She had zero upper body strength. She never had had arm muscles to amount to anything. And try as she might, the bones stool wasn't enough height to give her the leverage she needed to pull herself up.

She needed momentum.

She finally decided on an idea. She would get a running start and see if she could use the bone pile as a springboard. It was worth a try, at least.

As it turns out, bones don't make a good springboard. Every attempt was met with failure and her crashing back to the hard, cold dirt floor. Every time, she had to rebuild her mound, never managing to get the result she had hoped.

She was tired and, utterly stuck.

Feeling defeated once again, she laid in the corner and cried. She reminded herself it had been amazing that her spirit hadn't been broken. No matter what had been thrown at her, she hadn't lost hope of regaining the life she once took for granted.

She planned to sleep now and garner her strength because tomorrow she was getting out of this place.

17

AFTER

"**A**hem!" Chris interrupted.

Brianna jumped backwards twenty feet at the sound. She had gotten so lost in John's arms, she had forgotten her wits. It was something she couldn't afford to do right now, despite him being a very good kisser.

She shifted her eyes to her feet, which seemed to be the safest view at the moment. She couldn't bare to see what Chris' expression revealed. Or bare for him to see her blushing like a schoolgirl caught by her parents.

"Sorry to interrupt. I just wanted to let John know that we are all set for the morning. We should leave by 7 a.m. to catch the flight we chartered. And the boats will be ready and waiting," Chris reported.

She looked up at John who was nodding his head, making mental check marks on his list. He didn't seem the least bit fazed by what Chris witnessed.

She, on the other hand, was feeling mortified.

He had kissed her twice now. She had not only welcomed it; she was fairly certain she had been encouraging it. She cursed herself. It wasn't the time for getting swept up. They both needed a clear head, to focus. However, it was hard not to get swept up when a man like John was looking at you.

It was an understatement that she was going to be messed up for a very long time. She knew it was going to be difficult to trust people ever again. She would always be looking over her shoulder, fearing that someone might grab her at any moment. She would be suspicious that every person was trying to manipulate her.

It wasn't smart to get involved with anyone, even though her body seemed to feel differently concerning John.

"Brianna?"

She snapped her head up and realized they were alone again.

"You okay?" he asked.

"Yeah. I was just thinking," she replied. "We should actually talk about it this time. As much as I don't want to talk. I think we have to figure out what is going on between us."

He sighed, "Yeah, I think you are right."

There was a silence for a few minutes. They looked at each other sheepishly and then started laughing.

"So," she started. "Go ahead. Talk."

He laughed.

"Leave it all to me."

"Well you are the one who kissed me. Twice."

"Yes, and you complained vehemently, both times," he winked.

"Seriously, I don't know what is going on except that I like you. Obviously," he smiled.

"Well, I kinda figured that part out," she teased, trying to keep things light.

"You caught that, did you? Smart girl"

"Smart ass," she retorted with a smile.

He smiled again.

They got quiet again. It was awkward to have this conversation under normal circumstances, especially so early into an attraction. Given how they met and the circumstances, she figured that the awkwardness factor had been multiplied tenfold.

He turned to look out at the river. "I guess it isn't the best timing, given everything," he stated.

"No. I can't imagine worse timing," she agreed.

He turned to face her then.

"Tell me this though. Do you feel something for me? Or are you just thankful for me getting you away from the Doppelgangmen?" he asked.

She thought for a moment, hoping the answer would just burst out of her. When it didn't, she managed.

"Honestly. I don't know. Maybe a little of both, I suppose."

"Hmmm. Okay," he mumbled and turned back to the river front.

"It isn't that I don't like you. I do. I just don't know that it will be a good time for me. Likely, not for a while," she continued.

"I get that. I do," he paused. "I wasn't expecting you to

be either. Honestly. I was supposed to go in, get you, and then get out. But something has happened. It isn't just about saving you anymore. Not for me."

She didn't know how to respond to that confession. It was a sweet sentiment.

"Look, you don't have to say anything. I just...I am just asking you to think about it. Just don't rule anything out yet. Don't rule me out. Because when this is over, I do plan to take you on a proper date. You have been fair warned," he finished, a mischievous smile on his face.

"Oh, have I?" she smiled in return and promised, "I will think about it."

"Good. So...tell me more about this farm. Where was it? Did you have to bale hay or work with livestock like a real country girl?" he teased.

"Of course! I have even milked a goat," she bragged.

With that, the conversation about their tangible attraction had ended. They talked for a while about her childhood, their school days, and favorite films. It was completely random and she loved every moment of it. It felt better than normal.

Once again, when she was around John she temporarily forgot all other things. There was something about him that made her want to jump in, head first. Except she knew that jumping wouldn't be using her head at all.

He made her feel safe. That fact alone made all the difference these days. It was enough, for now.

It was getting late and she was tired.

"I think I may get some sleep. I don't know how much

use I will be to you tomorrow, but I might as well be rested," she told him.

He nodded, "You will be more help than you think. But don't worry about that for tonight. Sleep well."

"Well, goodnight," she said before heading towards the door inside.

"Brianna?" he interjected as she started indoors.

"Yeah?"

"This may seem like a weird request. But..." he hesitated.

"But what?" she prompted.

"It was stupid. I heard it in my head and it makes me sound creepy. Just forget it," he finished.

She walked back towards him.

"No. Please tell me. I really want to know now," she pleaded.

He gave her a skeptical look.

"I promise I won't think you are creepy. At least for the first ten seconds after you say it," she teased.

"Scout's honor," she pledged, holding her hands in the familiar gesture.

He laughed.

"You weren't a scout," he playfully asserted.

You don't know that. I could have been a scout," she responded.

"Nope. Scouts are boys," he stated.

"That is incredibly sexist," she joked.

"I know. I know," he smiled.

"Seriously, I want to know what it was," she said again.

"I was just going to ask to stay in your room," he started.

He gestured for her to hear him out when she saw her surprised expression.

"I wasn't expecting to have sex with you or anything. I just had the thought of being there to watch you sleep...in a non-creepy way. It is just with Annabelle being taken today and everything, I was feeling overprotective," he rambled.

She looked at him but didn't respond.

"See, I knew you would think I was a creep. Just scrap that. I just felt protective. Sorry," he apologized.

She sighed, "I don't think you are a creep. My answer is, yes. You can stay in my room tonight."

He rebounded quickly asking, "Are you sure?"

"Yes. Yes, I am sure," she replied.

She nodded her head.

"After everything we have been through in the last few days, I understand the thought. And I trust you."

He smiled, humbled, "Thanks for trusting me."

"So, I want to go to bed now. Are you planning to come up with me?" she asked.

"Yeah. Let's go," he replied as he motioned for her to lead the way.

Only stopping to drop off their beer bottles in the kitchen, he followed her to her room. The silence between them was awkward enough that she began to question her agreement of letting him stay.

He wasn't doing anything ungentlemanly, she was just gun shy. Despite saying she trusted him earlier, she was beginning to believe it was more 80/20.

He didn't try to make a move. He made sure to keep a healthy distance. She wasn't sure if he knew, but it was making her feel more comfortable. Again, he was putting her at ease without effort.

He didn't say a word as he began making a bed on the floor. She looked over and worried about him not getting any rest and then trying to lead them tomorrow. She imagined that floor would be uncomfortable.

She debated in her head if she should share the bed. She wasn't sure of herself. She thought she might freak out at the idea of a man being so close to her when she was asleep, vulnerable.

"Umm, John. Do you want to share the bed?" she asked.

He seemed to sense her fear and shook his head.

"Nah, it is okay. I will be alright. You will get more sleep this way," he replied as he plopped down on his makeshift bed.

"It isn't me getting sleep that is important," she remarked.

"It will be fine," he said as he turned over on his side, his back facing her.

She watched as he began adjusting, attempting to make his position cozy. He didn't say a word or look at her. If he was hoping she wouldn't feel guilty, he was failing.

She sighed.

"John. Seriously. You can't sleep down there," she insisted.

"Of course, I can," he argued.

"John, just get in the fucking bed," she demanded.

"Such language!" he teased.

She grabbed a pillow and threw it at him, hitting her mark of his head with excellent precision.

He laughed, only infuriating her. However, he got up and retrieved the thrown pillow before walking over to the bed. He glanced at her before he climbed into the bed, testing to see if it was truly okay with her. She gave her consent with a nod and held her breath, waiting for the panic to set it.

He simply adjusted himself and went straight to sleep. He didn't try to touch her or make any conversation.

She had waited in vain for an anxiety that never settled.

18

S he was jarred awake by the horrid sound of a bell ringing. It had been a long time since she had been roused from her slumber by a smartphone alarm. Instinctively, her body still rejected its meaning.

She opened her eyes to find herself sprawled across John's chest. He had one hand resting on the base of her back, but otherwise was detached from her. Seemingly, she had used him as a pillow. As she raised her head, she noticed the drool pooled on his t-shirt.

She was completely mortified. She pulled away from him and buried her head under an actual pillow. She prayed he wouldn't notice, but anticipated the inevitable teasing.

Miraculously, he didn't mention it as he removed himself from the bed. He stripped his shirt without a single smirk and began picking up the blankets he had left on the floor. She laid lazily in the bed, watching as he tidied up the room.

"You should probably get ready. We don't have much time before we take off," he said as he stacked the blankets on the edge of the bed.

"Oh! Wear some of those workout clothes I got you. And the athletic shoes. You will need to be able to move fast," he added as he exited the room.

She grudgingly dragged herself from the bed and dressed quickly. She felt a few knots in her stomach. She didn't know what to expect but one thing was certain. She was going back to the island today. She was consciously heading near the lion's den.

It was quite possibly a bad decision.

She pushed her doubts away and carried herself downstairs to the kitchen. She found the guys busy getting things together. John and Robert were packing bags while Chris and Ethan were somberly sipping coffee. The mood was as solemn as a funeral. They all seemed to know what was at stake.

She made her way into the kitchen and grabbed a muffin. Ethan poured her a cup of coffee before returning to his own. They drank in silence, gathering around the kitchen island. Although, Brianna realized that there really wasn't anything they could say. They were all at different levels of nerves for different reasons. The daunting task before them was likely a suicide mission.

Ethan was the worst. Dark circles had formed under his eyes. She was sure he didn't sleep at all. The frown seemed to have become etched into his face. He looked very different from the guy she met 36 hours ago. This man seemed broken, a sentiment she related to herself.

"Okay, we should have everything. Everyone ready?" John asked.

They all nodded their heads in agreement. For better or for worse, it had begun.

There was very little conversation the entire morning. Beyond the necessary logistics, she noticed the guys didn't even exchange looks between each other.

They didn't interact with her either. It seemed every man for himself mode as they were mentally prepared for their jobs. She, in contrast, could have used some guidance. She still had no idea about the details of her role.

John would only give non-committal responses when she asked. He had only indicated she was to stay in the rented boat and wait for them. If that was the extent of her role, she wasn't truly needed here. There had to be more to it.

She knew she was bait. They had planned to spend the day parading her around town, making sure that the Doppelgangmen or their contacts saw her. Except that was the part of the plan that baffled her. Why did they want these people to know they were coming? She had asked John about it, but he had stonewalled her. He had only replied that they knew what they were doing, to trust them.

He might as well have asked for the moon.

She was downright terrified about being used as bait. She was scared they may trade her for Annabelle. She was forced to rely, once again, on the decentness of virtual strangers to not take advantage of her vulnerability. And the thought was making her sick.

John noticed that she looked peaked during the flight. "Are you alright?" he implored.

"No, I am not," she managed. "Why am I being used as bait? It makes no sense unless…"

She couldn't finish her sentence. She was beginning to hyperventilate. He moved from his seat next to her and kneeled on the floor, grasping her arms in reassurance.

"Breathe. Just breathe," he urged.

She tried, but she was having a difficult time following his command. Her mind was jumbled. She was becoming utterly overwhelmed with fear. Her vision was blurring. It felt as if something was crashing down on top of her, restricting her body.

"Brianna. Look at me," he pleaded. "I won't let anyone hurt you. You have to trust me."

Upon hearing those words, she looked at him. Still struggling for breath, she stared deeply into his green eyes. She noticed for the first time that there were specks of gold mixed in with the green. It reminded her of the sunny pastures where she grew up. The grass would simmer in the light. It felt like home.

She had begun to steady herself. She had trusted him so far.

"Brianna. I got you," he promised her.

It hadn't felt right. She couldn't justify any reason for her to be put on display. She needed to understand.

"I can't see any reason for being bait. I am not going back there. And you are going to explain what you intend to do with me. Right now," she demanded.

He sighed and shaking his head.

"I have no intention of you going back there. I don't

want to scare you. But to be honest, there is always the possibility that they will be trying to get you again. But I am going to do everything I can to prevent that and still get Annabelle back. You aren't bait. Really, you are a decoy," he began.

"What?" she interrupted.

"The idea is they will be thinking we will make a deal for an exchange. But you won't be anywhere near there. I won't let you," he asserted.

"So, you aren't planning to offer me for her? You are actually going to steal her back while they are expecting a trade?" she reasoned.

"Yes. Using you is an attempt to draw them out," he explained.

"That makes me bail, John. Plus it sounds very risky. How do you plan to get them to agree to it?" she asked.

"We are betting they will approach us. And, well... We already sent word that we would be open to an exchange through our contacts," he responded.

"Again, what makes you think they will go for it? You seem so sure."

"Well, I'm not sure. But I think they will go for it. They want you back. They can't afford for you to be alive or free. You could expose them. They will try to neutralize that threat," he explained.

"I will do everything I can to keep you safe," John added when she didn't respond.

She nodded.

She didn't think it would work or maybe she hoped it wouldn't. But, she was breathing easier.

She realized that hoping it wouldn't work meant she

wished they failed in retrieving Annabelle. She immediately felt guilty and wanted to take the thought back.

It occurred to her that her captivity had made her selfish. She was only concerned for herself. In the past, she had tried to be generous and think of others. Now, she didn't. A side effect from spending almost a year isolated and not being able to depend on anyone. She didn't like this new quality of hers, even if it proved to be useful.

She spent the remainder of the flight contemplating her options. She was not going back to that compound. She needed a contingency plan that the guys didn't know about, a way to ensure her own safety. It would make her feel better to have a secret backup plan.

The only problem was she didn't know what she was going to encounter when they landed. Any idea she came up with would need to be fluid. Or she would need to spontaneously act, which was not one of her strong abilities. There was the disadvantage that her plans often went awry and her skills were insufficient. Today it would have to go differently since her continued freedom may depend upon it.

They arrived forty-five minutes later. It wasn't the main airport, but a different landing strip on the outside of town. It didn't take long for them to load into the waiting cars and head towards a hotel. John's plan was officially in motion.

The scenery was the same as it was a few days ago. It amazed her that she was back so soon. A reality that hadn't quite hit her yet. If she were honest, it felt more like the last week had been a dream. In her mind, she was still in that shed. John was just a mirage induced by boredom and desperation.

The hotel was a simple one. It wasn't one of the fancy resorts John had told her had sprung up on the south side of the city. It was a basic room, exactly what they needed to get ready. They wouldn't be staying overnight. If everything went according to their plan, they would all be on a plane back to Australia that night.

Once they got into the room, John handed her a stark white sundress, expensive black lace-up sandals, and some diamond jewelry she guessed was the real deal.

"Why are you handing me this dress?" she asked with a raised eyebrow, not attempting to masking her surprise.

"It is appropriate for where we are going. Besides, it will get more notice than those workout clothes. You can put those back on later. For now, we need you turning heads and this definitely will do it," he indicated with a smile.

It was the first time she had seen him smile that day. She was betting it would be only time it happened too. It was going to be a long day with an even longer night.

She took the clothes and went to change outfits. As she got ready, she gazed at her reflection in the mirror. The dress fit perfectly with an open back and halter top that framed her well. The diamond earrings and starry pendant necklace gave the look a touch of elegance and class.

Assessing herself, it occurred to her that it had been a while since she had really looked at her face. The face that got her into this mess. It was hard to not hate it now.

Like most girls growing up, she had been insecure about her looks. She was never one of those females who had been blessed with self-confidence or even the ability to fake it. Her role models had been a mother who had grown up playing sports in a house of brothers and an older sister who preferred being dirty in the outdoors than primping for anyone. She had been more feminine in nature, a quality that had left her figuring out the aspects of beauty on her own.

Any confidence she had before she was kidnapped had been hard won and self-taught.

She had never viewed herself as beautiful. She had thought she was somewhat attractive, pretty even. Now her self-esteem was non-existent. She hated her face with a vengeance. It had become ugly to her because it had been the root of her troubles. If she hadn't had these features, she would have been left alone.

Seeing her reflection was a reminder of all the bad things that she had endured. It haunted her.

It was also the face of a coward. When she looked at herself, she felt the disappointment of the girl who had sworn she was a fighter. Yet, when it had come down to it, she had failed to put up much resistance. She hadn't managed to escape in seven months. She had been defeated by the crusty old man. What a joke she had turned out to be.

She adorned the dress and sandals without further reflection. She didn't even do a last check to make sure she looked presentable. She figured that any effort she took to be attractive was a waste of time. She truly didn't care if she did.

She exited the bathroom to find the guys waiting on her. She noticed that only John was dressed similar to her. He was adorned in khaki shorts, a belt, and a tucked-in blue polo top. The others were wearing black pants and t-shirts.

The anxiety level in the room was high, worsened by the fact that no one would say anything. They all dreaded what was before them.

"You ready?" John asked, intrepidly.

She half-way laughed.

"Sure. I am so excited!" she mocked.

He rolled his eyes and grabbed his phone from the table.

"Alright, I have my phone. We are going to start making the rounds at key places. Call if you hear something. Ethan, you got this?" he directed to the guys.

"Yes. For the hundredth time. I know what to do. Go!" Ethan yelled.

John's face showed some skepticism, but he said nothing more. Instead, he motioned for her to follow him out of the room.

"The other guys aren't coming at all? Not even to shadow us?" she asked as they exited the hotel.

"No. We don't want them to know how many we have in our group. They would just increase their forces. It isn't exactly a sneak attack. And it is going to be hard enough. Like I said, we are relying on the fake out. They know we are coming so any information we can keep quiet, the better," he explained.

"This isn't what you had planned, is it?" she guessed.

"No, not at all. We were supposed to have more

people coming from Asia and the US. We are also down on the resources we have, weapons and such," he confirmed.

"So why are we doing this now?" she had to ask, despite knowing the answer.

"We don't have a choice if we want Annabelle to have a chance at living. It was actually brilliant on their part to grab her. We messed up there. We assumed they would try to grab you. But they found a way to force our hand," he explained.

"Aren't you a little worried they will just grab me while we are out in public? You were worried about that last time we were here. And obviously it was a concern in Brisbane."

"Yes, of course. That is why I will insist you don't leave my sight."

"Actually," he said, then he grabbed her hand to hold it as they walked to a convertible sports car.

She raised an eyebrow.

"What?" he had noticed her scrutiny.

"Fancy car," she commented.

"It is necessary," he replied.

Their drive to the first stop took less than ten minutes. It was a reminder of how small the island was, at least for driving. She assumed you could get anywhere in ten minutes.

He parked the car on the side of the street near some businesses. He glanced over at her, assessing her state before they got out of the car.

She was nervous. Still a little shaken from the debilitating, almost panic attack on the plane. She was trying to keep a clear head and not lose her nerve to go through with the agreed plan.

She reminded herself of Annabelle. It helped to envision her face and what she was likely experiencing. The guilt easily overcame any latent selfishness. It was all she needed to find the motivation to tuck her fear down deep and move her body out of the car. It also proved to be enough inspiration to hold her head high, faking a sense of confidence which didn't really exist in her.

Once again, John noticed everything about her. He came around the car and gave her a kiss on the cheek.

"I'm proud of you," he declared.

"Why?" she pondered.

"I know you are scared right now. But you aren't backing down," he explained.

"Not yet," she muttered under her breath.

"What?" he asked.

"It's not important," she denied. "What do we do now?"

He gave her a dubious expression, but he didn't push it.

"We are going to walk around for a bit. Window shop," he indicated.

"Window shop? And that is going to get notice?"

Now she was doubtful. She didn't understand how two seemingly unassuming tourists would draw enough attention for the Doppelgangmen to notice, much less their contacts.

"How is that going to work?" she asked.

"Well, typically what happens is people gaze in

windows and if they see something they like, they buy it," he teased.

It would have been funny in a different scenario. It was the witty, dry sense of humor that she always loved. In fact, it was one of the things she liked the most about John. And one of the things she didn't, his timing. She realized he was trying to lighten the mood, but it was too inappropriate. She imagined if Ethan were there, he would find it insensitive, despite the intention to ease tension.

"Hmmm," she responded.

He appeared to get the idea and offered his hand instead of another smart ass comment.

They walked hand in hand to a couple of upscale boutiques aimed at high end tourists. Brianna had to admit that if she had the means and was shopping for real, there were several items of interest. However, since they were faking it, her heart wasn't in it. She had to constantly remind herself to keep her shoulders back. She realized that body language likely didn't matter, the contacts would only care that she had been spotted in town. Except she wasn't going to give the crusty old man the satisfaction of thinking he had beaten her again.

They wandered around the city center for about an hour. Rarely speaking, neither had a lot to say to the other. He never let go of her. A public affection that was comforting.

He held her hand. He guided her with the touch of his hand to the small of her back. He paid attention and anticipated, just as he had since they met.

It was like a dream, a good one this time. She even

forgot a few times that they barely knew each other. For a moment, she had selective amnesia

Next, they pulled into a valet at what appeared to be an expensive resort.

"What are we doing here?" she inquired.

Granted she hadn't known what to expect that morning, but she didn't think the day would consist of all the five-star locations. She didn't know what to think about the show of money.

It was logical when she considered it. She had figured out a long time ago that the Doppelgangmen had financial means to keep her locked up in a mansion on a remote island of the Pacific Ocean. There was a staff of around twenty people, who wouldn't' come cheap given the circumstances. Plus John had mentioned they were connected worldwide and powerful. It was more the public part of the parade that was curious. Nonetheless, she played along as intended.

"We are going to eat lunch and make sure that we are seen, just like before. So, it is exposure," he responded. "Well, maybe more so here. The Doppelgangmen have a lot of contacts in this place according to our intel. Likely because this is where the most important people, the most affluent people, will stay when they visit the islands."

The valet opened her passenger door and waited for her to exit. She was barely out of the car before John was by her side, grabbing her hand once again.

She wasn't complaining. He had been affectionate all morning and she was getting used to it. They were going to need a talk after all the craziness was over.

"Act happy. Arrogantly, even. We want to piss some people off that you are here and they can't touch you."

"Why would we want to do that?" she asked confused.

"The 'crusty old man' as you call him. It will get his goat. He won't be able to resist coming after you, especially when he knows you are nearby. He will see you as more accessible."

"How do you know that?" she wondered.

"I just do," he said.

They made their way to a table at the center of the room. She wondered if he had arranged that placement, but she didn't ask. They were definitely on display here. It felt like it was the bride's and groom's table at a wedding with all eyes on them.

His shell of confidence didn't crack in the least. She, however, was a little unnerved.

It bothered her at how well he played the part. If she hadn't been told differently, she would have assumed he had come from money growing up. He had the spoiled brat routine down perfectly.

"It is a little unsettling," she told him.

"What is?" he asked.

"How good an actor you are."

He looked at her, never removing the grin from his face.

"Just doing my part, darlin'."

"Don't play it too well. I will start to think you aren't worth the trouble," she quipped.

"Oh, I think I already know your opinion of me," he winked.

She looked around the dining room, taking in the

fanciness of the place. It was a moderate sized room with about 20 round tables of varying sizes. Each was set with white linen tablecloths and light green napkins pitched as tents. Fragrant, bright tropical flowers adorned the center of every table. The smell of the orchids and coconut oil was intoxicating. It was the perfume of paradise.

She guessed it was the premiere resort. Judging from the patrons, it was definitely where the wealthy hung out. The room was almost full of people, which surprised her because the place seemed to be expensive. Granted, she didn't have knowledge of how successful tourism was in the Hale Island. She had never heard of it as a destination spot, but she wasn't exactly in the know with the hidden getaways of the rich.

She did know that places like this made her nervous. Even before she had been taken, she had never been comfortable around those with excessive wealth. She had encountered it when she had dealt with some of her company's clients. She had always felt out of her league. Being a country girl who had grown up in modest surroundings, she didn't know how to act around those people.

Her apprehension must have been apparent because John reached across the table to give her hand a squeeze. It helped a little.

She had assumed that the Doppelgangmen were well funded, but it was beginning to dawn on her what they were truly up against. The amount of wealth and power to keep just one woman in that complex with the size of

the staff must have been astronomical, at least by her
standards.

Add to it that they had to have paid off government
officials, contacts, and countless others. They had taken
girls across international lines. They had even murdered
some of them. There was no way that someone hadn't
noticed.

The fact that John had knowledge of them and was
still alive was proof. He couldn't have been the only one
over all the years to have insider knowledge, the only one
to deflect. Plus, there were several on the outside who
knew, beginning with the guys and Annabelle. Someone
had to have gone to the authorities before now. Yet, the
Doppelgangmen still existed.

"They aren't a small organization, are they?" she
abruptly asked him.

His eyes got big and his face paled. He grabbed her
hand again and silently shook his head to indicate this
wasn't the place. Like a scolded child, she dropped
her eyes.

He squeezed her hand, seemingly prompting her to
look up at him. But she didn't. She nodded her head and
kept her eyes low. She was growing tired of being
handled. She wanted some control over herself again,
some say in what she could say and do without fear of
being reprimanded.

The whole situation was daunting for her. She was
already filled with regret at her decision to come back to
these islands. From the minute she got on the plane, she
had been feeling the dread.

Every move, she was second guessing herself and her

resolve to follow through with her promise to John. Every part of her wanted to run for the door and make her way back to her previous life. She could let them handle it. She would feel guilty about not helping Annabelle, but she was beginning to believe anything she did would be worthless.

Her realization that these people were more connected than she had originally thought had made the urge to split increase by the second. Her anger had also grown. John was withholding a lot. She was certain of it.

He kept saying he "just knew things" and not giving her specifics. She hadn't been informed as to all the details. He had admitted that much. Piecing it together on her own, she knew he had alluded her one too many times for comfort. She was fed up with it. And he knew it.

"Brianna? Look at me, please"

"What?" she snapped at him.

He leaned back, crossing his arms across his chest. He acted startled by her apparent hostility, but he was obstinate to his core. He wasn't going to back down from her.

She continued to glare at him, her arms now crossed too. Her frustration was hitting a peak and she didn't want to be soothed or placated anymore. She wanted to know what she was facing. All of it, every single detail. And if she didn't like what she heard, she was leaving without any apologies. There had to be people on this island who would help her. If not, she would find a way to help herself.

The waiter picked that inopportune moment of their standoff to begin his service. He quickly realized his error when he took one look at the tension between them and promptly said he would come back.

John looked pissed now. She could understand why. To him, she was making a scene. She wasn't playing by the rules. She was having a spat. And now, at least, the waiter knew. It wouldn't be long before others took notice of their tension.

She imagined she had been annoying him. She was constantly questioning and scrutinizing his responses. Though in her shoes, she was putting her life and, more significantly, her freedom on the line. Again. Plus, she was always the last to be given an explanation, a limited one at that.

He took a deep breath and leaned forward.

"What is your problem? This isn't the place or the time," he whispered.

She also leaned forward. "I am the last to know anything, especially about what you are planning. You are using me, plain and simple. If I am the center of your plan and I am supposed to trust you, you should return the favor. You should trust me with the information. But it is quite clear from one moment to the next that you are keeping things from me. It stops now. Or I walk!" she responded more calmly than she felt and without raising her voice.

"This isn't the time for a tantrum!" he uttered with clinched teeth. "If you want to leave, then there's the fucking door."

Now, it was her turn to be flabbergasted. She hadn't expected that reaction. She thought he would do as he had previously done. He would reassure her, convince her to stay. Maybe give her a nugget of information to pacify her. Instead, he was telling her the opposite. He was saying that she wasn't needed.

It was a similar response to when she said she wanted to help them the first time. He had told her that she couldn't handle it. She didn't know what she should do. She sat there in defiant silence. His jaw set in a firm resistance. He wouldn't look at her anymore. He was serious.

"Why did you bring me back here if I wasn't wanted?" she managed to ask.

He turned to her.

"You were wanted. Are wanted. But I really don't have time to constantly do this with you. I realize you have been through a lot. I get it. It is hard to trust me or anyone. But we need for you to be in or out. Not halfway. It is 100% in or out. And we have to know which you are immediately. You are already jeopardizing everything this very moment. There is a lot riding on all this and we can't afford any more of your mini meltdowns," he sighed.

"I think you should go to the bathroom and think about it. Make a decision and if you are ready to suck it up and do what is required of you without bitching about it then come back to the table. If not...well, I wish you well in your journey back home and return to your life," he threatened.

She didn't know why it shocked her so much as she sat there mulling over what he said. John had been hot and cold since they had met. One minute he was supportive, caring, and affectionate. The next he was being completely selfish by leaving her at the police station alone to look like a crazy person or by rejecting her when she tried to get involved. However, he was right about one thing. She had to make a decision. So she did.

She got up from the table, nodded her head at him, and abruptly left the restaurant.

19

AFTER

S he reached the front door within seconds and headed down the palm tree lined driveway towards the road. She didn't have a car of her own, but her legs worked. She would just have to walk. She hoped it wasn't too far since these designer sandals weren't meant for marathons.

Still steaming and distracted from her argument with John, she didn't notice at first where she was going. She was vaguely aware of the direction to town. So, she steered her feet that way.

The setting was quite beautiful for a walk. It reminded her of the tree lined plantations of the southern United States. Except there wasn't any Spanish moss draping from the limbs.

The trees were stunning. They were absolutely massive and could rival the redwoods of Northern California. She assumed they had been there for hundreds of years.

It was easy to believe that she was in a perfect paradise until she had reached the end of the road. From there, she could see the real essence of the islands.

The vegetation was still breathtaking, but the structures that she saw in the distance were deteriorating and shabby. The whole island was a standing contradiction. It was a mix of old and new, a stark contrast between the resorts and the indigenous buildings. On one side, you had the extravagance of money and on the other you had the simplicity of poverty. The majority of the islands were the latter from what she had seen.

She started down the road towards the buildings, hoping it would take her to the main city center. Luckily, she was partly correct. Within ten minutes of walking, she was on the outskirts of the city. She guessed it couldn't be more than ten more minutes to the center.

Although, she wasn't sure what she would do when she reached the center. She had been thinking during her stroll about what her next steps should be. She had cooled off from the disagreement with John and began to regret her decision. She hadn't intended to leave John high and dry. She had just been so angry with the lack of transparency. She understood if he couldn't tell her some things, but the cloak and dagger routine he had going wasn't conducive to building trust. She needed to have more confidence in him and the situation before she could dive in head first.

She needed more confidence in herself.

As she got to an alleyway between the first buildings of the city, she felt that familiar paranoid feeling of being watched. She looked over her shoulder and noted there were some random cars on the street. But there was no movement. Perhaps she was being insecure again, or more so now that she was on her own. She had to remind herself that there was absolutely no evidence that anyone was following her. There weren't any suspicious people or vehicles. Of the people she saw, no one paid attention to her at all.

"Hmmm. So much for John's theory of standing out," she thought.

She made her way down the alleyway and found herself on a busy street. She weaved her way through the people milling around the sidewalks. She didn't interact with any of them, but she did nod her head at the few street vendors she saw along the way.

The streets were mostly scarce until she got further into town. As more people started to emerge, she felt a little more at ease. She was enjoying the anonymity of a crowd.

Except she really didn't. She kept looking over her shoulder, searching for signs of something nefarious. She didn't know what she was looking for in each of the stranger's faces. It wasn't like wicked people would have a flashing sign over their heads saying "beware." No matter how much she reassured herself, she just couldn't completely shake the apprehension.

She began trying to remember if the faces she saw were the same each time she looked. She thought it would help quiet her mind if she could disprove anyone was trailing her. However, it proved more difficult than she had believed it would be.

She scrutinized every face and discovered it wasn't easy to remember so many people at once, especially if she wasn't actually meeting the person. She was becoming more confused with each passing glance, which in turn increased her angst. It was impossible. How was she to know who had been there before, going about their day versus someone who was blending in to keep an eye on her? Wasn't that the point, to not be noticed?

Then, she had an idea. She popped into the nearest store and ducked into a corner by the window. She would wait to see if anyone's behavior was suspicious from her sudden change in direction.

At first, she saw nothing except people continuing to do their job or shop. There wasn't anyone lurking around or attempting to find a crack in the sidewalk interesting. In fact, no one acted the least bit conscious that she had unexpectedly entered the store.

Suddenly, her breath caught in her throat. There were two guys who began loitering on the other side of the street. They weren't being conspicuous, but there was something about them that made them stand out to her. It seemed obvious that they were waiting for her to re-emerge onto the street. She was certain these two had been stalking her.

The store was filled with souvenirs from the islands, knickknacks that fueled the economy. She just saw them as a shield as she crept her way to the back of the store. She was only looking for a way to slip out without notice by the two semi-permanent fixtures outside the front. However, when she reached the back of the establishment there wasn't a back door. She even checked for windows in the bathroom like they did in movies when someone wanted to escape a bad date. No such luck was to be found. She would have to brave it.

Her only option was to exit the way she came. She would try to lose the men in the crowds if she could find a crowd in this city. And there was no time to second guess herself. She left the store in a hurry. She made her way down the streets at an almost run, dodging all the people she encountered.

At first, she just moved. She didn't stop to look behind her. She didn't check to see where she was going. She just put one foot in front of the other as quickly as she could. She ignored the pains shooting from her mid-calves and the agony as her feet screamed. She just kept chanting in her mind, "run, run, run."

She didn't check to see if they were following her. Although she didn't have to look, she already knew that they were.

After a few minutes of weaving between people, she finally dared to pause.

They weren't there. She squinted and rose on her tippy toes. Still, she didn't see them. She had been wrong. There was no sign of the two men she had seen on the street earlier. She was surrounded by anonymous faces. And she was just an insignificant being amongst them. A thought that made her feel glorious.

She sighed her relief and continued on her way. She shouldn't have been far from the city center now. She still wasn't sure what she was going to do once she got there.

But, at least, she wasn't in the danger of being kidnapped again.

Her heartbeat had started to slow and her breath was coming easier. Smiling to herself, she began strolling along with a solace she shouldn't have felt so soon.

Her mind returned to the events of the day. It didn't seem possible that she had been on a flight from Brisbane that morning. Now, having broken with John, she was making it just fine on her own. Minus a few hiccups. But it was enough that she was free and alive. Despite being alone.

There was a bit of bitterness in that fact. She had come to believe that she wouldn't survive without him. She had liked having him around. He was dependable and resourceful. She wasn't. She had tried relentlessly to escape the compound that had held her. She had failed, time and time again. It had taken a man's graces to get her out of her hell.

It was a sad reality, a hard pill to swallow. She had prided herself on not being weak. She had talked a good game as a strong woman. But when it came down to it, she had been as useless as the ornaments she had pretended, not so long ago, to be.

It was a revelation that she wasn't a badass. She had led herself to believe that she was. So, it should have come as a shock. It should have jolted her, inspired her to revolt against the idea of being helpless. Instead, she had calmly accepted it. She had needed a man to save her.

It had been this truth that had caused her to rebel. Now was her chance to reclaim some semblance of her independence. She would make amends to John later.

But she had to prove a point first, if for no one except herself. She could make it on her own. She knew she could. She would repeat that to herself until she believed every syllable.

Without warning, she felt a jerk of her body backwards. A hand clasped over her mouth, not that she could scream since the air in her lungs was expelled with the force of her crashing into the chest of one of the men who had been tailing her.

She knew what this was, she didn't question it. She had fully experienced it before. Except this time, she was determined there would be a different outcome.

She didn't waste any breath on screaming. Just the opposite. She immediately began kicking and thrashing. She wiggled and squirmed and used every bit of energy she had to begin pushing their combined momentum backward.

She took a deep breath to strengthen her final shove. To her utter joy, the increased force propelled him against the brick wall with a thud.

The impact was audible. Their bodies reverberated against each other, effectively loosening his grip. He grunted from the pain that radiated throughout his body. But she didn't care. Let him hurt.

She bounced her body from his. It had worked. She had used the impact to ricochet off him. She was free.

She did not pause for a second. She took off at a sprint from the alleyway.

The other man was fast on her heels. He was quick. He had closed the slight lead she had had. But she had also learned from past failures. She immediately began zigzagging as he reached for her, throwing him off balance. She sprinted from side street to side street. The unpredictability of her path seemed to be working as she intended. It slowed him down, somewhat. The gap between them was increasing.

She was flat out running now, dodging a few bystanders along the way. In her peripheral view, she noted the faces in the crowd showed confusion. She didn't blame them. They didn't know if they should run too.

She, however, was already growing tired. A few minutes at this pace was feeling like an hour. Pain was shooting from her right side, her calves were cramping, her breath was labored. She had to stop, at least momentarily.

She slowed and did a quick check behind her. They were still coming.

"Fuck!" she shouted.

She picked up her pace again, weaving in and out of people. She couldn't keep this up. The pain in her side was growing more intense by the seconds. It would be disabling soon. Her legs were on fire, her feet were throbbing. She needed a place to hide.

She increased her stride despite her body's protest. Then quickly made her way to the side of the street, looking for an opportunity. She jumped into the first alleyway she could find. Her eyes frantically looked for a place to cower. Straight ahead she spied a dumpster which could do the trick.

She tucked herself behind it, praying they had been far enough behind that they didn't see her hiding herself.

She would find out in a minute if she had finally gotten lucky.

She sat and she waited. Shaking from both fear and exhaustion, her thoughts ran rabid. She needed to calm herself. She knew she should regain her breath and be ready to bolt again. It wasn't over yet.

She sat perfectly still, closed her eyes, and focused on clearing her mind. She concentrated on taking deep breaths that would slow her heartbeat. If nothing else, she had to minimize her recovery time.

For the first time, her continued freedom depended on her alone. She had no one left to help her. The weight of that reality truly hit her. She wished John was there.

"Good God, what have I done?" she thought.

She had been so hell bent on demonstrating her strength, her independence. Now she was realizing how dumb that move had been. She had succeeded in demonstrating her stupidity.

"I am such an idiot," she quietly criticized herself.

She opened her eyes and looked closely at her current situation. She was hiding behind a dumpster. She had spent the last hour without a plan or direction. Then she had been discovered and was running for her life. She was tired. She was frightened. She was sore. And her feet were bleeding. She had been too damn stubborn. Or just plain stupid.

She had started the morning with someone beside her, protecting her, looking out for her. Someone who had been kind and patient. Someone who made her laugh occasionally, during a time that was far from funny. Someone she already missed just being there. She had made a mistake leaving him. She knew that now. The guilt and sadness which flooded her emotions upon this realization was overwhelming.

Suddenly, she heard scraping sounds. And then there was the clinking of a glass bottle that rolled away as it was inadvertently kicked. A knot formed in her throat.

It was fairly obvious that someone was coming her way. She only prayed it wasn't the men who had been chasing her. But she had no choice. She had to remain still. If she looked and it was them, she would reveal herself. It was a risk she wasn't willing to take.

She sat in dread. The tears began to form in her eyes. She knew she had screwed up big time. Now, she just may pay the price.

The footsteps got closer and closer. Whoever it was would be upon her in a minute. But she didn't dare move an inch. She held back the whimper she desperately wanted to let out. She held her breath as she waited.

She saw the gun before she saw the man. It was at that point she knew who was coming. She knew she was done. She hadn't gotten far enough ahead. They had obviously seen her attempting to hide because she wasn't able to run anymore.

Except they had taken their time to enter the alley and had their weapons drawn. They were ready for her to resist. Not that she could blame them, as she had already proven them right.

Knowing an attempt to run again would likely result in getting her shot, she slowly pulled her knees up to her chest. They were before her now and she was staring up the barrel of two guns.

No one said anything at first. Their eyes darted from each other to the weapons commanding the situation. One of them motioned for her to stand up. She had no choice if she wanted to live. So, she cautiously obeyed.

She didn't want any sudden movements to be misconstrued as defiance. She would cooperate with them, as long as they had the advantage of a semi-automatic weapon.

She had made her way to her feet and was leaning back against the alley's wall. She awaited further instructions. None were given.

She barely registered what had begun to happen because it all moved so fast. Hardly on her feet and she heard screams from the street and the sound of feet attacking the pavement. In her peripheral she saw flashes of color quickly approaching their position behind the dumpster. Someone was interrupting their standoff, rather abruptly. Then she heard it, the piercing, distinctive sound of a gun being fired.

The two armed men before her dropped into a heap on the ground. Her eyes filled with a blur of red as the blood splashed on her face and pooled at her feet. Tremors began running throughout her body as she reacted to the horror of witnessing these men's murders first hand. There was a paralyzing fear that she would be the next victim of a bullet. With her eyes now clinched shut, she waited for a similar fate to the one she had watched play out moments before.

"Brianna. You're safe."

A voice broke through her barriers as she had prepared for the end.

Her eyes popped open to see John and the guys standing before her, concerned expressions on their faces.

"You okay?" John implored.

She didn't bother to stop herself. She flung her body towards him and wrapped her arms around him in a hug. She clung to him and began weeping from relief.

He was there. They were there. He had saved her once again. She was safe in his arms.

She felt as his arms came up around her, holding her chest to his, providing strength in his grip. He nuzzled her neck and tightened his hold to ease her shaking.

"Shhh, shhh. It is alright. You are okay now. I'm here," he soothed.

Those words did provide comfort, more than he knew. She knew that she couldn't fight these guys on her own. She had tried and failed.

As much as she had prided herself in the past as being completely independent, she wasn't. No one was. She needed people's help sometimes, evidenced from the last seven months and, especially, the last hour. It had been a hard truth to learn, but she had finally got it.

She pulled back from the embrace while maintaining her proximity to him. She wiped her eyes and looked at each of the guys. They all regarded her with a sympathy versus a scornful judgment at the predicament she had gotten them into with her stunt. They had killed two men because of her.

She looked down at the greying, lifeless bodies and felt numb. It amazed her that she felt nothing for these creatures. It was almost as if she was living in a video game and these kills weren't real. These guys would regenerate when they exited the scene and reset to chase another player.

Except it wasn't a video game or a movie or any alternate reality. It was as real as the blood that spattered her white dress. It was smeared across her legs and painted on her face when she wiped the tears away. There was no escaping it. She had caused these men's deaths the way she had caused Mark's. She bore some, if not all, of the responsibility for ending their lives.

While part of her screamed that it would have been them or her, she knew human life could never be disregarded so easily. Even if they had been bad guys, which she suspected they were given their occupation. It didn't excuse it. She didn't want to become jaded to killing people. Perhaps it was necessary for her survival that these men die, but she didn't want to forget they were once human beings.

Lost in her thoughts, she didn't immediately notice that John was evaluating her state.

"Are you okay?" he asked, concerned.

Pulled from her reflection, she replied honestly.

"Not really. Can we get out of here please?"

"Yeah, let's go," he indicated to the group.

They didn't clean up the bodies. The men were left just as they fell. Sprawled on the ground, almost like trash that had missed the dumpster.

She assumed the local authorities would investigate. She worried about how causally the guys had walked away from murder, and more so, what would become of an investigation once these men were found. However, she hadn't seen any police or any authoritative, uniformed people. It made her question whether the Doppelgangmen owned the islands, if there was any law there at all. Given the reach of their influence, she knew it was possible there wasn't.

They didn't exit the alley the way they had entered. John led them farther up the alley to where it split into some additional side streets. Keeping a firm grip on her hand, he navigated them through a maze of side paths and back ways that she could barely remember all turns they had made. It didn't matter though. They emerged on a main road within a couple of minutes.

He steered her to stand behind him as a shield, nodding at her appearance. She was covered in blood stains, which were indicative of malice. If there were local law enforcement agents around, she would definitely pass as a suspicious person given her state.

He nodded to Ethan before pulling out his cell. The group backed into the opening of the alleyway to wait as John spat out directions and their location. It amazed her how well he knew the town and how connected he appeared to be. A black van showed up within minutes to collect them, making her wonder even more who he had called. He was definitely a man in the know. But then again, it wasn't too surprising since he kept an apartment there.

The guys jumped into the van without hesitation. She required a reassuring look and a pull on her arm before she got into the vehicle. It was less resolve than she had shown in the past, which was progress.

John said nothing of her slight resistance. And she

didn't question their actions either, at least not aloud. To be honest, she was still a bit shell shocked from the events at the dumpster.

As they rode, she replayed the scene in her head. Over and over, the images repeated. She marveled at how the guys knew where to find her behind the dumpster. A reminder that made her grateful they had. She had feared she was not long for the world when they had showed up.

A quiet settled over the car and no one said a word for the duration of their trip into the countryside. It was dusk. The sun had already somehow set without her noticing it. Not that she would have. It stayed daylight for very long intervals on the islands these days. Yet, it would be dark soon enough and, then, time to begin their mission to get Annabelle.

She felt a tap on the shoulder from behind. It was Robert, who was handing John and her a backpack. Still in a daze, she opened it to find her black workout clothes. It was the indication that she should get ready.

She did a survey of the guy's clothes. Minus John, they were already dressed for the evening in head to toe black gear.

She didn't bother asking if she should change here. John already was. So, she just started the process of trying to not expose herself any more than necessary. Though at this point, she wasn't sure she had a care for modesty.

What was concerning to her were the blisters she saw on her feet. The hard running in those lace-up sandals had done its toll. Not all the blood on her feet belonged to the dead men resting in the alley. Slowly removing the sandals now, the damage was now visible.

She leaned over and tapped John, whose attention had been diverted to their outside surroundings. When he looked over, she nodded in the direction of her hurt feet. Without a spoken word of acknowledgment, he reached into his bag and pulled out a first aid kit. It was a preparedness that made her internally laugh.

"Of course, he had supplies," she thought.

He reached for her left leg first and laid it across his lap. Quietly, he began cleaning the wounds and adding ointment to them.

The cleaning part stung and she grimaced as he did his work. Soon enough, he had dressed the injuries with bandages and, curiously, had wrapped both feet as if she had sprained her ankles.

"Why did you wrap them?" she asked.

"You may need to do more running at some point. I don't anticipate it, but the wrap will keep the other bandages in place and provide some support. Your feet are going to hurt from all the running in the flats, regardless. This should help ease it a little," he explained.

"Ah okay. Thanks for that," she returned.

He started to say something else when the van pulled to a stop. He shrugged off any potential comments and hopped out without a backwards glance. The guys followed and began walking away. She looked around as she exited the car and saw they had arrived at an old dock.

It was a heavily wooded area with the tree branches cloaking the full view from the road. It provided a cover for obscurity. She imagined the locals were the only ones who knew of this place.

They made their way to the two boats sitting in wait. The wood planks of the dock were dated and beginning to rot. She worried with each step that it would break beneath her feet and she didn't particularly want to add wet to her list of complaints right now.

The boats, however, were a stark contrast to the shape of the docks. Two gleaming floating objects that appeared as if they had been taken from the showroom floor. They even shined despite the lack of sunlight to highlight them. Again, she pondered how connected these gentlemen were to have obtained two brand new motor boats on short notice.

"They certainly rescued people in style," she surmised to herself.

Robert and Ethan got into one boat while Chris and John climbed into the other. John held out a hand to help her into his boat before joining Chris to unpack the gear that was waiting for them at the stern of the boat.

They pulled several guns from one of the bags and began checking them. Systematically, John and Chris laid each weapon down on the bench after they had finished their assessments. By her count, there were ten handguns and two rifles on the boat with them. She looked over at the other boat where it appeared that Ethan and Robert were doing the same preparation. She guessed they had matching equipment.

The guys were all in the zone, checking and rechecking chambers and ammunition. She noticed their gadgets included knives, night goggles, and miscellaneous objects like duct tape and rope. They were well prepared, like a team of vigilantes. The only question she had was how far would they go to achieve their goal.

She knew they were capable of killing. At least they were when one of their own was being threatened as she had been. What she didn't know for sure was if they planned to barge into this place with guns blazing. Plus, she wasn't certain how she would feel about that.

Mostly, she felt uncomfortable at the thought they would just start firing without being provoked. She had been under the impression that they would attempt to sneak Annabelle out. Seeing all this firepower made her doubt that this was their plan. And she wasn't confident they would tell her the truth if she asked.

The whole situation was spiraling and she was feeling powerless to stop it. She understood why they killed those men earlier. They were pointing guns at her. It was likely they would have pulled the trigger because, as John had pointed out, the Doppelgangmen couldn't afford to have any loose ends. Although she didn't agree with the principle of it, it had seemed justifiable.

This scenario didn't.

"Brianna, can you come here a second?" John interrupted her thoughts.

She walked over to where they had inventoried and assessed their tools. He picked up a 9 MM and offered it to her. At first, she stared at his outstretched hand and didn't grab the weapon.

"Have you ever been around guns before?" he puzzled from her reluctance.

Somewhat offended by the remark, she took the gun from his hand. She quickly checked the safety wasn't on before turning her back to him. Her eyes darted around for a target before deciding to shoot the bark off one of the nearby trees.

She took aim and squeezed the trigger, hitting the narrow bark of a young palm tree directly at it is center.

When she faced him again, she found a huge smile on his face. After she raised her eyebrow at that reaction, he began to laugh.

"Brianna, you could have just said, 'yes, I know how to use it.'"

She noticed she had gotten the other guys' attention too. Except they were not amused based on their expressions.

"What the fuck?" Ethan demanded.

"Someone could have heard that! She may have just given away our position. Why are you fucking laughing? Is this a joke to you?" he yelled.

Ethan truly seemed pissed in that moment. His face was red, his teeth were clenched, and she swore she saw steam coming from his ears. Unlike the cartoon characters she had witnessed with that reaction, it was anything but funny.

John, as usual, was taking it all in stride.

"Dude. It is okay. I picked this location because of the privacy. If that wasn't safe then neither is us going through the gear out in the open. Trust me, it is fine," he indicated.

Ethan did not appear pleased, but he said nothing else. His face remained stone cold and his body tensed.

He was obviously still pissed. He turned his back to John and busied himself checking equipment he had already examined.

John simply shrugged his shoulders, focusing his attention back on her while Robert and Chris subtly observed their interaction. They watched the two of them like it was a TV show they couldn't bring themselves to stop binging.

"Where did you learn to shoot like that?" John asked her, not bothering to hide his reverence.

"I grew up on a farm. And my grandfather was big on guns. I never cared for them though," she remembered.

"You don't like them?" he probed.

She shrugged her shoulders.

"But you shoot well. That tree is at least ten to twenty yards away. That is pretty good for handgun accuracy," he informed her.

"I know. But I still don't really like them," she reiterated.

Now, it was his turn to shrug as he delivered the news.

"Noted. But I may need you to use your skills in a few hours."

"I am not going to kill anybody," she insisted, raising her voice to make sure she was heard.

They all returned her assertion with blank stares. He walked over to her, placed a reassuring hand on her arm, and calmed her.

"I don't expect you to kill anybody. Nobody here expects you to murder someone in cold blood," he started. "But you need to be willing to defend yourself."

He paused.

"I am glad you can shoot like you do. Please don't get me wrong. I want to be able to protect you. But we will be far too busy getting Annabelle out and trying not to get ourselves shot too. None of us will be effective if we have to worry about you as well."

She averted her eyes instead of arguing with him. This time, she understood where he was coming from in his viewpoint. She had stormed off like a child earlier today and had landed herself into a load of trouble. And he and his guys had saved her from her stupidity.

She had never agreed with killing people. The exception to that rule in her mind was only when her personal safety was at immediate risk. Self-defense was a circumstance she believed would justify taking a life.

She knew logically that had the guys not taken the actions they had, she would have had a 95% chance of being dead right now. Worse, her body would have remained behind a dumpster for who knows how long. In this case, she believed these deaths had been warranted.

Then it occurred to her again. How did they know to find her in that alleyway, behind that dumpster, at that exact moment?

Perhaps they had been following her since she left the restaurant. Maybe they saw those guys stalking after her, so they kept close enough to protect her. It also made sense given John's connections that he could have gotten a tail on her as soon as she left him at the table. He had had a large enough network to arrange a transport in a matter of minutes, so she guessed he could have easily kept an eye on her whereabouts from afar.

"I never asked. And don't get me wrong here either because I am so grateful. But how did you know where to find me? Were you following me as soon as I stormed out of the resort? Were you making sure that I didn't get myself dead or worse?" she finally questioned.

"Yes, I was making sure you didn't get dead or worse. Although I am not sure what worse would be," he joked.

He reached his hand toward her neck and held the pendant necklace he gave her that morning in his fingers.

"This has a location device in it. So, yeah. The guys started tracking you the minute you left me at the table. I'm sorry but I couldn't jeopardize your safety or Annabelle's from you being taken again. Though, I will admit when I gave it to you this morning, I didn't think we would need to enable it so soon. I didn't anticipate you walking out like you did."

She couldn't believe her ears. He had planted a tracking device on her without her knowledge or consent. While it had ultimately saved her life, it was creepy. She hadn't known.

It had been her primary grievance since meeting John. He wasn't forthcoming with important information. In fact, he wasn't upfront about anything. He would only tell her what he thought she needed to know, usually when she directly asked.

She also didn't know how he felt about her. Despite a few kisses and some serious flirtation, she was only certain he would protect her from physical danger. She was clueless about his intentions otherwise.

She decided that she wouldn't bring it up at this moment. It truly wasn't the right time to complain about a device that had prevented her from being shot. She didn't plan to argue his methods or his whole cloak and dagger routine. And she definitely wasn't going to ask him if he liked her. There were more important matters at hand.

For now, she would nod her head and make a mental note to revisit it. All of it.

"I get that. And, for the record, I figured out that acting the way I did, storming off... I regretted it. Almost immediately," she admitted.

"Almost immediately?" he winked.

She smiled.

"Even before they pulled their guns on me," she added.

He smiled before getting up to return to the guys who were going over their items again. Chris and Robert had begun arguing about a missing item. John was intervening. She was constantly surprised at his patience to deal with all the pressure and stress he was encountering.

But she decided to tone it out since it didn't concern her. She wanted a moment to herself. A second in time that didn't involve running or arguing or thinking. Just peace. Or a minute to fake it, at least.

It was less than an hour to go before they attacked a group of well-trained men who would gladly shoot them dead on sight. She didn't know if she had it in her to pull the trigger, whether it be for defense or otherwise. As she mulled it over, she secretly concluded that she couldn't kill someone. She didn't have it in her. She just hoped she wouldn't also hesitate if it was a matter of self defense.

She thought of Mark then. When he had attacked her, she had fought back. She hadn't intended to kill him, not that she could have with a wine glass as her only weapon. But she wondered, if she had had a gun or knife or an object that could have seriously injured him, would she have used it?

She had been so enraged by what he had intended to do she believed she would have been capable of almost any violence that night.

"Yes, I could have killed him myself," she thought.

The difference was he had attacked her after they had had a personal relationship. He was a known entity. He wasn't a stranger doing his job.

Then again, their job was evil. They were paid to kidnap and hold women hostage. Their job allowed them to physically abuse and kill, if necessary. While she was there contemplating their existence and the pain their families would feel if she ended their lives, they would most certainly drop her without thinking twice.

She was hoping that this perspective would make her less hesitant if the time came. It was the lie she was telling herself to psyche herself up.

She sat back and watched as they finished their preparations. John made phone calls while the other guys talked amongst themselves.

Except for Ethan. He hardly said a word to anyone. He seemed solemn and she knew why. It was obvious to anyone how much he loved his wife.

She had witnessed it in the way he had looked at her, in the expressions of the photos on their walls depicting their life together, in the way he had spoken about her, and, mostly, in his fierce determination to get her back.

She had admired it. It was the kind of devotion she had hoped for herself, back when she had hoped for such things. These days the most she managed was survival. It was truly astounding how perspectives change.

Now, she wasn't sure she would ever imagine a happily coupled existence for herself. There was no ever after for her future. Too much had happened. She was weary to trust anyone, even the handsome man who had acted as if he was someone who cared.

20

S he was jolted from her thoughts by the roar of the engines. She hadn't even noticed when they had finished with their preparations. But it appeared they were ready to go because John motioned for her to move to the bench. He was at the wheel, Chris and Robert were already seated in the back. They were both just waiting for her to take the spot between them.

Ethan was driving the other boat. His eyes already locked on the horizon despite their still stationary position. She wondered why Ethan was in a boat by himself. She would have guessed he was the most likely to lose his head, given what was at stake. She wouldn't have trusted him to be alone for fear he would go rogue to save his wife.

John knew him better though.

Almost as soon as her butt had hit the white leather seat, the boat jetted off into the wind. They bumped along on the water as the boat picked up speed. Her hair was thrown back and the wind chilled her face despite the hot and humid air.

Ethan was close on their tail, his expression one of pure anger. However, she supposed that hatred for the Doppelgangmen could serve him well tonight.

The dusk was fading quickly into the night. A fact not lost on the guys since they handed her some night goggles. Although, she had noticed they hadn't put them on themselves.

Chris and Robert were staring into the abyss, seemingly unconcerned as they made the journey to a volatile circumstance. She knew some people fed off the adrenaline of these situations, some who were even addicted to the rush. These guys didn't bat an eyelash. If she didn't know better she would have mistaken them for trained military. They were as calm and composed as ever.

She was the opposite. As they skipped across the ocean, she did her best to hide her fear. She desperately wanted to look brave. She was tired of feeling scared and weak. There was only so much vulnerability one could have. She had hit her quota, with herself.

She quietly scolded herself when her eyes began to water. It didn't take long for her to be exposed as a weepy mess, once again. As the tears slid down her face, Chris offered her his sleeve. It was a kind gesture that made her remember how fragile she was to them.

Since they had met her, she hadn't been her normal self. In fact, she had been acting like a frightened child. She knew it would be some time before she felt like herself again. She hoped one day they would get to see her the way she really was.

She had been surprised at how accepting they had been towards her. She was even more shocked at their willingness to put their own lives on the line and tolerate her earlier antics.

That was a testament to John and the kind of person she suspected he was deep down. It also showed what type of people these guys were.

It scared her to imagine what they thought of her. They said nothing, of course. Just as they had not commented on anything she had said or done thus far.

Luckily, they didn't alert John to her new tears either. She didn't want to try justifying the tears as only the wind stringing her eyes. She didn't believe she would be convincing. Mostly because she couldn't convince herself.

It didn't take long for them to encounter a series of small islands that were within view of each other. It occurred to her as she looked from one to the other, it would be truly remarkable to be able to recognize the differences amongst them.

It was then she realized John wasn't using a map to lead them to their destination. It was impressive that he knew the way well enough he could navigate blind to where they were going. She assumed that was one of the reasons the group sent him in to get her from the shed in the woods. He obviously knew what he was doing and his way around. There were no doubts he was the leader among them, in all instances.

She looked up again, noting that the islands had become grey silhouettes. The darkness of the night was descending and, soon, they wouldn't be able to see at all. John pushed up on the throttle and joined them in the back of the boat. She also heard the ceasing of the other engine as Ethan pulled up close to them.

She didn't have time to blink before the guys began stripping down to wet suits and changing their shoes for rubber boots adorned with hiking soles. John also changed to a wet suit he had pulled from one of the bags.

The men then dressed their chests with handgun holsters, strapping their weapons into place. They positioned the night goggles on their heads and checked the contents of the backpacks.

Again, she imagined that was what it was like watching a Navy SEAL team prepare for battle.

She wasn't dense to the fact that they didn't give her a wet suit. For the moment, it was as if she was non-existent.

She sat awkwardly as the boat swayed in the water and wondered once again what her role would be. It was obvious that she wasn't going into the fray with them. Or maybe she was going, but with less gear to prepare her for the elements. But that didn't seem to be a likely scenario.

A familiar lump was present in her throat. This time, however, she wasn't saying anything. She had to trust whatever John had planned. He knew what he was doing. He had always come through for her despite her regular opposition. The last thing these guys needed was her messing with their focus by voicing any sort protest about being left behind.

She would sit silently and wait for instructions. She promised herself she would, at least, try this time.

John pulled out a walkie-talkie and radioed Ethan.

"You set?" he simply asked.

"Yep," Ethan's voice crackled in return.

He looked back at the other guys, "Radios only if absolutely necessary."

They both nodded their understanding.

John walked over and kneeled before her. She had her head bowed, afraid to make eye contact. He grabbed for her hands with both of his and held them in his own, patiently waiting for her to look at him. Despite the dread, she raised her head enough to share an intimate exchange with him.

"So, I imagine you are scared right now, especially since we haven't told you the full plan. Which is partly for your safety and also because the plan is very fluid," he spoke softly.

She nodded before he continued.

"You are going to stay in the boat when we get to shore. We will leave you with a gun. We all thought it would be better, and more efficient, if we go without you."

It felt as if she was being told she couldn't go to a party by a concerned parent. She felt rejected and, somewhat, scorned. She wanted to be part of the rescue, she realized. She wanted to help get Annabelle out of the hell she had endured. She wanted to do what she could to prevent other Doppelgängers, or anyone, from being subjected to these people. She wanted to fight back.

"Why?" she inquired, meekly.

John sighed.

"We can't risk it. We can't trust you won't decide to abandon our mission and do your own thing again. Sadly, you are a liability now."

She felt her eyes watering again.

She had become a liability. She had done that with her stupidity. She knew without reflection she had only herself to blame for it.

It hurt.

She told herself that she wouldn't have been overly helpful anyway. She could shoot a gun, but she had only practiced with inanimate objects. When faced with a living, moving being, she couldn't be sure her aim or her ability to actually pull the trigger would be any good. She also couldn't count on her not getting scared and running away if she encountered the Doppelgangmen head on.

John had a valid point. She knew it, but she still didn't like it.

"Is there anything I can do to help?" she requested.

"Yes. Please stay in the boat. I want you to be down and out of sight," he started.

He reached up and cupped her face with his hand, gently caressing her cheek with his thumb. She leaned into it, closing her eyes and embracing the feeling of safety for a second.

"Brianna?" he softly called her name.

"Hmmm…" she mumbled.

"Please stay on the boat. I don't want to worry about you," he whispered.

She nodded her head in understanding. He pulled his hand away and stood. He gave the guys a nod as he went back to the boat's throttle.

It was go time.

He powered up the boat to half speed and steered it toward one of the landmasses shadowed on the horizon. It only took a couple of minutes for them to make it to shore. John brought the boat up close to the sand and Ethan pulled up next to him.

In a flash, Chris and Robert jumped from the boat and made their way to the edge of the trees with their guns drawn. They were on high alert and ready to defend if their approach had been noticed.

John didn't look at her as he grabbed his pack and leapt from the boat. He and Ethan anchored them to the sand with a rope attached to the bow. Then, she watched as they moved up the beach to where Chris and Robert were waiting. Silently, they slipped between the trees and disappeared.

At first, she watched the forest, listening for the signs of a battle or for the guys' return. Yet, the silence that met her in response was deafening. It was quiet and it was dark, reminding her of the lonely nights she had spent in the shed. Those nights had been the epitome of alone. A feeling she hadn't been keen to repeat.

She moved from her seat to the floor of the boat. John had asked her to stay hidden and wait, so that is what she intended to do. They had left her a handgun that she held tight against her chest, as if it were a security blanket.

It didn't take long for her senses to be heightened. Her eyes had adjusted to the darkness and she raised from her spot on the floor to peek her head over the rim of the boat. She stared into the woods, finally able to see the outlines of the trees and branches. There were faint sounds of movement by what she assumed was animals. Her ears then began discerning the whistle of the wind through the barks and the rustling of the leaves.

She looked back out at the ocean, watching the cresting of the black waves as they came to land. She could smell the seawater and feel the crisp mist on her face.

It would have been an extremely peaceful environment under different circumstances.

Suddenly in the distance, she heard popping sounds like firecrackers had been set off, followed by yelling. She poked her head up farther and looked for indications of life, but was met with more darkness.

She squatted farther down, but kept her view of the forest. She was certain she heard what sounded like gunshots, the noises of a fight. They had to be coming back this way soon.

More gunshots rang out, except this time she saw brief flashes of light in the near proximity. She wasn't sure what the flashes were exactly, but her adrenaline had skyrocketed. She cowered back down into the boat and prayed the guys would be back soon. It wouldn't be long before they would be out of here.

Then it occurred to her that they may not make it back. What would she do then?

Panic had started to set in and she crawled her way to the dashboard. She frantically searched for a key to start the engine. She needed a way to save herself and get the hell out of here, if it came to it.

She found none.

"Oh shit!" she cursed.

She scrambled to the back bench and started to rummage through the guys' bags. She desperately tried to remember which one belonged to John. Soon, it didn't matter. All the contents of every single bag was scattered on the vessel's floor.

He had to have taken the boat key with him.

"Fuck, fuck, fuck!" she angrily whispered to the night.

She sat there, defeated. There was still no sign of the guys emerging upon the shore. It had been several minutes since she had last heard the gunshots and they had to have been gone for at least fifteen minutes. She didn't think it should take that long. It was a bad omen.

She needed to find an escape because the Doppelgangmen would be after her next if they had truly taken out the guys. They would descend upon her and she would be a sitting duck with no way out.

She decided she should check the other boat for a key. Perhaps Ethan hadn't taken that one with him. But she had to move quickly. She didn't know how long she had before the worst happened.

She grabbed the handgun before jumping out of the boat. When she landed on the left side of the hull, she was knee deep in water. She immediately regretted not thinking her plan through a little, because she realized that Ethan's boat was on the right side.

Not wanting to waste any more time and needing to make up for her error, she started moving to the front of the boat as quickly as her water-logged tennis shoes would carry her. Her muscles ached within a few minutes as she struggled to move her legs from the resistance of the sand and water.

She dug her heels in and pushed harder.

She was finally making some quick progress towards Ethan's boat when two figures ran out of the woods onto the beach. Brianna stopped in her tracks, not able to see either of these people clearly in the dark.

They, however, did not slow their trajectory towards her. As they neared, she saw that these were two of the Doppelgangmen and they had their guns leveled at her. She panicked. She had forgotten until they were within striking distance that, she too, held a gun in her hand.

She had enough time to aim the weapon at the forehead of one of the approaching guards, but her hesitation in squeezing the trigger cost her. In rapid sequence, he knocked her arm upwards and grabbed her other wrist, spinning her towards him.

Her back was pressed against his chest and he had a firm grip on her body. Still, she began to squirm.

He didn't waste any time in fighting her. With a quick blow to her head, she had crumbled to the ground.

21

AFTER

She was vaguely aware of being dragged a few feet onto the beach. As the water gently crashed over her body, she sensed there were people standing over her.

She heard voices, but she couldn't make out what they were saying. She was having trouble staying present in reality. Her head was pounding so hard, she questioned whether the man had split it open with an axe. The pain was radiating throughout her body. When she opened her eyes, her vision was bleary and bright. There were colorful spots everywhere.

The next thing she remembered, she was being carried. It was reminiscent of when John had carried her from the woods not so long ago. Only now, she feared it would be the opposite outcome.

She knew she was being taken back into the hell.

She was in and out of consciousness. Except she was

aware she had been thrown onto the floor like a sack of potatoes and transported somewhere. It was déjà vu.

She processed very little on her boat journey beyond the beautiful clarity of the night sky full of dim stars. Given her situation and how she imagined the Doppelgangmen felt about her, she worried that this would be the last beautiful sky she ever saw. She didn't believe they would make the same mistake twice.

She didn't know who was in the boat with her, but she was mindful that there was someone guarding her. When she started to rouse her head, she noted a gun was promptly stuck in her face. She laid back down.

Her orientation of time was off, mostly because she felt as if she had been hit by a truck. Every second felt like an hour, so she had no way of knowing how far away they were taking her from the guys, from John.

The thought of the guys just then brought fear into her heart. She had no idea what had happened to them. It hadn't been a good sign when the Doppelgangmen had showed up on the beach as they had.

It was the logical conclusion that something had gone very wrong. She allowed herself to consider the possibility she wanted to block out.

What if they were all dead?

As soon as the idea of John being dead occurred to her, she felt the bile rise up in her throat. She doubled over and threw up on the floor, retching until she was dry heaving from the lack of contents in her stomach. The tears began to stream when she imagined not seeing John's face again. She was flooded with emotion that left her feeling raw.

She was realizing how attached she had grown to him over the last week. She didn't want to believe he could be dead, despite it being the most likely scenario. He had promised he would protect her. He had told her that they would be okay.

It didn't seem like he would be keeping his word this time.

She laid on her back and let the tears flow. She didn't bother trying to conceal them or attempt to stop crying. She didn't have the strength to pull herself together anymore, or the will power.

The images of each of the guy's faces were flashing through her mind. She was the cause of all their deaths. She had been the reason Annabelle was taken. Her attempts at escaping the house had also ended in death.

The body count on her head was becoming too much for her to bear. If only she had just died herself in that shed, some of those people, good people, would still be alive. There would still be somebody working against the Doppelgangmen, fighting for their demise.

It was in those moments she truly began to give up. It had come to a point where she had felt it was over. She would stop denying it now. She could stop struggling against it. There was nothing left but the acceptance of the aftermath and the inevitable fallout to come.

She had reached that point. She didn't care anymore what they did with her. Although she was hoping her fate would be a swift one.

It was her best guess that they would kill her and find another Doppel as a replacement. From what John had told her, she must have been amongst a handful of possible choices. She had to have been somewhat disposable. After all, she did end up in the shed, left to die.

Maybe they would put her back there. Or perhaps she could provoke them to shoot her so it would be a quick and definitive end.

Either way, she would soon find out because the boat pulled up to a dock. The bright, orange lights illuminating the marina hurt her eyes. But at least she was more conscious now, as she had begun to take in her surroundings.

She shifted her body to a sitting position and watched as two men hopped onto the wooden structure. They tied the boat off while the driver killed the engines. She turned her head to see the last remaining passenger in the boat. To her horror, she recognized him.

It was Ethan.

"Oh my God," she said aloud in disbelief.

She knew he had heard her because he had looked directly at her as she spoke. However, he didn't show any signs of remorse. He simply ignored her, climbed onto the dock, and disappeared into the night.

If she hadn't felt sick before, she was undoubtedly ill now. Her shock was overwhelming. She had been hand delivered to the Doppelgangmen by one of their own.

It was also a wretched act because it meant John and the guys were most certainly dead. John would have never willingly let Ethan betray them.

Then it clicked. Where was Annabelle?

Even if Ethan didn't care about her, he loved his wife. He would have never left Annabelle on that island. There could only be two possibilities. Either she was already dead when they arrived or this was his plan to exchange Brianna for her.

Perhaps the island had been a trap. A rouse he had participated in to get his wife back. But she didn't have time to figure it out right then.

She was being hoisted to the dock by one of the guards. They led her down a lit path to a waiting ATV and drove her through a familiar forest. The house that haunted her dreams shined bright on its hill. She was back in the crusty old man's clutches.

Gloating, he was there at the front porch, expecting her arrival. The sight of him sent shivers down her spine. She had thought that she would never have to face him again. It wasn't a pleasant thing to be wrong in that belief.

She walked up the stairs to face him, but his triumphant spirit was too much. He was so downright giddy that it made her ill.

Then, he spoke, "Hello, my dear."

His sly smile was the definition of creepy and condescending to her. He side-stepped and held his outstretched arm toward the house.

"I believe you know the way, my dear."

She sighed and strolled through the doorway. She had resigned herself. She had already reasoned it would all be over soon. If not, she was promising to make sure of it herself.

But first, she had to find out what had happened to John. She owed him that much. Perhaps she was a masochist at this point, but she needed to know what had become of all of them. She also wanted to know what

Annabelle had experienced and what had made Ethan do what he did.

She walked, unencumbered, to her old room at the top of the stairs. She had been free for a week, but it had already felt like this place was part of a very bad and distant memory.

She smiled at that realization. She knew that the only reason these hallways felt like a dream was because of John.

It hadn't been just one thing John had done. Sure, he had gotten her out of this place for a little while. But it was how he had made her feel normal again that resonated. They had talked about things, shared stories of their childhood. He had gone out of his way to make her feel comfortable. It had been his kindness and patience that she had needed the most.

She sat on her bed, looking around at the blank walls once again. Her eyes averted to the corner where Matt's body had been left as an example of misbehavior. All evidence had been cleaned away, but the lesson was still present.

She wasn't sure what her next move would be, but she wasn't going to play by their rules this time around. She knew she had very little time left and she no longer cared about her fate.

Her mind was clear.

She would not waste away in a shed with an indefinite death date. She would motivate them to act. If they intended to kill her, or even if they didn't, she had made her decision. She was going to die fighting instead of spending another night in that room.

With her mind set, she got up and walked downstairs. She carried herself with the confidence of a woman who had nothing left to lose. She headed down the hallway towards the library, passing a guard on her route. She didn't flinch. She didn't stop. She did, however, notice the surprise on the guard's face before he started to follow her. Yet, she wouldn't be deterred by him or anyone else. She was on a warpath.

She searched each room, but somehow, she knew where she would find him. She barged into the gallery.

She was right. She had found exactly who she had been wanting to confront.

He was standing in front of one of the portraits, sipping a whiskey as casually as he would at a dinner party.

"So, when exactly did you decide to sell out your friends?" she accused Ethan.

He had been caught off guard by her outburst. He had dropped his drink, spilling its contents on his clothes. His face, however, hadn't registered any reaction to her question. He simply stood there, wiping his shirt and pants to remove the excess liquid.

Shaking his head in disgust, he frowned his contempt. He was a stark contrast to the warm guy she had met days ago. It wasn't the same guy. The man before her was cold and calculating. In his every move and gesture, he schemed. He finished dabbing at his pants and gave her his full attention with a scathing look.

"What do you think you know?" he scolded.

"I know you are here. I know you brought me to them. I know John would be pissed if he were alive to see it. I know what he would think of you. You betrayed him," she yelled.

She didn't care about the consequences of screaming at him. It didn't matter what they did to her now. In her mind, her fate had been sealed on that beach. Or maybe beforehand. She figured she should, at least, get to speak her piece. Whether it meant anything to anyone else or not, it mattered to her.

He seemed more amused than pissed. The smirk that covered his face was the pinnacle of arrogance.

"Hmmm," he mumbled, slightly shaking his head.

After a pause of silence, he gave her a tight lipped smile.

"Well, I guess it is a good thing he is dead then."

She charged at him, causing him to jerk backwards. Her arms flew up in a rage, ready to tear his eyes out.

He lost his balance as he stumbled in reverse, his hands crossing his face to guard it. Seeing an opportunity immediately, he defensively grabbed her wrists as she was pouncing to strike. Shifting the momentum, he pushed her arms down to her sides and regained his stance.

In an instant, he had turned the tide and was now in her face. His temper had flared.

Nose to nose, his pupils had dilated. His eyes were filled with restrained hatred. His breath was hot on her face. His grip on her wrists was cutting off the circulation.

"What the fuck do you even know?" he repeated.

They were in a standoff. Except she refused to back down this time, knowing where it would likely lead. She knew she would be struck down in one way or another.

However, her resolve didn't falter. She wouldn't be intimidated anymore.

He still radiated with anger. But she didn't cower. She mustered all the energy she had to hold her ground. She boldly stood taller and pushed him back with her body.

Surprisingly, it worked. He conceded a little, withdrawing his face and lessening his grasp enough to allow blood to flow again.

"You don't know anything. You are pathetic. A disgrace to the face," he reeled against her.

"Well, this isn't what I expected to find," Annabelle interjected.

Brianna spun on her heels, utterly paralyzed by seeing Annabelle standing in the doorway of the gallery. Ethan, on the other hand, hadn't wasted any time. He quickly discarded her and their confrontation. He had run to his wife and already had her tightly tucked into his arms before she could blink.

Annabelle was alive. And standing there unharmed.

Judging from their reunion, she safely assumed Ethan had traded her for Annabelle. Not that she blamed him for his motivation. Their hug would make most people envious of the closeness they shared as a couple.

But if his wife had been here, then why did they invade the other island looking for her?

Ethan seemingly had known where she had been the whole time. He wasn't the least bit shocked at her appearance in the room.

Had he planned to double cross the guys from the beginning? Could Annabelle's disappearance been a ruse to make it easier to get Brianna back into the fold?

Brianna was very confused. She had so many questions. For the moment, the most important ones were revolving around John.

"Is John still alive?" she demanded, interrupting them.

They pulled back from each other and looked at her. Annabelle looked completely confused while Ethan's disdain had returned. His regard for her remained scathing, to the say the least.

"Why would you think John is dead?" Annabelle earnestly asked.

"Isn't he?" she looked at Ethan.

Ethan didn't answer, choosing instead to stare back at her.

Brianna wasn't going to let it go. It wouldn't be that easy for him. She wanted his wife to know what kind of man he was. She nodded her head towards him when she responded.

"Because they were on a mission to save you from a place you obviously weren't being held. And the guys didn't come back. Only Ethan did. With the Doppelgangmen guards," she explained.

Annabelle looked at Ethan, who still said nothing. She gave him a curious expression which he combated with a nonchalant smile. Abruptly, she shrugged her shoulders and they left the room.

Brianna was flabbergasted.

"A shrug! What the hell?" she exclaimed.

It was insulting. Surely their long-term friend deserved better. She wasn't going to be blown off despite her inferior rank in the house. She marched out of the gallery, determined to make them talk to her. She had to know what had happened on that island. She had more respect for John than to let him be forgotten so quickly.

But as usual, she was too late for answers.

She was stopped in the doorframe by the sight of two guards flanking Ethan and Annabelle down the hallway. She slipped back into the gallery and peeked her head out to watch. The body language said it all. It was not a friendly interaction. The guards had grabbed each of their arms and was leading the couple away, under protest.

Reminding herself that she had nothing to lose, she quietly trailed behind as the guards led them towards the front door. She crept along, staying close to the walls to use any furniture as cover.

She snuck all the way to one of the front windows and peered out. They weren't far ahead of her as she witnessed the couple descending the front steps to the yard.

Still being manhandled, she wondered where the guards were taking them. It wasn't as if there was an ATV waiting to escort them from the property. The only option was the woods.

"And the shed," she thought in horror.

Suddenly, her show was interrupted. She jumped at the sound of the crusty old man's voice.

"Enjoying the view, sweetheart?"

She closed her eyes tightly, hoping that she had imagined him. But a quick glance behind her confirmed she had been discovered.

"Why don't we get you a front row seat. I don't want you to miss anything," he insisted.

He, once again, held his arm out to gesture the direction she should walk. They headed outside to the front lawn where a few guards and the couple had gathered.

"I wanted to make sure Brianna saw everything," the crusty old man explained to the guards, whose expressions showed curiosity at their arrival to the scene.

"After all, this is all for her," he finished before motioning for the them to proceed.

22

AFTER

She watched in horror as the guards made Annabelle and Ethan kneel at gunpoint. The fear of what she was about to witness overtook her. Even more surprising was how compliant the couple had become in the span of a few minutes.

There were no more protests as the two got on their knees. There were no outbursts or pleas for savaltion. They didn't even bow their heads. Neither of them seemed concerned in the slightest about a gun being in their face. There was only submission.

It was odd and exceedingly disturbing. It was like watching a ritual sacrifice occur. The sheep were very much aware they were going to be slaughtered.

She was horrified. She had seen enough violence and death for an entire lifetime. The last thing she wanted was to watch an execution. Despite her dislike of Ethan and his actions, she didn't want to see him die. Or Annabelle.

In fact, she refused. She turned to walk back into the house when the crusty old man yanked at her arm to pull her backwards. She jerked back from his grip, stumbling to the ground in her effort to evade him.

They all stopped to look at her sitting on the ground. All their eyes were casting judgment, as if she was the strange one for trying to walk away.

"Who are you people?" she rhetorically asked.

But she didn't start crying or becoming hysterical as she had in the past. She was way beyond any response like that now. Nor did she wait for them to react.

She simply got to her feet. She looked pointedly at the crusty old man and turned to walk away. She headed towards the house. She didn't care what they did to her. She was done with all of it. Even if the crusty old man had hollered at her to return, she wouldn't have.

She was almost to the steps when it all exploded.

It started with a single gunshot.

Then a fire rained down in all directions. She threw herself to the ground. As more and more shots rang out, she began to crawl towards the porch, finally curling up between the side of the stairs and the house's foundation. She wasn't sure how much protection it would provide, but she didn't have time to get back inside.

However, there was one advantage from this spot. She could see what was happening on the lawn as it played out.

It was dark and difficult to make sense of everything. Upon first glance she saw several bodies on the ground. She imagined they were dead or too scared to move. She heard the popping of rifles firing behind her, meaning there were defenses in the house. She could also see several guards using the trees and the night as cover. She didn't know where all these extra guards had come from because there was only a handful before the shooting had started. She also guessed the gunfire had originated from inside the woods given how the guards were positioned behind the trees.

There wasn't much else she could discern. It was happening too fast.

Then as quickly as the gunfire had started, it ceased. Silence engulfed them. A quiet that was more terrifying than the bullets whizzing past her body.

They all waited. No one moved, unsure what was next.

A million thoughts went through her head, "Should she risk moving to get better cover? Who was attacking the compound? Could it possibly be John?"

It had to be John. No one else would open fire on the guards, especially at the exact moment his friends' lives were at stake.

It occurred to her that maybe this was a part of the plan. Perhaps they had known that Annabelle was here at the house and staged a trade. It seemed a possible scenario, if not the riskiest one imaginable.

"That has to be it!" she thought.

It certainly made more sense than Ethan going rogue and betraying his friends. He was smart enough to have known better. He wouldn't have trusted the crusty old man to keep a promise. He would have figured out that trading her for his wife wouldn't result in them walking away unscathed. It was never going to be that easy.

It would also explain why they hadn't been fighting their impending execution. They had to have known that John and the guys were planning to step in for them.

She considered it to be the only explanation to what was happening around her now. It was a rational conclusion.

Except there were only three of them against a multitude of guards. She estimated during her tenure at the compound, there had been somewhere around twenty different guards in rotation. She had often wondered where they were housed. She had concluded after observing them that they had switched off every couple of days.

But tonight, she had seen more of them on site than ever. The crusty old man had obviously known they were coming, just as John had predicted. They had increased the security so the odds were even worse than they had anticipated.

The only question was just how outnumbered was John's team. Even if they had taken out a few guards with their initial shots, there were still too many to fight. The advantage was to the Doppelgangmen.

The silence grew long. It had been almost ten minutes since the last shots were fired. There was still no movement.

She began to panic. She prayed the odds hadn't caught up to them too soon. The cease fire and lack of a raid by John's guys didn't speak well for that hope.

The guards using the tree shields had begun signaling. An indication that they were about to sweep the woods. They believed they had gotten their attackers. They just needed to confirm it.

She needed them to be wrong.

They had begun to mobilize, several of the guards disappearing into the forest. They moved like a military squad, fluid in their motions to work like a team. The others made their way back to the lawn to investigate the bodies that lay there. They stayed low to the ground, checking and rechecking their every step.

She stayed where she was to watch it all unfold.

Four guards grabbed the crusty old man and moved him to the house in two by two formation. They didn't bother to check the others for life.

They weren't going to leave her outside either. The last two guys of the formation stopped before her, screaming for her to cooperate as they tugged her from the ground. She didn't want to go into the house anymore, but it seemed to be the safest bet to avoid any crossfire.

Once they were through the doorway, the guards began locking down the house. It became a fortress before her eyes. Wood shutters hidden behind the curtains were outstretched over the window panes. The front door was reinforced with a long, horizontal metal bar.

"Should we escort you to the safe room?" one guard asked the crusty old man.

"No, I think we are fine for now. Get one of the staff out here to tend to me," the crusty old man ordered and motioned to his bleeding leg.

"Yes, sir," the guard obeyed.

She wasn't sure what she should do.

She stood there, watching as the crusty old man was mended. Momentarily, she had the insane thought of intervening. She was contemplating a way to exacerbate his injury so he would bleed out. Except the guards were still ready to defend him.

"And you aren't that person," she reminded herself internally.

With each passing moment, her disappointment grew. There was continued silence from outside. There wasn't the slightest sign of a threat now. She believed her last hope of surviving had just come and went. If John and the guys had somehow survived, it was obvious they had given up. It was also likely that Ethan and Annabelle were now dead. She was stuck here for the foreseeable future.

Although, she expected that her future would be a short one. She assumed she would joining the list of the dead very soon. It was a merely a matter of time before she ended up back in the shed, if she wasn't outright killed for her prison break.

After a while, she headed up to her bedroom to wait out her fate. She entered the room with a heavy heart. When the attack had started, it had created a glimmer of hope. A hope which wasn't quite dead, but lessening with each single breath.

She laid on the bed and stared up at the ceiling. It wasn't just the sounds that had stilled. She felt numb. Every movement, every thought seemed to be a dream. Reality wasn't reality anymore.

In many ways, it was a comfort. The last week had

been non-stop motion. An adrenaline ride that had reminded her she was alive. It had been a gift. A re-taste of freedom before it all ended.

She was tired now. Her mind was exhausted. Her spirit was broken.

She had heard it said before that hope dies last. After being disappointed so many times before, she no longer believed it to be true. She was resigned. Her hope was finally gone while she lived on.

Then she heard it. A series of pounding sounds that shook the walls. Each boom got louder and louder. Each vibration more turbulent. She got to her feet and went into the hallway where she heard the frantic movements downstairs.

Paralyzed, she debated the best option. The house seemed to be coming down all around them.

23

AFTER

She didn't flinch. She didn't attempt to find safety. She did the reverse. She calmly walked down the stairs into the destruction.

As soon as she descended the stairs, she noticed the disarray. There were pieces of the ceiling littering the hallway. Glass was scattered on the floor from the broken wall frames. She moved forward, stepping over two guards' bodies as she made her way through the mess.

The front door was intact but there was a gaping hole between it and one of the windows.

"Not much a fortress," she scoffed aloud to no one.

Not far from her, she heard yet another boom and the sounds of crashing. Instinctively, she ducked expecting more of the ceiling to come down. When it didn't, she cautiously headed towards the commotion.

Every so often, she stopped to listen. She heard the sporadic popping of what sounded like gunfire and the scuffling sounds of people running.

However, she didn't see a living being. The only other people she had encountered were the dead guards.

She was a little confused, but she wasn't frightened. Nevertheless, she was careful as she followed the direction of the sounds. She tiptoed, hugging the wall. She made it slowly down the long hallway leading to the library and gallery. On the way, she saw a few more bodies. It seemed that the guards had been taken out, one-by-one.

"This has to be John!" she realized, almost giddy at the idea of seeing him again.

She had to admit it. She was impressed. She would have bet against those guys. She had doubted in their ability to take out a few of the Doppelgangmen in ideal circumstances. Yet, she seemingly had to disregard her incorrect assumptions. They had effectively stormed the castle and succeeded.

She wasn't immune to the amount of violence and death that her rescue had required. However, she appreciated that these weren't exactly the good guys. She could attest to it firsthand.

These were men who had done nothing as she was abused, mentally and physically. One of them had even tried to go as far as to sexually assault her. She had been property. Treated as being insignificant besides the features of her face matching someone else's. She didn't spare a pause at their corpses. They hadn't earned it.

She heard voices when she got closer to the library. More importantly, she heard John.

"Well, where are you keeping her, old man?" he calmly demanded.

His question was met with silence.

She knew she could answer his question by bursting into the room and throwing herself into his arms. It was what she wanted to do. Instead, she hesitated. She wasn't certain why but she didn't speak up or waltz into the study.

She just didn't. She stayed still to listen.

"I will find her whether you tell me or not..." he insisted.

"Indeed. What will you do with her?" the crusty old man asked.

John laughed, heartily. A laugh that sent tremors down her spine. It sounded evil, even for John.

"As opposed to you, old man? For starters, I don't have to keep her hostage to keep her with me," he claimed.

He was taunting him, using her as the salt to pour into the crusty old man's wound.

"Perhaps. But does she know who you are?" the crusty old man shot back.

It took a moment for John to respond.

"She knows me," he replied.

"And does she know what we are?" the crusty old man followed up.

Again, it took a moment for John to respond.

"She knows part of it. She will know more with time," he answered.

It was difficult to understand what was happening between the men. It was out of context for her. She couldn't see their body language or hear their tone. She didn't know the dynamic between them. Her mind was jumping to conclusions and completing imaginary scenarios.

She needed to see them interact to understand why John was taking the time to toy with the crusty old man versus coming immediately to find her. If she was his sole concern, why hadn't he looked for her first. More importantly, what was it that the crusty old man thought she didn't know.

He was mocking John in return. He was implying that John was still keeping stuff from her. Given her limited experiences with John and his secrets, she believed it was a plausible threat that the crusty old man had just made.

She decided now was her moment to interject. Unfazed, she strolled into the library. However, she was caught off guard by what she saw when she entered.

John was sitting on the couch relaxed, his feet on the coffee table. A gun was in his hand, but his arms were lax across his chest. Ethan was in the corner, leaned up against the bookcase, his gun held at his side.

The crusty old man, however, was on the floor. He did not look relaxed. His face revealed signs of someone who had been severely beaten. His forehead had an open cut.

Brianna didn't know what to think. She stood in the doorframe without speaking. John looked up and was on his feet as soon as he saw her. With a concerned look on his face, he cupped her cheek again.

"Hi," he whispered tenderly.

She looked at his familiar face, his comforting eyes. She didn't understand what she should believe when she had walked into the room. An old man was crumbled on the floor, in pain, and John had been lounging casually on the couch.

It was cold. It was not the guy she had grown to trust, the guy upon which she had become dependent. Just as Ethan wasn't who she had thought, she feared that John wasn't either.

It wasn't that she felt bad for the crusty old man. Sorry was the last thing she felt for him. It was the worry that John wasn't as good natured as she had assumed.

She had determined beforehand that the guys didn't have difficulties with killing people. They had done it a lot in the last 24 hours and had acted justified in their actions.

She just wasn't sure if it meant something to be so at ease when basically torturing another human being. Even when it was that particular human. If he could be so unfeeling, was it possible he could turn on her too?

He was still waiting for her to respond to him, a perplexed expression on his face. She looked deep into his eyes, searching for signs that he wasn't who she had thought.

Except she saw the compassionate and caring man she had been getting to know. The man who had been concerned with her safety and well-being more than anything else. It was the same John as before. So she leaned into his hand. She wanted to let him know she was still with him.

She then glared at Ethan, who equally returned her scorn.

She was planning to let John know about his friend. Perhaps he would just confirm that Ethan had been doing as he had been instructed. But she wasn't going to assume it and let Ethan get away with a double cross if that wasn't the case.

She next turned her attention to the crusty old man. He was defeated. But, she had a few things to say to him.

She kneeled in front of him, getting closer than she ever had. He was staring at her, an arrogant defiance in his eyes. She was filled with more rage than she had believed possible.

Many of those long, lonely nights in confinement, she had imaged having an opportunity to confront him. Yet, her mind was suddenly blank. Looking at him, she no longer thought he was worth it. He wasn't worthy of the breath or the regret from retaliating. He didn't get to take her dignity too. She just wanted to leave it behind her and never look back.

She turned to John with one question.

"If he lives...will they still come after me?"

John sighed.

"Yes. But, it is likely they will be after you for a long time anyway."

"And if he dies?"

"I don't understand the question," John remarked.

"What happens if he dies? You said they will still come after me no matter what. I want to know what is next, if he dies," she clarified.

She looked over at the crusty old man, who was listening intently to what she was asking. She realized that her internal debate about the value of his life was now public knowledge.

She didn't care.

This was a man who had toyed with her for months. A man who told her she wasn't valuable. Someone who had said she was only as good as the face she had inherited. He had hoped she would have been easier to control. He would have preferred she had died in those woods. He was evil and she most certainly despised him.

She had wrestled with the idea of taking a human life when it was the guards. Guards who were only following orders for the most part. But as those men fell, one by one, she discovered she didn't have any issue with it.

This man was another matter, entirely.

The debate, however, wasn't whether she should be the one to end it. She didn't care if he died. It just wasn't going to be at her hands. She already knew she didn't have it in her to pull the trigger. The real question was whether she could ask someone to do it for her and live with the consequences.

John hadn't answered her previous question. He seemed to be choosing his words wisely.

"It doesn't matter what you do to him, honestly," John finally stated. "I get it. The desire to cut off the head of the beast... But, unfortunately, he isn't that head."

She nodded and looked at the crusty old man with more disdain. He hadn't been the boss. Yet, he had treated her as if he were in charge. He had thrown his weight around. Anything to make her feel smaller.

Knowing this made her angrier.

"He isn't the one in charge?" she repeated.

"No. Not exactly," John answered.

"Who is?" she insisted.

"Brianna, this isn't really the place to discuss it," he

started. "Trust me, I will fill you in. But not at this exact moment. We should be getting out of here anyway."

John was interrupted by diabolical laughter.

"You think you can trust him?" the crusty old man threatened.

She whipped her head around with that accusation. The crusty old man quietly smiled at her. He was trying to cast doubt. She knew it, but she couldn't help herself. She quickly looked back at John to gage his reaction.

He didn't look panicked, guilty, or even remotely untrustworthy. Rather he seemed amused at the insinuation.

But before she had time to truly process John's reaction, she saw Ethan moving in her peripheral vision. He walked up to the crusty old man, raised his gun, and shot him dead.

She jerked back in horror, noting John's similar response. He said nothing, but he had the same shock registered on his face. Neither of them could fathom what they had just seen.

"What the fuck!" John yelled before storming out of the room.

Ethan leaned over the body, examining it. Then he shrugged his shoulders and sat on the edge of the desk. His gun resting on his thigh, he stared at Brianna with contempt.

She didn't like the idea of being alone with him. Except she couldn't pull her eyes away from Ethan or move an inch from her spot in the room. Probably because she was afraid to turn her back on him. He might shoot her too. She knew he wanted to kill her.

She couldn't make sense of any of Ethan's actions or John's blanketed acceptance of them. Ethan had betrayed John. He had traded her for Annabelle. Unless that had been part of the plan, she found it difficult to forgive.

She debated asking Ethan again since they were alone. A thought that was quickly discarded because of the continued hatred he was radiating towards her.

"I am going to find John," she announced, hoping he wouldn't turn the gun on her.

"And I am supposed to care?" he mocked.

She was confused. But she would figure out Ethan's anger later. She needed to find John first. She was ready to get out of here.

He wasn't in the hallway. So, she made her way from room to room and discovered he wasn't downstairs.

She was getting worried. In fact, she was growing frantic. Where did he go? She rushed upstairs to search those rooms, finally finding him in her old white wall bedroom.

He gazed over his shoulder when he heard her approach. He didn't say anything. He turned his head away from her and continued to stand there, staring at the white walls as if it were a complex work of art he was trying to analyze. He gave the impression of being lost and upset.

"Are you okay?" she asked.

He turned to look at her again. No emotion registering on his face.

"Yeah. I just don't know why Ethan did that," he explained.

"Yeah, I know. I wasn't expecting him to do that

either...or do any of the other things he has tonight," she told him.

His face showed an interest in that statement.

"What do you mean? What did he do tonight?" John questioned.

She moved closer and sat on the edge of the bed. She waited for him to sit beside her before she began.

"Well, for one, they knocked me out and brought me back here. Was that part of the plan?"

He sighed before responding.

"No. Not exactly."

She raised her eyebrow and waited for him to elaborate. He sighed again.

"When we got to the other island, we found it only had a few guards. And no Annabelle. And before we knew what was what, Ethan was gone," he added.

"He was gone alright. He was handing me over. And he was so...smug about it. He didn't care about me. I am not sure Annabelle did either," she related.

As she told John, she felt a surge of anger. She was getting mad. John put his hand on hers to calm her. He waited only a few seconds before he responded.

"Brianna, he saw an opportunity to save his wife. Can you really blame him for taking it?"

She showed her doubt.

"Look, I am pissed at him. I am. And there will be words about it later. But...I have known him for a long time. And Annabelle too," he continued.

"And you just forgive him so easily? We could have all been killed. But he didn't care," she retorted.

He shrugged with a sullen expression.

"I didn't say that. It's complicated. And we need him right now."

"You effectively stormed the castle. What did you need him for?" she scrutinized.

He stood, fidgeting. He was, obviously, annoyed she wouldn't let it go.

He didn't answer her.

"How did you manage it anyway? A siege without a calculated plan? It was so well executed and well timed. If that wasn't the plan in the first place, how did you do it?" she persisted.

"Brianna! None of that would have happened if he had not helped us. He helped set the explosives that brought this house down. He helped us take out some of the guards. More importantly, he didn't fight against us when we showed up. Plus, he just killed your arch nemesis!" John defended.

She was utterly confused. Ethan was being praised for not fighting against them? She understood there was history between those guys, but she didn't think his actions were noble. She was absolutely certain Ethan could not be trusted. She was beginning to have her doubts about John's judgement too.

"I think we should be going now. This place gives me the creeps," he said as he walked to the door.

He waited in the doorframe for her to join him.

Defeated, she sat there for a minute. Despite the crusty old man's death, she knew it was far from over. John had even warned that he wasn't the ultimate leader.

She was betting the Doppelgangmen would come after her sooner than later.

Even if they didn't, there were still too many unknowns for her to rest. She was afraid it would be a long road before she was truly safe and at peace.

She didn't know what was next. She had guessed she wasn't going to get the answers she needed tonight. John was being cagey again. Nevertheless, she met him at the door, ready to go.

When they got downstairs, she saw that some of the bodies were gone. Once they got to the hallway, she discovered it was Chris and Ethan who were cleaning up.

"What are you going to do with the all the dead bodies?" she wondered aloud.

"We are going to dump them in the ocean," John informed her.

"Why?"

John gave her a bemused expression, "Because we don't have time to bury them."

She smirked at him in return.

"Why move them at all?" she asked.

His reply was a quizzical look.

"Look, there is damage everywhere. Hell, there are holes in the damn house! Clearly, you can't hide what happened here," she reiterated.

John smiled.

"We aren't trying to hide anything. We are showing some respect for the dead since we have a little time. Besides we knew some of these guys. It is the least we could do," he made clear.

"You are showing them more respect dead than they ever showed me alive," she muttered.

John ignored her and started helping the others.

"So, there won't be more of the Doppelgangmen coming here?" she rambled.

She could tell she was annoying them. Each of their faces bore the exasperation they clearly felt. Only John demonstrated the patience of a saint. He dropped the feet of the body he was moving to come reassure her.

"I will be right back guys. Just give us a second," he indicated.

He motioned for her to lead the way to the front hallway where they could sit on the stairs.

"Brianna. I think maybe you should go sit outside and wait for us. We will come and get you when we are done loading. It shouldn't be long," he said, starting out of the room before she could argue.

"What?" she protested.

Abruptly he turned back into the room and charged at her. His eyes were on fire. He was pissed.

"Enough! That wasn't a request. Stay here," he yelled at her before leaving her in the front hallway.

She was pissed too. How dare he yell at her?

She had a right to ask questions, a right to know what was happening. She had been flying blind the whole time. She never truly knew what was going on. John was the only one telling her things. But he was always withholding, keeping her on a leash. She was tired of it.

She made a decision right then and there. She would reclaim her independence. Even if she had to do it all on her own, she would find a way to make it. And the first chance she had, she would be on a plane back to the States.

It was time. She needed to get some distance from these guys if she was ever to regain any semblance of control in her life. She needed some space. Otherwise, there would continue to be an imbalance of power. She would be treated like a child, indefinitely.

That wasn't who she was nor who she wanted to be.

She walked to the front porch and spied as the guys brought more casualties from the lawn and the edge of the woods. Their path was lit only by flashlights and the residual light of the house. She watched in the darkness as they carried the bodies to a small trailer being pulled by an ATV.

The whole scene was surreal. Of all the strange events of the last year, this one took the prize for the weirdest.

It was the middle of the night now. She didn't understand what the hurry was, or as she had told John, the point of it. It felt as if she was watching a post-apoptotic TV show and this was the post-attack clean-up.

"It wasn't good to leave the corpses lying around," she supposed. "They had to ensure that the evidence was destroyed...minus the structural damage to the house and the blood stained floors."

She rolled her eyes.

It was silly. It didn't make any sense. But she was reprimanded when she questioned it, so she was determined to keep her mouth shut. For the time being anyway.

She didn't go into the yard. She stood and silently observed as they finished their work.

They knew she was there. At least, John did. When he came out to help them, he turned his head in her direction immediately. She wasn't quite sure, but it felt like he had noticed her. He was always anticipating her moves before she made them.

He didn't react. He simply helped his friends. When they were done loading, he walked over to her, effectively establishing he had seen her. As he approached, he didn't seem annoyed or pissed anymore. But she was a capable adult. It was time she acted that way.

When he was before her, she discovered her anger from earlier had faded. Like a couple after their first fight, she wanted to forget it ever happened.

He was John. As complex as the next human, but someone who had proven he cared. She only needed to find a way to assert herself and keep her resolve to break free.

"We're finished. You're ready to go, I imagine," he stated.

"Yeah, more than you know," she said as she descended the stairs.

He held out his hand to her.

"Okay, let's go then."

She didn't' hesitate. She grabbed his hand in return. She had been learning for a while to take comfort where it could be found. If she didn't, she would have lost any semblance of sanity. She would have lost herself. And then the Doppelgangmen would have won.

That was what John was for her. He was a safe zone, someone she could lean on. She felt like her true self was returning when she was around him. The fighter was emerging against the odds.

It was a feeling she didn't anticipate would change anytime soon. A feeling she wanted to keep. It was the one good and constant thing in the chaotic mess that had become her life.

He ushered her over to the same ATV that had brought her back from the dock. She hadn't seen in the darkness, but the others had been waiting. They were all there, except Annabelle.

Robert and Chris were already positioned in an ATV cart. Ethan was alone again, driving another ATV with the trailer hitched. John was waiting for her to slide onto the back of their four-wheeler.

She didn't acknowledging any of them. It was a somber mood and no one was speaking.

It was Ethan who led their way back to the docks, transporting the dead behind him. If she thought watching them load the bodies was bizarre, the journey of that trailer topped it.

The lights on their ATV cart were dim, but one thing illuminated extremely well. Long blonde hair was cascading down over the rear tail light. If there had been any doubts about Annabelle's fate, they had just been answered.

She felt sick to her stomach.

Annabelle was another person who was dead because of her. The stack of the bodies on that trailer was resting on her shoulders and the weight was overbearing.

The guilt over Annabelle was the greatest she had

experienced. Annabelle had been kind to her. She had tried to help her, help them all.

Ethan's behavior in the study made more sense now. Brianna still didn't plan to forgive him or begin to trust him. She just understood better.

Ethan had obviously loved his wife. She thought again about the photos she had seen of them in their home. Always smiling and acting goofy. They had been happy, in love. They were each other's world. It had been obvious to anyone who had observed them.

Then, they got dragged into the mayhem.

As much as she was feeling, she could only assume John felt exponentially more. He had known the couple for a long time. Plus, it had been his idea to try to break the Doppelgangmen.

She didn't know how big the organization was overall, but these guys had taken out at least one site. Temporarily.

Although, they had partly succeeded, the price of victory had been too high. It was a small consolation for Annabelle's death.

24

AFTER

The ride had been short and quiet. No one had uttered a sound. The only noise was the humming of the engines and the cracking of the earth as they had driven over it. Once they had reached the docks, she saw several boats were anchored. The orange glow of the lights gave the atmosphere an eerie feeling.

Chris and Robert hopped from their cart and headed straight to the back of the trailer. They began unloading as soon as Ethan had parked it. They seemed anxious to have their task completed. She couldn't blame them for that sentiment.

John sat there with her for a moment. He didn't say anything. He simply put his head in his hands and slouched over.

He bared the burden. It was on him and he knew it.

It was the first time she saw the vulnerability he had worked so hard to hide. Right then, she wished she could ease some of the pain. She reached out and stroked his back, reassuring him that she would support him the way he had her.

He turned his head, looking at her intently. She saw the strain in his eyes. He had done this for her. It had all been for her.

"Are you okay?" she asked.

"No, not really. But I have to be," he replied.

With that, he got up and joined the others in carrying the corpses to the boats. She remained on the ATV, watching as they worked.

Annabelle was left alone until the end. Seeing it was time, John silently held the guys back to give Ethan some space. Their heads were bowed in respect and shame. They had failed their friend.

Ethan went to retrieve his wife's body. Although she didn't particularly care for the man, she pitied him. It was a horrendous sight to witness. His distress was conveyed in his every gesture. It was unquestionable he was broken.

His gait was slow as he walked to the trailer. He stood there for quite a time, staring down at her. He gazed at her as if she were a fallen angel. He was mesmerized by her, even in death.

It seemed forever before he slowly gathered her up into his arms. Silhouetted by the orange dock lights, he transported her to a separate boat.

It was a heartbreaking image she knew she would never erase from her mind.

She slowly made her way to the guys. Slipping her hand into John's, she lowered her eyes with them. They were giving Ethan his privacy. It was a funeral and a husband's last goodbye.

Ethan took a while letting go, but he finally rejoined the group. He gave John a slight nod before quickly returning to the boat with the majority of the human disposal. Chris and Robert followed, climbing into the boat with him. Without another word amongst them, the engines fired up and they were gone in a flash.

"Well, that was heart wrenching," she commented awkwardly.

"Yeah. It was," John nodded. "Now comes the harder part. You and I have to go dump her."

"What?" she shrieked.

"We are going to go dispose of Annabelle's body," he confirmed.

"Why would we throw her into the sea? The guards make sense. Kinda. But Annabelle? Why won't there be funeral and stuff?" she questioned.

"It isn't what Ethan wants," John explained.

"What about her other family? They don't get a say?"

He didn't respond immediately. His facial expression revealed he was choosing his words with caution.

"Look, I agree with you. Her family should be able to say goodbye. But Ethan has asked we do it this way. Maybe he doesn't want her family asking too many questions or knowing what she was involved in," he rationalized.

"They didn't know?"

He didn't respond.

"Still, they have a right to pay their respects," she insisted.

"I didn't ask his reasons. I am just respecting them," he stated.

He had shown her the courtesy of not rejecting her argument too quickly. But he wasn't really considering going against Ethan's wishes. Nevertheless, he heard her out. He nodded his head in understanding before he walked to the boat where Annabelle's body was waiting. He got behind the wheel and didn't look back at her. He just patiently waited for her to suck it up as she had done before.

She begrudgingly joined him in the boat and they were on their way.

They didn't talk as they bumped along into the darkness. It was both calming and disturbing. The wake of the boat cutting through the water made rhythmic lapping sounds. The cold, brisk wind numbed her face. She looked up at the dark sky and marveled again at the clarity of the stars.

In all other regards, it was a beautiful night.

John brought the boat to a stop fifteen minutes later. They exchanged a look, but neither moved from their spots. It was clear that they both dreaded doing was required of them.

"At least it is peaceful here," she offered.

He gazed up at the sky.

"Yeah, I guess," he said.

"Should we get this over with?" she muttered.

She moved over to Annabelle's head, planning to grab that end. She leaned down in preparation when something caught her eye. She noticed Annabelle had been wearing a necklace. She bent forward and squinted, trying to get a better look in the darkness.

Her heart caught in her throat. She didn't need a closer look to know. It was the exact same necklace that she had around her neck. Annabelle had been wearing a necklace with GPS capabilities.

She froze as he came up behind and stood over her. Not sure if he had seen her inspecting the necklace, she didn't make any sudden movements. She wasn't sure how to react, but she knew she should play coy until she sorted out what she had just realized.

"Actually, could you grab the feet? That will be the lighter part," he suggested, apparently oblivious to what she had seen.

She took a deep breath. She would have to process everything later. It was not the place or time for her to freak out. She needed to be deliberate now. She couldn't afford to lose her cool for several reasons.

"Lift on three," he directed. "One. Two. Three."

In a swift motion, they heaved the corpse over the boat's edge. Annabelle instantaneously disappeared into the blackness. She was gone in the blink of an eye.

Brianna continued to stare at the water, already trying to reconcile what she had discovered. If Annabelle had been wearing the necklace, then John had lied. They all had lied. They had to have known much more than they had told. For starters, they had to have known where Annabelle was.

She couldn't trust any of them.

John was still standing beside her, staring into the abyss himself. His face was as stoic as her own. For a time, they said nothing. Both lost in their thoughts. Although she doubted he had a clue about her mind at that moment.

Finally, he spoke.

"Now that that is done, what do you think about staying out here for a couple hours? Just until the sun comes up."

She didn't turn to face him nor did she respond to his suggestion. She suspected her response wouldn't matter anyway. She assumed the question had been rhetorical. John had a way of doing what he wanted.

He also had a way of convincing you that what he wanted was what you wanted too. It was a talent.

She quietly went and sat on the bench at the back of the boat. Now, it was her turn to stare at the Milky Way. She didn't speak. She was too lost in contemplating what it all meant, sorting between what she knew to be true and the things of which she couldn't be certain.

Surprisingly, she wasn't angry. Confused. Suspicious. But not angry.

She wasn't sure what she would say to him. They were alone in the dark, on the ocean, rocking back and forth in silence. It could be the perfect moment to finally get some answers. Or the absolute worst time to show her doubts.

She noticed then that he was watching her. He had turned his back from the horizon and was leaned against the boat's side. His eyes were trained on her, almost predatory.

"Are you still thinking about earlier?" he asked when he realized he had her attention.

"A little," she answered, truthfully.

He sighed and then came over to the spot beside her on the bench.

"Which part?"

She shrugged her shoulders.

He side-bumped her.

"Tell me," he probed.

"All of it. I am just worried, I guess. I mean, what happens now?"

He laid his head back and sighed.

"Well, we go back to Brisbane tomorrow. After that, I'm not completely sure."

"That is reassuring. You have a plan, at least," she teased.

He half laughed and gave her a genuine smile.

"A man with a plan," he said, absentmindedly.

There was a pause of silence.

"I want to go home," she confessed.

"Home, home?" he clarified.

"The States, yes. How soon after we get to Brisbane until I can go?" she asked.

"There are few things we need to do first. But no more than a day or two. Then we'll go back," he replied.

"We? As in together?" she questioned.

She felt his eyes on her again, waiting for her to look at him. He waited until she did before responding.

"Yeah, I thought so. Is that not what you want?" he asked.

Despite everything, it was hard to trust him. He had proven himself by protecting her. But he wasn't perfect. He had definitely made some mistakes. He had withheld a lot of information and acted sketchy. He had also lied to her outright on a few occasions, as was likely the case with Annabelle's necklace.

On the flip side, he had saved her many times. He could have left her there when Ethan had traded her. Instead, he had risked his life and tortured his conscience to come after her. Several people had died to ensure her continued freedom and he had taken the responsibility for it.

She knew she wasn't afraid of him. Even when he had had flashes of anger, she wasn't frightened. Not for a minute. He had never tried to hurt her. He had done the opposite at every opportunity.

"Could it make the lies and the holding back forgivable?" she contemplated.

First, she needed some answers.

"I don't know," she replied. "There are some things I need to understand."

He didn't resist.

"Like what?" he prompted.

She took a deep breath.

"For starters. I need to know more about the Doppelgangmen," she began.

He hesitated. In classic John fashion, he tried to thwart her.

"Do you really want to know? Cause once you do, you are a bigger target, a bigger liability. The more you know, the bigger the bullseye," he warned.

"Yes. I really need to know," she stood her ground.

He didn't respond immediately. He waited a few

minutes, making Brianna doubt he intended to tell her anything.

"Are you going to not tell me?" she demanded.

"No, I am going to tell you what I can…I am just choosing my words wisely Like I said, they didn't tell me much at first. Most of what I know has been learned second hand, after I left them," he prefaced.

She nodded, waiting for him to continue.

"I don't know all the history. You had to be a part of the inner circle for that information. Which takes years. But they have been around for centuries. I don't know why your face is important to them exactly. I do know you weren't the first to be kidnapped. And a few came willingly, supposedly. Anyway, they use these women for different things. I know that…breeding them is part of it," he trailed off, clearing his throat.

Her disgust was apparent. She wanted to vomit.

"So, the crusty old man?" she managed.

"No, I am not sure of that. Maybe. But it is more likely you were meant for someone else. Not him. I suspect that the higher ups don't know you were even taken," he related.

"Why?"

"Just a hunch that I have. Based on what we have heard, or haven't heard from our contacts."

"I think I am going to be sick," she stated.

"I'm sorry. But I did warn you," he reminded her.

"Is there anything more that you know?" she redirected.

"I know they are well connected, well-funded. I told

you that before. They are very powerful. And it is all very secret," he answered.

"Yeah, you have said that before. How do you know this?"

"I was one of them, you know. When I got out, I didn't burn all the bridges I had. And we have made some connections over the last few years who have told us more about it," he explained.

"You have been working on it for years?"

"Yeah, I thought I mentioned before. Three years to be exact," he clarified.

"How have the police or authorities or whoever not arrested these guys? If this has been going on for so long..." she wondered.

"They buy them off. They convert them. Blackmail. Various means. Same as with the mafia and other criminal organizations. It is too big to take down at once. You must do it piece by piece. And I am not sure there are even resources dedicated to it. Most authorities haven't heard of these guys because they are very careful and they fly under the radar."

She gave him a confused look, one that conveyed her question.

"We are pretty sure they have people in the government. Well, governments. Plural," he indicated.

"But you don't know why my face?"

He flinched, just slightly. But it was enough that she noticed it.

"No," he said.

She was about to start an argument, to challenge that

he knew more about why her features were important to them when he abruptly stood.

"You already know the majority of what I do. And before you complain, you don't need to know anything else. You already know far too much," he cut her off.

She was annoyed. But she decided not to push it. Not yet. She would get more answers in time.

While he might be cunning, she was definitely persistent.

"How long until we head back?" she changed the subject.

"A couple of hours. It is almost 2:30 a.m.. Sunrise will be around 5 a.m. Do you want to sleep a couple of hours?" he offered.

"Yeah. But what about you? Don't you need some sleep?" she retorted.

"Well, there is only one bench," he commented. "Unless…"

"Unless what?"

"Unless, you wouldn't mind sharing the bench," he finished.

"Uh, sure. I don't mind sharing with you," she hesitately agreed.

He came back over and slowly positioned himself across the back of the bench. There was enough space for her to lie there too, but only if it was in his arms. Knowing this already, John held out his arm as an invitation. She hesitated for a second, ultimately resigning her nerves on the matter. It wasn't him she was afraid of, but the intimacy with someone she didn't fully trust yet. He was still hiding things.

After she awkwardly laid down, he gently put his arm over her. She was stiff as a board. He then unexpectedly buried his face into the back of her neck, letting out a long, hot breath that sent tremors down her spine. But it had the surprising effect of relaxing her. Her muscles loosened and she sank into his arms.

He didn't speak again. However, she felt his rhythmic breathing, the warmth of his body. Those seemed to be words enough, conveying comfort and safety.

He just held her. He didn't try anything else, convincing her once again he was one of the good guys at heart. He was giving her the time she needed.

"We can go back to the States together," she stated after a bit.

His response was simply stretching up to kiss her on her forehead.

For the first time in a long time, the outlook was encouraging. She drifted into a short, peaceful slumber.

When she woke, the sun was rising. She sat up and watched the light illuminating the water in beautiful orange and pink hues. John was starting to stir from her movement, proving he was a light sleeper.

The view of him was almost as beautiful as the sunrise. A strand of his dirty blonde hair had fallen over his brow. The low sunlight made his skin glisten, highlighting the three o'clock shadow of a beard.

She returned her gaze to the horizon and didn't notice when John had opened his eyes. When she eventually realized he was awake, she wondered how long he had been that way. He was staring again.

He pulled himself into a sitting position, reached up

and held her face. He paused briefly to look into her eyes before he pulled her into him. He gave her a long, sensual kiss, making her flush with each lingering brush of his lips.

It was not the start to the day she had been expecting.

25

S he didn't know how long they kissed. She had lost track of time. When he finally broke it off, his face hovered in proximity of hers for a few seconds.

"We should get back," he said as he got up.

Without further discussion, he started the boat and sent them on their way. She cleared her mind, not bothering to overthink it. She had decided she would resume thought at another time. For now, she merely leaned back and enjoyed the ride.

Again, she was impressed with how well he navigated without a map. It didn't take long before they reached the same dock they had left the day before. She saw the other boat was already tied off. However, the guys were nowhere in sight.

As they pulled in to anchor the boat, she joined him at the wheel.

"Where are the guys?" she inquired.

"I imagine they're on their way back to Brisbane already," he shrugged. "Maybe they came in last night. Ethan is good at navigating in the dark. And he isn't normally one to linger under the best of circumstances."

"So, how exactly are we getting back? I don't see a car."

He smiled.

"It is called a cell phone. You see, it lets you call people who drive these cars that come to pick you up. Much more effective than a smoke signal, but much less fun," he teased with a wink.

"Ha. Ha. Very funny," she mocked in return.

They parked the boat and John made a quick call. In no time, a car showed up to take them to the airport. Or so she had thought. As they pulled to a stop at a nondescript building ten minutes later, her confusion increased.

"What are we doing here? Aren't we going to the airport?" she questioned.

"Yes, we are. I just need to make a quick pit stop. Pay someone. It won't take long. Stay here," he explained.

She didn't ask any more questions. Mostly because he was out of the car before she had even wrinkled her forehead.

She leaned forward and watched as he knocked on the door. The door opened without another person becoming visible and he disappeared inside. It was all very mysterious.

"Do you know where he is going?" she asked the driver.

"Ma'am, I am not authorized to say," he replied before stepping out of the car and leaning against the driver's side door.

"That is one way to avoid answering someone," she said to an empty car.

She reassured herself that she and John were a united front now. At least, his body language had conveyed they were together. It had seemed as if he had finally taken down some of the walls he had been using to shield her.

He had been affectionate all morning and had rarely released her hand. She also noticed they had begun mirroring each other, a sign that they were in sync.

She would try to trust him. Despite her bafflement at the unscheduled stop, she knew he would tell her what she needed to know. She had to believe in him.

They were parked outside a dingy wood building that was once painted white. Surrounded by trees, it looked more like someone's backyard shed than a meeting place. It was the classification of the term 'shady'.

"I will be right back," he had said before hopping from the car.

Still it had been, maybe twenty minutes, before John was in his seat again. She never saw another person. He didn't offer any additional information, as usual.

She was extremely curious who he was paying. And why. But true to her promise to herself, she didn't ask. Not quite yet.

They went back to the private airstrip where a chartered plane was waiting for them. There was still no sign of the other guys.

"Will I ever see the guys again?" she asked.

"Yes, of course. Why wouldn't you?" he responded.

"I just wasn't sure. Aren't we headed back to the States almost immediately?"

"Yes, tomorrow or the day after. If I can get everything together when we get back to Brisbane. Either way, you should see the guys tonight at Ethan's house," he clarified.

"We leave tomorrow?" she reiterated.

"Yes, I hope so," he affirmed. "Why?"

"Just checking," she replied.

"Hmmm. Okay," he said before boarding the plane.

The flight back to Brisbane was considerably shorter. They spent the majority of the time cat napping, the fatigue from their night catching up to them. In fact, she had difficulty keeping her eyes open. She was also becoming a permanent fixture in John's arms because that is where she had ended up.

If there was a silver lining to everything that had happened, it was these moments. It was finding him. Or, truthfully, it being found by him. She was grateful, more and more, it had been him and not someone else. It was truly remarkable how much had changed in the span of a week.

Once they had landed, they were in a taxi heading towards the outskirts of the city. John was preoccupied again, likely going through all the things he needed to get done before they left Australia.

She was excited though. She was relieved to be going home in less than 24 hours.

She had thought back at the compound she would go

at it alone, regain her independence. But since John had opened up about what he knew of the Doppelgangmen, she had been rethinking the whole distancing herself. It had been a turning point in their budding relationship and, perhaps, he could help her rebuild. She was beginning to believe he would reveal the rest of his secrets with time.

She was also coming to grips with the fact that her life would never be normal again. She would remain a target, just as John had predicted. She preferred to not fight the Doppelgangmen alone, mostly because she had finally accepted that she wasn't the greatest at it. She had admitted to herself, in some measure, she needed help. She wanted John to be that person.

The taxi stopped outside an undistinguished warehouse. It's metal exterior was brown, blending in with all the other warehouses in this district. There was truly nothing spectacular about the neighborhood or the structure they were visiting.

John paid the driver and waited for her to climb out of the back seat behind him.

"I guess I am coming in this time?" she inquired as the taxi rolled away.

"I sure hope so, considering the taxi just left," he teased. "Actually, we are here for you. You need to be here."

"Wait. Why? What are we doing?" she wondered aloud.

"Travel documents," he stated.

"Wait, what?"

He grabbed her hand, dragging her inside the warehouse. The interior was nothing like the outside. Sleek and modern, they had entered an industrialized loft that was absolutely breathtaking.

They were immediately greeted by a young petite woman with glasses. Her hair was jet black and braided down her back. She was dressed in jeans and a cut-off, grey Ramones t-shirt. She wore several necklaces around her neck. She was pretty in the adorable way.

Her face lit up when she saw John. He released her hand to hug the pretty little thing, smiling in return.

"Hey John!" she exclaimed. "How are you?"

"Oh great, she is peppy too," she thought to herself, jealousy flowing through every part of her body.

The girl radiated bright and shiny. As opposed to her, the bearer of gloom. Everything Brianna touched these days was dark, not the sort of thing that attracts a guy's attention for the long haul.

She had always had the opinion that most guys wanted easy breezy without a lot of baggage. And she was far from being hang-up free anymore. She didn't like the girl on the spot. Probably because of the way she was looking at John as if she wanted to devour him.

She didn't know what to think of herself. She had never been the type to be jealous. It was a new emotion and she suspected it was because of her attachment to John. It was definitely something she intended to rectify in herself as soon as possible. She didn't like herself for it.

"Raven, this is Brianna. Brianna, my pal Raven," he introduced.

"Hi," she greeted her with a handshake.

"Hello," Raven dismissed her immediately, refocusing on John.

"It is so great to see you! What brings you by? Not that I am complaining!" she flirted.

He motioned to Brianna, smiling when he did.

"I need a passport for her. We are going to the States tomorrow and she doesn't have a valid ID," he explained.

Brianna was surprised.

"They were going to get fake documents. They were not going to the authorities to let them know she had been found. He was planning to sneak her back into the States," her mind whirled.

"Sure thing," Raven replied, the disappointment evident on her face. "Brianna, come with me. I will need to take your photo."

She followed the girl to the back of the loft, into a room filled with computer screens. Raven pointed to a blank wall painted a light grey. There was a stool in front of it and a camera on a tripod across from it. Her instructions were self-explanatory.

It didn't take long for Raven to snap her photo and usher her out of her IT lair. Brianna wandered back into the living room and found John making himself comfortable on the couch. She had the impression he had spent some couch time at this loft with Raven. She hoped she was wrong. She wasn't prepared to deal with any more insecurities at the moment.

"Why don't you wait here with John. It will only take an hour or two," Raven indicated from behind her, startling her.

John looked up from a laptop he was using. His eyes

darted from her to the couch spot beside him. Brianna went over to sit next to him, glancing over to see what he had been looking at on the computer.

"I am looking at our possible tickets for tomorrow," he confirmed.

"Ah okay," she muttered.

She wasn't positive it was the best time to question, but she needed to know what the big picture was. She hesitated before she asked.

"Where are we going in the States?" she asked.

"Seattle, for the beginning," he told her.

"So, I am not going home first," she supplied.

"Eventually," he started, turning his body to face her. His face serious.

"I am going to take you home, but there are some things we need to do first. If that is alright?"

She thought about it for a minute. She shrugged her shoulders to show her uncertainty.

"Brianna. I thought you wanted to go with me. I certainly want you to be with me," he let her know.

"I don't have to guess that we aren't going to the police to tell them what happened to me. Since we aren't even trying to get my real documents..." she stated.

"No. I wasn't planning to inform anyone that you are alive. Not just yet. We need to fly under the radar for a bit longer. Are you okay with that?" he informed her.

"I guess I have to be," she responded.

He noticed her instant sadness and reluctance. He reached his arm around her, positioning himself so she could burrow into him. She sunk into his side, laying her head on his chest. Her doubts were returning.

A little bit later, she was being shaken awake. She hadn't meant to doze off, but the sleep deprivation was still getting to her. She was sprawled out on the couch and John was kneeling in the floor at her face. Her eyes were still heavy and she was dazed. She had slept hard.

After he had helped her up, he handed her a new passport. It seemed she had slept long enough for them to finish doctoring up her fake travel documents. She flipped through it, noting there were a few stamps to make it look as if she had travelled with it before. The only accurate information was her first name and photo. Otherwise, it was a completely new identity.

She stared at it. The surreal factor was kicking in again. She wasn't sure she was completely comfortable with this plan, which she didn't know fully what it was. She had hoped that John would let her know what she needed, when she needed to know it.

As it was, he hadn't volunteered information yet. Or he was waiting for her to ask. One of the two always seemed to happen before the other.

When they had said their goodbyes to Raven, they called a cab. Once outside, she was shocked to see that it was already night. She had slept much longer than she had realized. It was getting late now.

She didn't ask where they were planning to go next. It didn't really matter, she was along for the ride.

Except John received a call on their way to wherever.

She couldn't hear what was being said on the other end. She only saw how irritated John was becoming. He redirected the driver and, at last, offered her an explanation without prompting.

"We have to go to Ethan's house. He is acting strangely and I need to calm him down," he provided.

"Were we not going there before?" she asked.

"We were. I just wanted to run a few more errands first. But it will be alright. It can wait until the morning," he clarified.

"What is going on?"

"That was Chris on the phone. He said that Ethan has been in a mood all day. They just wanted to know how much longer we would be. I think it may be getting on Chris' and Robert's nerves," he answered.

"I just want to go see what is going on," he added upon seeing Brianna's worried expression. "Nothing to worry about."

"Do you think he is dangerous?" she finally managed.

"Ethan? No," he said, purposefully.

Within ten minutes they were pulling into Ethan's driveway. She looked around when they got out of the taxi, not sensing a hint of the dread. The river front house was as peaceful as the last time she was here.

As they walked to the side entrance, John suddenly stopped. He rapidly turned around, wrapped his arms around her waist, and pulled her into a kiss.

In classic John fashion, his lips made her weak at the knees. Then he abruptly pulled away as quickly as he had grabbed her. His grin at that moment was also enough to make her weak. She felt it everywhere in her body.

"What was that for?" she laughed.

"No reason. Just wanted to do it as a reminder before we get caught up in the annoying bullshit."

His smile widened.

"C'mon," he directed.

Any worries she had had earlier about Raven were put at ease for a second.

They entered the living room a minute later. Chris and Robert were slouched on the couch, drinking beers. They were also engrossed in some televised sporting event. They looked perfectly content in their apparent laziness.

"Where's Ethan?" John interrupted their concentration on the game.

"I don't know. Brooding somewhere, I suspect," Robert replied.

Chris simply hunched his shoulders.

"I am right here," Ethan said as he walked into the room.

Before anyone could blink, Ethan raised a gun and opened fire. In a flash, he had splattered Chris and Robert across the couch. Their bodies slouched over. Their blood oozed out, staining the couch a dark red. Their beers crashed against the wood floor, spewing the yeasty beverage onto it.

Everything had blurred as John had pulled her towards him and down to the ground. They used the furniture for cover. They scrambled around the back of the couch on their knees, moving as fast as they could. Tears were already streaming down her face. She couldn't believe what was happening. She knew that Ethan was unhinged. But John had insisted he was alright.

Her breath was as rapid as her heartbeat. It was making it difficult to think clearly. She was in flight mode.

The room was silent minus the cheers from the sports program. The sounds coming from the television could be used as an advantage for their survival. She hoped it would mask their movements. Except she couldn't tell where Ethan was either.

It was not a good sign.

She looked up at John, who was intently listening for signals of activity from Ethan too. His focus was solely on keeping them alive.

The flickering images from the TV was the only light the room had to combat the night. It was dark. Very dark. She could barely see the worry lines on John's face. Though, this time, they were surely there.

He hadn't expected it. Ethan had been his friend. He had known he had been upset about Annabelle but he hadn't seen this response coming. It was obvious from the absolute shock over Ethan's latest actions. His face still showed his disbelief.

She, on the contrary, had predicted it. She wished she had said something more about her concerns. It was too little, too late now.

They heard footsteps again. Ethan was moving. And so were John and her. They scrambled towards the front of the couch, staying low, using the shadows to distort their shapes.

They had to get to the door. If they had a chance at all, they had to get out of his house.

The footsteps had stopped again. Although, she knew he was still there. She could hear him breathing now.

Her eyes were beginning to adjust as well. She could

see John more clearly. She saw a fear in his eyes for the first time ever. As they waited for Ethan's next move, she wished she couldn't see John's reaction. It was more painful and scary that he was shaken. She had come to rely on him being solid, unfazed in these situations.

Even more frightening was when she took her eyes from John and saw Chris's blank stare focused in front of her.

He was dead. It was almost certain that Robert was the same.

She looked around the room, expecting to see Ethan's outline. But he wasn't there. He was nowhere in sight.

She didn't understand why they weren't leaving.

"Had John seen something she hadn't? Was Ethan blocking the door? Why were they still stationary?" she rambled in her head.

She grabbed John's arm and squeezed it.

He looked at her then, an opportunity she used to silently urge him to lead them to safety. Without words, she pleaded with him.

Seemingly understanding her request, he nodded his head in the direction of the door the exterior.

He held up three fingers to indicate they would run on his count. She affirmed with a nod of her head and readied herself to go.

Slowly, his fingers disappeared. It was now or never. They took off.

Unexpectedly her back foot slid in the beer and blood that had puddled on the floor as she bounced up to sprint. She stumbled, falling back down.

She didn't waste a second.

She rapidly got back to her feet and moved her legs as fast as they could go. Training her sights to the path in front of her, she immediately crashed into Ethan's back three seconds later.

He had stopped running, although they were maybe ten feet from the door.

She looked over his shoulder, seeing now that Ethan was blocking their way. His gun was pointed on his longtime friend.

He didn't look human anymore, just a hollow shell of vengeance. The same man who had shot the crusty old man without provocation. The man, who without warning, had just killed two of his friends. The man who was prepped to shoot two more former alliances.

He hadn't said a word. He hadn't tried to explain himself. It had made him all the more terrifying.

He simply stood there.

John had his hands up in surrender. He was using his body to shield her. It was the only way to protect them at that point. He was relenting, hoping that Ethan would be sensible.

John had no weapon, no way to defend them. He had to know it would be over as soon as Ethan decided it was.

They didn't breathe, fearful of what would be the thing to make up Ethan's mind. She couldn't figure a way out of this one. The only hope was if Ethan snapped out of it, if he realized what he was doing and spared John.

"A long shot," she thought.

But as they stood off, Ethan's face began to soften. She couldn't believe what she was seeing. He was slowly lowering the gun. He also took a side-step back, effectively giving them passage.

But John hadn't moved. Maybe, knowing his friend, he had believed it was a trick.

She saw it differently. To her, this was their opportunity. Good or bad, their only hope was to make their feet move towards the door. He was letting them go.

She nudged John's back, encouraging him to get them out of there while he still could.

Ethan finally spoke.

"I guess things didn't quite go as you had planned. Did they, John?"

He gave him a sly smile.

"John. What a ridiculous name that is."

Finally, John made his body go. He leaped in the direction of Ethan.

"NO, NO, NO, NO!" she screamed in repetition.

A blast rang out, followed by the sounds of agony. She scrambled to figure out what was happening as John dropped to the floor. Brianna stood paralyzed. Like a deer in the headlights, she was powerless.

Ethan, however, was not frozen. He aimed his gun at her and fired.

She heard the sound of the shot before she felt it. Then, a warmth accompanied with the searing pain overcame her. She felt it in her torso. A fiery hurt that rapidly radiated to all parts of her body.

She felt the strength of her legs give out. She fell to her knees, then crumbled to her side as she rolled over onto the floor.

It was the most excruciating feeling. More than she

had ever imagined it would be. She struggled to not faint from the pain. She just wanted it to stop.

Milliseconds felt like hours until she became numb. Her vision was blurring, her heartbeat slowing. A calm was setting in. She knew it was likely an indication that her body was shutting down. She wouldn't be conscious soon. Or maybe she wouldn't even be alive much longer.

The world became a distant place from her current reality. She was only aware of heightened sounds, which confirmed it was the senses that are the last to go when dying.

She heard everything. The ticking of the clock. The scraping of Ethan's shoes upon the floor as he toured each of his victims. The cheers from the fans at the sporting event that was still playing on the television. And the grunting of John from pain.

John was still alive. She could hear him. She knew it was him. He was hurt, but he wasn't dead. At least, not yet.

But there wasn't anything she could do about it. She was on her back, staring at the ceiling. She had no will to move. Surrounded by white noise, a peace was setting into place. She was truly numb now.

She laid there. Marveling at how quickly it had all gone down. Without fanfare, without a big speech. It was all so anti-climactic. It was over just as things had been getting started.

She struggled to keep her eyes open, to remain somewhat alert. She wasn't long for this world. She knew she would be fading soon. There would be no more fighting.

She heard one last gunshot as she slipped out of consciousness. The thud that followed made her wonder if it were Ethan, ending his own life. She didn't have time to contemplate it though. It was too late to help her. The hope had died.

26

AFTER

F lashes of red, yellow, and purple penetrated her closed eyelids. The light was blinding even though it was blocked. Slowly, she pried her lashes apart to be met with a dark figure, silhouetted in the overhead fluorescents. Every image was a blur. It made her head hurt.

She squinted to get a better look just as the sight of a mask approaching her face appeared. The air around her was suctioned away as the mask attempted to create a vacuum. The sudden lack of oxygen sent Brianna into a panic. She started to scream with a cracked voice.

"Help!" she tried but the syllables were indiscernible.

She thrashed in her bed, finding that her arms and legs were heavy with fatigue. But it was to no avail, there was no stopping it.

The mask crashed down over her nose and mouth, just as she let out another scream. The air escaping her lungs was quickly replaced with oxygen from the apparatus. The quick exchange of exhaling and inhaling made her choke.

The pain radiating throughout her body was overbearing. She had been hurt before, even frequently in the last year. Yet, it didn't compare to what she felt now.

Everywhere throbbed, a dull ache in every inch of her body except one. In her left side, the pain was more acute.

She imagined it to be the same as if someone had opened her insides and poured acid into her open cavity. Ironically, she finally understood the meaning behind that euphuism about salt in the wound.

She was in the hospital. She was aware of that much. The details of the how and the why were still fuzzy. So far, she couldn't process anything besides the fire she felt in her side. The slightest movement sent spasms through her entire body that made her nauseated and faint.

"It is best to not move," she heard someone say, as if she hadn't already figured it out herself.

She looked up at the person at her bedside. Their human features were becoming clearer as her eyes adjusted. It was a female nurse, a reassuring sign she was safe.

However, it didn't appear this nurse had anticipated her need of drugs. She had to find her voice, however raspy it may be.

She reached up for the mask, fumbling in her attempt. Luckily, the nurse understood the movement and lifted the oxygen mask to the side. She leaned her ears forward to Brianna's mouth to hear the request over the air currents.

"I need something for the pain," she managed.

"Sure. I will get you something," the nurse replied, as she reached to the pump at the head of hospital bed.

Within a few beeps, Brianna was dazed, but still conscious. She wondered why the nurse hadn't thought of it before she had asked. It would have saved time.

She was grouchy. She knew it. She also felt she had a right to be a little bitchy. She had been kidnapped, held hostage by a crusty old man for months, and thrown in a shed of bones to rot because she had disobeyed.

Then she had had a glimpse of freedom, a taste of hope before it was all ripped away. Now, she was in the hospital with a hole in her side and zero drugs to numb the pain. She had earned a moment to complain.

The events of her life were becoming clearer. She had been through hell. And she was still breathing. It was labored breath at the moment, but it still meant she was alive.

John.

She suddenly remembered. And Ethan. Chris. Robert. Their faces were flashing into her mind.

"Were they okay?" she wondered.

She didn't quite remember what had happened. She racked her brain to recall the last events of her memory. But her brain hurt too much.

She wanted sleep. She needed sleep.

The drugs continued to take effect as she struggled against the weight of her eyelids. She quickly decided she wouldn't fight it. She would let herself rest this time.

When she awoke, she could figure out everything, including what had happened to John.

As quickly as she thought his name, his face appeared before her. It was almost as if she had conjured him into her dreams.

She realized it was a dream immediately because the images were on a loop. Like the repeat function of a gif, she saw the corners of his mouth inching up into a smile, over and over again. It was both a comfort and a torture.

Her entire body cried. There wasn't a part of her being that didn't feel the pain. She tried to crack open her eyes once again, but they fought her. Her body would not cooperate anymore.

Then she heard it. His kind voice, cutting through the hurt.

EPILOGUE

Faith had had a blast. Her ears were still ringing from the bass that had pumped into the concert hall. Her friends had even scored front row spots. She had never been that close before and her body was tingling from the vibrations.

She smiled as she thought of how the lead singer had touched her hand during the show. Her friends had been a little jealous, as they were the ones who had waited hours outside in the cold, wet Portland weather to make sure they were first. However, it was a short lived envy that died as quickly as the next song had started. They had danced and flirted the night away.

She was grateful for those girls. College life had lived up to the hype because of them.

They had met in the required freshman English and had bonded over a love of music. Four years later, they were staples of the concert scene and bonafide hipsters. They certainly had come a long way from their days in the dorms, listening to Faith's old turntable and planning the shows they were going to hit.

Now, Faith had her own apartment.

She had begged her parents to help her pay the rent so she could live off campus. A decision she was regretting as she put her purse down and looked around an empty room. She missed those cramped days of dorm life and coming home with the girls. It was an ache she was sure would get worse next year when they were forced to go their separate ways to find jobs.

It wasn't that she didn't like her one-bedroom place. It was that she was lonely. It was the also the first time in her life that she didn't have a boyfriend. If she had known that Josh was going to break up with her, she might have rethought the apartment idea. She had expected it was to be their place together. She had made up her mind about it when she had signed the lease. He, however, had made other plans with Marcy Keller, a fact that still made her bitter.

"I won't go there tonight," she told herself.

It had been such a great night. She had sorta met a new guy anyway. Well, they had made eyes at each other. She wasn't actually sure she would see him again, but he had been a gorgeous distraction. And he had spent the night staring at her. It had been a huge boost to her recently fragile ego. She felt confident she would have a new boyfriend sooner than later. A better guy was waiting around the corner. Until then, she would relish her girlfriends and their good times together.

As she looked around her apartment, she realized she would need to clean this weekend. The place was a wreck and she would be lucky if she had any clean clothes for class in the morning. She began shifting through the ones she had thrown on the couch, smelling some of them to determine how clean they were. It seemed the weekend would include laundry if these garments were any indication. There was nothing wearable.

It was Friday classes tomorrow, so she decided she could get away with wearing her pajama pants. She had been doing this routine a lot this semester. She figured one more time wouldn't hurt. Then, she would do laundry and start anew again. It was time to pull herself from her flunk. Tonight had reminded her what it felt like to have fun, a reminder she had desperately needed.

She gathered up the clothes she had tested and took them to the hamper in the bathroom. She decided she could do the rest tomorrow after she got home. It was late, so she would just go to bed tonight.

"Worry was for the morning anyhow," she remembered her mother always saying.

She quickly brushed her teeth and washed her face. Then she turned off the bathroom light and went to check the locks in the living room.

Once she saw everything was secure, she grabbed her phone from her purse and turned off the lights here as well. She headed to her bedroom in the dark, having already memorized the way in her small space.

As she opened the bedroom door, she stopped in her tracks. She thought she heard something or sensed someone was there.

Frightened, she didn't dare to move. She listened closely and strained her eyes to see in the dark. She was too far from the light switch at that moment, but she realized she did have her phone in her hand.

Slowly she lifted it to her face and clicked the side button to illuminate the home screen. Instantly, she traced her finger up from the bottom of the screen and found the flashlight function. Pausing only a second to listen, she tapped the icon.

Light filtered out of the phone, showing her the path in front of her. She noticed she was shaking because the light beam wasn't steady.

"You are being silly," she thought as she swung the light towards the wall where the bedroom switch was.

She had just taken a step when she heard the sound again. There was movement. She was sure of it. She made her mind up quickly and took a mad dash for where the light switch was.

As she reached the wall, her body was slammed into it with an impact that felt like a stomach punch. She grasped for breath and felt pain pulsing in her right shoulder.

She felt him behind her then, towering over her. His hands were on her. He covered her mouth with one hand as his other hand pushed her towards the wall to brace her. She tried to turn to face him, but he already had her body pinned by pressing his up against hers.

She began to panic. She didn't know what to do. Her heart and brain were both racing.

"Should she fight him? Or should she wait to see what he did next?" she frantically questioned herself.

She didn't have an answer. For the moment, she remained frozen.

Then she felt a prick in her arm. He had given her a shot. She was being drugged. She knew she was in serious trouble.

He suddenly lifted his hand from her mouth and loosened his grip. She turned around to see the gorgeous stranger from the club staring down at her, a sinister smile on his chiseled face. She opened her mouth to finally scream for help, to beg for her life, or simply ask why he had chosen her.

But before she could utter a sound, her world went completely black.

To Be Continued

ABOUT THE AUTHOR

Ally comes from a long line of strong Southern women. Encouraged to read and dream at an early age, she was always making up stories that she would re-enact with her Barbies.

After she completed ten long years of education, she finally began to pursue her passion of sharing her stories with others. She currently lives in the United States, but she is always leaving on adventures abroad. One day she plans to retire from her nomadic ways.

Until then, she continues on her quest to find all the beauty left in the world. She has a loyal doggy friend, Levi, and a temperamental cat, Tinkle.

ACKNOWLEDGMENTS

I wanted to acknowledge those who made it possible to finish this first journey.

I wish to thank my mother. She instilled a passion for reading at an early age and encouraged me to be creative. This sentiment was also echoed by my grandmother and aunts, who believed in education and pursuing a woman's independence.

Next, I thank Daniel, Jaime, Ranee, and Mandy, who always stood by me and gave me encouragement when I needed it. However, a special thanks goes to Kelly, who braved a double space nightmare and never stopped believing in me.

Finally, I am indebted to my brother. He gave me a soft place to land when I jumped off the proverbial cliff.

I love them all and cannot begin to express my gratitude in their support. I owe them all this dream.

www.ingramcontent.com/pod-product-compliance
Lightning Source LLC
Chambersburg PA
CBHW020334180626
46812CB00001B/199